Published by Ink
www.inkubatc

Copyright © 202

Elena Frost has asserted her right to be identified as the
author of this work.

ISBN (eBook): 978-1-83756-596-2
ISBN (Paperback): 978-1-83756-597-9
ISBN (Hardback): 978-1-83756-598-6

LET'S PLAY DEAD

ELENA FROST

INKUBATOR
BOOKS

PROLOGUE

Pretending to be dead is much harder than it looks.

I played my first corpse when I was ten years old. My brother, Daniel, and I were cadavers in a primary school production of *Burke and Hare – the Musical*. Not great casting for Danny, who, thanks to his ADD, spent the whole play twitching. I've played a few corpses since – Cordelia in a production of *King Lear*, a murder victim in *Silent Witness*, and a drug addict in *Casualty*.

It sounds pretty obvious, but the most important thing is to control the breath. It's one of those things that the more you try to do it, the less successful you are. I've found it's helpful to concentrate on your back ribs rather than your chest or stomach if you want to breathe shallowly. And, of course, you've got to try your best not to swallow, or flinch, if other actors are still moving around on set.

But as difficult as it is to play dead on the stage or on film, it's just a job, like any other. It's harder when the stakes are higher.

It's harder to play it for real.

CHAPTER ONE

I hold my breath as Bella patters past my hiding place. The table above me is groaning with wedding presents – crystal glasses, a Fortnum and Mason hamper, Le Creuset pans. People have been generous. I hope the table won't collapse under the weight of their generosity.

'I'm coming! I'll find you, Mummy!'

Sitting here, crouched under the table, I have to be careful not to squash my corsage or any of the dozens of delicately appliqued flowers on my dress. That's the problem with shopping for wedding dresses with your four-year-old daughter. More is most definitely more. Instead of the chic, understated sheath dress I had envisioned, I ended up with a frothy confection of tulle and Brussels lace. If I'm honest, I'm secretly rather thrilled with it. It appeals to my dramatic side.

'Have you seen my mummy?' Bella asks an unseen person in the room on the other side of the tablecloth.

'I don't know.' The answering female voice is kind. Probably one of the hotel or catering staff. 'What does she look like?'

'Like a princess.'

My heart swells with love.

'Let's go and see if we can find her, shall we?'

I fake a sneeze. A loud, stage ACHOO!

'Mummy!'

The corner of the tablecloth is flung up. Bella pokes her head in, her pale redhead's complexion pink with excitement.

'Found you!'

'Oh no! You're too good at this.'

She looks around my refuge, wide-eyed. 'Can I come in, too?' She shoulders her way in before I get the chance to answer, and plonks herself down on my skirt. I was trying to keep her occupied and out of mischief in the lull between dessert and the toasts, but it seems she's got me into mischief instead.

'Have you seen the bride anywhere?' I hear Alex's voice on the other side of the tablecloth. 'My wife?' I thrill at his words.

There's a pause before he speaks again.

'Where can my two special girls have got to? They can't be hiding from me, can they?'

The woman Bella was talking to has clearly tipped him off where we are. I put my finger to my lips. Bella stifles a giggle, eyes round.

'Oh no. If I can't find them, I'm going to have to eat all of that delicious wedding cake on my own.'

Bella's eyes meet mine in consternation, her face a battleground of emotions.

Alex continues, implacable. 'And it's cream and white chocolate. Bella's favourite.'

'We're here!'

His words have the desired effect. Bella bursts out from our hiding place. I clamber out after her, trying not to put either of my heels through my voluminous skirts.

'Oh, my goodness!' Alex feigns shock, clapping his hand to his heart. He winks one of his dark eyes at me, making my heart thump. 'Whatever were you both doing in there?'

'Hiding!'

'From me?'

He picks Bella up and whirls her into the air, ribbons trailing. She squeals in pleasurable fright. He puts her down again.

'Run in and find Uncle Danny. We'll be there in a minute.'

She does as she's told, satin slippers flashing over the carpet.

Alex turns his dark eyes to me. 'Are you ready for the speeches?'

I nod.

He frowns. 'You've creased your dress.'

'Just a little bit. And it was worth it to keep her busy.'

He brushes a strand of hair off my face and tucks it behind my ear. 'Whatever am I going to do with you, Mrs McMahon?'

'I can think of a few things.'

He kisses me. A long, luxurious kiss that thrills me down to the toes of my silk shoes. As we pull apart, I see the woman Bella was talking to earlier, hovering on the edge of the room. Her face is a mixture of admiration and envy. I don't blame her. I have no idea what I've done to deserve this gorgeous, gorgeous man.

'Shall we go in, Mrs McMahon?' He grasps my hand.

In the main reception room, they've finished clearing the pudding plates and have started serving the champagne and cake. Danny is sitting with Bella on his knee at the top table. He catches my eye and grins. I suddenly realise how flushed my face must be, how dishevelled I am. I grin back at him and stick out my tongue.

We take our seats. Alex taps his knife on his glass.

'Can I have your attention, everyone?' The room quietens as our guests in their wedding finery jostle for views over the floral arrangements. 'Thank you. Has everyone got their champagne and cake?'

I beckon to Bella, and she slides off Danny's knee to come to sit on mine.

'As you all know, the first speech is traditionally made by the father of the bride, but in the absence of Lisa's father, Kenneth, who is sadly no longer with us, her older brother, Danny, will do the honours.'

There's a lot of applause and a chorus of appreciation as Danny gets to his feet.

'Thank you.' He pushes his glasses further onto his nose and clears his throat.

The room settles into an expectant silence. My own mouth has gone dry. I know he's been dreading this.

'Before I begin, I should probably warn you I'm not used to public speaking, not like my show-off sister, who's always happiest when she's centre stage.' He nods at me and grins. 'Sorry, sis, but it's my turn now.' Laughter. 'First, I'd like to thank you all for coming to share this wonderful day with us. I'd like to thank Suzy Wilson, the wedding planner, who's done such a great job, and the caterers, ditto. Let's have a round of applause for them.'

Everyone claps enthusiastically. Danny waits until the applause dies down before speaking again.

'As most of you probably know, this isn't Lisa's first rodeo.'

The room is suddenly very quiet. I hold my breath. Where is he going with this?

'When David died three years ago, it turned Lisa's world upside down. But she dealt with it with grace and strength, giving her daughter, Bella, the best, most loving start imaginable.'

Tears prickle my eyes. I blink them back.

'Lisa and I were womb-mates. Aka twins. We've been together for every important step of our lives – our first steps, our first day at school, our first spliff ...'

There are a few whistles at that from the sizeable police contingent in the room.

Danny continues, '... And, more recently, hot yoga at seven a.m. every Thursday.'

Laughter.

'I have to say my yoga moves are a bit ... eccentric. But Lisa tells me it will do me good, and I believe her. She is usually right. Or so she likes to tell me.' He pauses. 'Three years ago, I saw my usually indomitable sister knocked to the floor. But she picked herself up; she carried on. I never dreamt, the day I introduced her to my boss, that her life was going to change forever. That was only eight months ago, Alex, but I can honestly say I've never seen my twin sister so happy. Lisa, you deserve every good thing in the world.' He raises his glass. 'To the happy couple.'

'THE HAPPY COUPLE!'

'May your marriage be long and sickeningly happy. From

now on, you will be taking every significant step together. I will miss you, sis. But I won't miss the hot yoga.'

There's laughter, cheers and applause as he sits down. He meets my eyes, red-faced. I nod at him and wipe away a tear. Thank you, I mouth.

Alex stands up.

'Thanks, Danny. I have to say, I think you should stick with the yoga.' He raises his glass to my brother with a grin. 'Looking good, Danny boy.'

More whistles and hoots, but the noise dies down quickly. Ten years older than me, tall and broad-shouldered, with a hint of silver in his short-cropped dark hair, Alex is the kind of man who can command a room without even trying. Many of the men present are his subordinates, Danny's old work colleagues.

'I'd like to start off, as is traditional, with a few thanks. First of all, to all of you for coming to help us share this wonderful day. As most of you are probably aware, neither I nor Lisa have any family apart from Danny and my sister, Georgia, who unfortunately can't be here today. So to all of you – thank you. We wouldn't have a single wedding gift without you.'

Laughter. Everyone raises their glasses.

'Next, I'd like to thank our maid of honour, Willow.' Everyone looks at my friend, sitting beside Danny, the pink streaks in her hair clashing joyously with the pale aqua silk of her dress. 'Willow is Lisa's oldest friend. This whole shebang wouldn't have been possible without her. To Willow.'

'WILLOW!'

I beam at her. If her answering smile is a little tight, I pretend not to notice.

Alex continues, 'And of course, today I'm not only marrying one beautiful lady, but will now have two in my family.' He raises his glass to Bella. 'To my gorgeous new daughter, Bella.'

'BELLA!'

Bella squirms with pleasure on my lap. I kiss her cheek. The room settles again as Alex's face grows serious.

'The day I met Lisa started much the same as any other. I had paperwork to do. Backsides to kick.' He smiles, but his sombre expression forestalls any further response from the crowd. 'And I had to attend the annual ceremony of the Police Bravery Awards. One of my officers, PC Daniel Bellwood, had been nominated. As you all know, Daniel won the award. And quite rightly. But it was me who was the real winner of the night because Danny introduced me to his sister.'

He turns to look at me with such warmth that I blush pink, heat spreading down my neck and across my chest.

'As he introduced us after the ceremony, I found myself looking into the most extraordinary pair of green eyes. Bells rang. Sparks flew. The rest, as they say, is history.' He hesitates. 'As Danny so poetically put it, this isn't my first rodeo either. Like Lisa, I've also suffered a terrible loss. I think it says a lot about the resilience of the human soul that we've both decided to give it another go. It isn't my first rodeo, but it is, most definitely, my last.' He raises his glass to me. 'To my beautiful bride, and cowgirl to my cowboy, Lisa McMahon.'

'TO LISA!'

When everyone has finished the toast, he sits down beside me and kisses my cheek. I take his hand and squeeze it. The best-man speech follows, from Alex's friend Mike, who he's known since police college. After that, conversation flows freely. Danny gets up to go and chat with his friends, and Alex takes Bella off to show her to someone on the other side of the room. Willow shuffles along to sit beside me.

'Congratulations.' She kisses my cheek and hugs me.

'You still think I'm making a mistake?'

'No.' A blush suffuses her elfin features. For a fellow actress, Willow is one of the worst liars I've ever known. She's a Northerner, never shy of saying whatever comes into her head, even if it's to a bride on her hen night. 'I'm so sorry, Lisa. I know I should have kept my gob shut.' She looks suitably contrite. 'It's just you've known him such a short time. I was worried you were rushing things.'

I take her hand and squeeze it. 'You're right. We are rushing things. But somehow, it just … feels right.'

She kisses my hand. 'Then that's okay by me.'

'Anyway.' I grin at her. 'It's done now. For better or worse.'

We both hear a commotion at the door and look towards it. A dishevelled, dark-haired woman in a hoodie – definitely not one of the guests – has pushed her way into the room. She looks agitated. Luckily, Alex is only a few yards away from the door. I see him frown, then move swiftly to intercept her. They exchange words. I can't hear what is said, but their faces are tense. Alex signals discreetly to Tommy Becker, one of Danny's burly ex-colleagues, who is sitting nearby. After another brief exchange of words between the woman and Alex, Tommy escorts her from the room.

'What was that about?' asks Willow. 'Do you know her?'

I shake my head, mystified. Alex catches my eye and heads back to the top table. Willow relinquishes her seat to him. He takes my hand.

'Who was that?' I ask.

'Nothing to worry about. I'll tell you later.' He tugs me gently to my feet. 'Come on, I want to introduce you to Bill.'

Assistant Chief Constable William Glover is Alex's boss at the Met. A tall man with the lean features of an aesthete, he looks more like an academic than a senior policeman. We find him talking to his wife, Kathleen, at their place at one of the tables. They both get to their feet as we approach. Even though Bill was also, technically, Danny's boss, he's too high up the chain to have much to do with the sharp end of policing. I've never met him before.

'You look stunning, my dear,' says Kathleen, a round-faced, elegant woman of indeterminate age who smells deliciously of Coco Mademoiselle. 'Your dress is gorgeous. Elie Saab, isn't it?' Her voice has a soft Irish burr.

'It is. Thank you.'

Bill Glover takes my hand and kisses it. 'Lisa, Alex is a lucky man.'

Alex winks at me. 'I know how lucky I am.'

Bill smiles down at me. 'You should know, Lisa, your husband will go far. With you beside him, the sky's the limit. You can't underestimate the importance of having a good woman beside you in this job.' He puts his arm around his wife and hugs her to him. The look they exchange is so tender, so lovingly complicit, I catch my breath. I hope Alex and I still look at each other like that in a few years' time.

'I hope you'll save a dance for an old man later,' Bill says to me.

'I'd love to.'

'Then it's a date.' He gives me a cheeky wink. Kathleen tuts and slaps his arm playfully.

We leave them to finish their champagne.

Alex leans to whisper in my ear as we walk away, 'Don't be fooled by the charming-old-gentleman routine. That man has nerves of steel.' He sniffs. 'God, you smell delicious. I can't wait to get you alone.'

His words send a thrill of desire through me. 'Down, boy. We have hours to go, yet.'

'I'll be counting every minute.'

CHAPTER TWO

'*Is not this man jealous?*' Willow stuffs T-shirts and skirts into her suitcase willy-nilly, not caring if they'll crease.

'*I ne'er saw this before,*' I reply. '*Sure, there is some wonder in this handkerchief! / I am most unhappy in the loss of it.*'

'"*Tis not a year or two shows us a man. / They are all but stomachs, and we all but food; / they eat us hungrily, and when they—*'

'*Hungrily* or *hungerly?*' I interrupt her. 'The text says *hungerly?*'

'Does it?' She takes the script from me. 'So it does. I'll have a word with Greg. See if he'll let me fudge it.'

'Fudge Shakespeare? He won't. Greg Toksvig's old school.'

'Bugger. Okay, then ... *to eat us* hungerly, *and when they are full, / they belch us.* Do you think I'll need another jumper?'

'You have five already, Willow. No, you won't need another jumper.'

'I'll take one, just in case.' She grabs one off the many multicoloured piles on the floor. Willow's ramshackle bedsit is tiny, stuffed full of vintage clothes and costume jewellery – little more than a giant wardrobe with a window. She rams the sweater into her suitcase. 'You know how draughty rehearsal rooms can be.'

'I do.' I try to keep my envy from showing on my face. Willow is away for two months, playing Emilia in a co-pro of *Othello* with the Bath Theatre Royal and Hackney Empire, and part of me – quite a large part – wishes it was me. I haven't done any acting since David died. I haven't needed to, financially, and my head hasn't really been in the right place, but I've missed it. David was freelance, and he used to work from home, looking after Bella while I was away working. Alex is far too busy to do that, and I don't want Bella to be brought up by a nanny, even though Alex says we can afford one. When I said yes to Alex's proposal, it was in the full knowledge that my acting days were probably over.

'You will come and see me, won't you?' asks Willow, wrestling with the zip on her now overstuffed suitcase.

'Course we will. Maybe towards the end of the run. We'll give you a couple of weeks to get in the swing of things.'

Something flickers on Willow's face. Disappointment? She really is laughably easy to read for an actress.

'Surely you don't mind me bringing Alex?' I say. 'We haven't been able to have a honeymoon yet. A couple of nights in Bath will be lovely. Georgia has offered to look after Bella.' Georgia is Alex's older sister, a scarily well-groomed barrister in her early fifties. She wasn't able to make it to the wedding because she was tied up in a court case in Brussels. If I'm honest, I'm slightly intimidated by her, but she seems to adore Bella as much as Alex does. In fact, Bella is with her now, shopping.

Willow catches my eye and pulls a little face. 'Take no notice of me. I'm being selfish, wanting you all to myself. I keep forgetting you're a brand-new bride.'

'Not so brand new anymore.' Alex and I were married three weeks ago. Bella and I moved in the day after the wedding, into the house he used to share with his late wife, Polly. When we first had the discussion about where we would live, Alex was adamant we could buy somewhere new together, but actually it doesn't bother me. To be honest, I'm a little dazzled by the luxury of it all. It's a detached new build in a gated development. Each of the four bedrooms has an ensuite, the kitchen is state of the art, there's a huge utility room and even a dedicated cinema room. Alex had one of the bedrooms decorated for Bella, complete with a tented bed and enchanted forest mural. Bella and I were living in a converted Victorian flat in Clapham that used to leak when it rained and crumble randomly when it didn't, so it's lovely not having to worry about draughts and woodworm. And I could hardly deny Bella her own enchanted forest, could I?

'Earth calling Lisa.' Willow is grinning at me. 'Come in, Lisa.'

'Sorry. Miles away.'

Willow looks at her phone. 'Bugger. Give me a hand down with this lot, will you? The taxi's due any minute.'

After she's double-checked she's not left the gas on or a random tap running, I help her haul her bulging suitcases out of the flat and down the stairs.

'This is the key for the door down here, and this is the key for the flat. The flat door can be a bit sticky. You have to jiggle the key. Oh, and ignore next-door's cat if it tries to convince you it's a stray. Everybody feeds it. It's as fat as a hippo.'

'I'm not going to be living here,' I remind her. 'Just popping in every now and then.'

She nods. 'I know. And I know what a sucker you are for animals. If you see the cat, ignore it.' She smirks. 'Even if it looks at you *hungerly*.'

After I've waved Willow off in the taxi, I go to find my car in the side street where I left it. It's a lemon-yellow Fiat that I've had for years, and, as knackered as it is, I can't imagine driving anything else. We rattle southwest together, out of the city and towards Twickenham.

This is the first time I've ever lived so far out of town. I've always thought of Richmond and Twickenham as a bit twee, with their leafy river walks, quirky shops and olde worlde pubs. But on closer acquaintance, I've come to appreciate them. They're something of an oasis, particularly if you have a little girl who loves feeding ducks.

My new home isn't far from Strawberry Hill. I use my remote control to open the gates onto the development. The estate is small, with a couple of low-rise apartment buildings flanking the road, which then turns into a horseshoe leading to three detached houses. The verdant grounds are beautifully landscaped, with strategically placed cameras that are a constant reminder we aren't *so* far from the city. I can see why the development appealed to Alex. Given his job, he's more security-conscious than most people.

The middle house is Alex's. Ours. I feel a thrill of pleasure as I steer my car through the gates and park up in my usual spot on the drive. The house is in darkness, but security lights flash on as I get out of the car, lighting my way to the front door.

It's silent in the hall, the kind of hush you only get from well-carpeted luxury. As I hang my coat in the closet and slip off my shoes, I can smell cedarwood mothballs and furniture polish. Although I balked at a nanny, Alex insisted on keeping his cleaner, Mrs T. She comes twice a week and keeps the place neat as a pin. She brings fresh flowers too. Lilies today. I admire them as I switch on the hall lamp and tidy my reflection in the mirror. My hair, as always, needs attention, the red curls springing in all directions now they're freed from the tyranny of my beret. I tidy them as best I can, pushing them behind my ears. But I'm not too worried. Alex loves my hair.

The kitchen hums with a low-key efficiency. I put on the overhead lights and go to the fridge to see what there is for supper. I don't need to worry about feeding Bella because Georgia promised to give her something before Alex picks her up on his way home. That's just as well because there isn't a lot to eat in the fridge. Some tomatoes, cheese and a head of lettuce. I had meant to shop for groceries this afternoon, but was sidetracked by Willow's departure. Oh well, I suppose we can order in, as it's just the two of us.

I get the take-away menus from the drawer by the sink, then flick through them, indecisive. Do I fancy a curry or something a bit more subtle? Malaysian, perhaps? With a sigh, I look up.

There's a face at the window.

I almost hit the ceiling. The woman stares at me for a long moment, her pale face framed by wild, dark hair. Then she hurries to her left, towards the front door.

The doorbell rings before I can reach it. I open the door on the chain to peer out at her.

'Hello?' I'd say she's about forty, dressed in jeans, a

hoodie and a red beanie. Now I can see her more clearly, there's something familiar about her. 'Can I help you?' I can't put my finger on where I might have seen her before.

Her face twists awkwardly. 'My name is Keira,' she stammers. 'Keira Benson. Polly's sister.'

'Polly?' My mind doesn't make the connection at first, but when it does, I'm dismayed. 'Polly! Oh.'

'You're Alex's new wife.'

'Yes.' Now I remember where I've seen her before. She was the woman who gate-crashed the reception, who was escorted out by Tommy Becker. Alex never did explain who she was, and I simply forgot to ask him about it. But now I'm baffled. Why would Alex be so inhospitable to his dead wife's sister? I can understand why he might not invite her to the wedding, but having her frog-marched out seems extreme.

I realise we're still talking through a two-inch gap in the door. Remembering my manners, I take the chain off.

'Sorry if I scared you,' says Keira. 'At the window. I didn't know if there was anyone in.'

'That's okay.' Why couldn't she just ring the doorbell, like a normal person? But, of course, I don't say that. 'Alex isn't here, I'm afraid.'

'I know.' She glances around, jittery. 'It isn't him I've come to see.'

'Oh?'

She doesn't elaborate, but her face twitches with emotion.

'Why don't you come in?' I show her into the kitchen and then feel immediately awkward. She looks around as if she were in a dream. Caresses the marble countertop with a finger. This was her sister's kitchen, every inch of it planned and installed by her. I can barely remember where the teabags are kept.

'Would you like tea? Coffee?' I ask dutifully.

She shakes her head and tugs off her beanie, revealing more of her dark, greasy hair. Whatever it is she wants to talk to me about, she's taking an awfully long time to get to the point.

'I'm sorry about Polly,' I say, to fill the silence. 'It must have been a terrible shock. It was a car accident, wasn't it?'

'No.' She twists her beanie in her hands, agitated.

'No?' I'm confused.

'It *was* a car. But it wasn't an accident.'

'Sorry?'

'Alex killed her.'

All the breath goes out of me.

'He made it *look* like an accident. He's very clever.' She grabs my hand. 'That's why I've come. To warn you.'

I prise my hand from her grip. It's clear now why Alex had her escorted from the wedding. I'm going to have to tread very, very carefully.

'I'm sure you're mistaken,' I say as gently as I can. 'Alex wouldn't—'

'He would. He did.'

I shake my head. 'Alex adored Polly. He's still grieving her.' I know that's true. Alex and I were both broken when we met, but gradually, gradually we've been helping each other to heal. Only a couple of nights ago I found him sobbing over one of Polly's old cardigans he'd found in the back of the airing cupboard. I don't care what this woman says, my husband is *not* a murderer.

'I'm sorry, but you're mistaken.' My voice is firm. 'You

might believe what you're saying is true, but your grief for your sister has muddled you. Disturbed your mind.'

'That's what my doctor says.' Keira frowns and shakes her head. 'But it isn't true. I know what I know. No one will listen.'

I don't know how to respond to that.

She stares at me, dark eyes vivid in her white face. 'What would you say if I told you I can *prove* it? I can prove Alex killed Polly.'

We both hear wheels on gravel – a car turning into the drive. Alex! My heart leaps with relief. Keira looks panicked. Presses something into my hand. A piece of paper with an address on it.

'Come and see me,' she begs. 'Please! I'll prove it to you.' She hurries to the door. I'm torn. I don't want her in the house. I want her safely away, and yet ...

'Don't go, please,' I call after her. 'Let me help you!' God knows, she needs help. Serious help. But she's already gone, through the hall and out, leaving the door wide open.

Tyres crunch to an abrupt halt. A car door slams, and a few moments later Alex hurries in through the door, carrying Bella and shopping bags. His face is pinched with anxiety.

'Lisa! Was that Keira I nearly ran over on the drive?' He puts Bella and the bags down. Bella scampers off into the living room. 'Are you okay?'

'I'm fine.' Even as I say it, I know it's not true. My heart is still thumping, and I need to sit down. Alex follows me through to the kitchen.

'How did she get in?'

'I let her in. Why wouldn't I?' I sit heavily on a chair. 'Why the hell didn't you warn me about her?'

'Oh God.' He runs a hand through his hair. 'I'm so, so sorry. I never thought she would come here.' He frowns. 'She must still have her key card for the gate.'

'Mummy!' Bella appears in the doorway, hopping with excitement. 'Auntie Georgie bought me a new dress.'

'Did she?' My eyes meet Alex's in an unspoken communication: later. I hold my hand out to Bella. 'Come and show me. Quickly. It's nearly bathtime.'

Bath and bedtime take longer than normal because once I've let Bella try on her new dress, I can't get it off her again. I have to bribe her with the promise of hot chocolate to get her into the bath, then into her pyjamas and then into bed. I have to admit the dress is beautiful – linen, hand-embroidered with flowers. It isn't frothy enough for a party frock, but it's still far too good for everyday wear. I have no idea when Georgia thinks Bella will wear it. How much money has she spent? Is she embarrassed by Bella's clothes?

When I get back downstairs again, Alex has made a start on supper, turning the tomatoes into a sauce for pasta. We both know this still isn't the right time for explanations, so we work together in silence as I make Bella's hot chocolate.

'I'll take it up,' he says when it's ready, wiping his hands on his apron. 'She'll want a goodnight kiss.' He heads out.

As I'm cleaning the worktop, I see something red on the floor underneath one of the counter stools – Keira's hat. I realise she must have dropped it in her hurry to get out. I pick it up as Alex comes back into the kitchen.

'She's fast asleep,' he says, 'with Teddy Pea.' Teddy is Bella's favourite toy, a disreputable-looking teddy bear in a vibrant shade of green. He's horribly threadbare and only has one eye, but she adores him. He was my childhood toy, but ever since Bella first clapped eyes on him, they've been inseparable. Alex holds the hot chocolate out to me.

I shake my head. 'No, thanks. So?'

He looks at me, dark eyes intense. 'I think we need something a bit stronger before we start.' He pours two glasses of red wine from the bottle beside the hob and gives one to me. As he does, he spots what I have in my hands.

'What's that?'

'Keira's hat. She dropped it.' I prompt him again. 'So?'

'So.' He perches on a stool at the counter opposite me. 'Keira. She's Polly's younger sister, and she's always had ... problems. She was hospitalised a couple of times in her twenties for depression and mood swings. Her doctors eventually diagnosed borderline personality disorder. When I met Polly, Keira was on meds, which kept it more or less under control. She still had her ups and downs – you never quite knew which Keira you were going to get, the life and soul of the party, or ...' He hesitates, decides not to go there. 'But she was functional. And in spite of everything, Polly adored her. They adored each other.'

He takes a long swallow of his wine. 'She didn't take Polly's death well. It was a shock to all of us, of course, but ... Keira ... I think something broke.'

I sip my own wine. 'She says you murdered Polly.'

'I know.' Alex's expression is bleak. 'I think she honestly believes it. She needs someone to blame, and I'm the obvious target.'

'She says she has proof.'

'Proof?' He gives a bark of bitter laughter. 'What proof can she have? The accident was nobody's fault. Except, if I'm brutally honest, Polly's. She'd been drinking. The coroner said she was almost twice over the limit when she died.'

I flinch. I had no idea. I'd seen news stories about the crash, of course, but none mentioned Polly was over the limit. Presumably Alex had managed to pull strings to keep that quiet.

'I wasn't even there.' His face crumples suddenly. He puts his hands over his face. 'I should have been there.'

Poor Alex. I go to put my arms around him. He kisses my cheek. 'It's okay. I'm okay.'

'She needs help, Alex.'

'I know.' He wipes his face on his sleeve. 'I know. I've tried to talk to her doctor, but ... I'm not an actual blood relative. There's only so much I can do. It's hard. She's fixated on this ... this fantasy ... and it couldn't be further from the truth. I loved Poll.' He looks at me with brimming eyes. 'I loved her, Lisa.'

I hug him hard. 'I know you did.' My heart is breaking for this brave, strong man who's had so much to bear.

He makes another attempt to pull himself together, scrubbing his face with his hands. 'I'm sorry. I should have told you all this sooner ... I should have warned you.'

I kiss him. His lips are salty with his tears.

'I've done what I can for Keira,' he says. 'But ... I have to protect you and Bella. I didn't know she still had a key card to the estate. I'll get it cancelled. I'll get someone to have a word. Tell her to steer clear.'

I nod. That would be a relief. But ... 'Do it gently, Alex. For Polly's sake.'

'I will. I promise.'

I kiss him again. This time he kisses me back. His kiss

deepens, and his arm tightens around my waist, pulling me to him. There's a desperation to him, an urgency it's impossible not to respond to. White heat courses through me, turning my legs to jelly.

We lose ourselves in each other.

CHAPTER THREE

'She needs help, Danny.'

'You want to be careful with mental-health stuff, Li. You can't just go swanning in there like some kind of saviour.'

I nod. If anyone knows what he's talking about when it comes to mental health, it's Danny. Danny was invalided out of the police force because of his PTSD after the stabbing incident that earned him his bravery award. He's still receiving treatment for it, still having nightmares and panic attacks, although it isn't something he likes to talk about.

'Has she been back at all?' he asks.

I shake my head. There's been no further sign of Keira, which is a relief. Alex must have done what he promised, and got someone to have a word with her. I haven't asked him; in fact, we haven't mentioned her again. Even so, she's been living, rent-free, in my head during the two weeks since her visit.

Danny crams another biscuit into his mouth and speaks around it. 'And really, it isn't any of your business, is it? It's between her and Alex.'

'I suppose.' I don't take it personally. Danny has no filter between his head and his mouth. 'No! No!'

I jump up and rush to stop Bella's new spaniel puppy, Figgy, from chewing the leg of one of the bar stools. I gently prise the puppy's jaws from the wood and put him back in his fenced-off area – an improvised enclosure – in the corner of the room. I know he won't stay in there for long: he has an almost supernatural talent for escape.

Bella was delighted – beside herself with joy – when Alex turned up last weekend with the new addition to the family. I have to admit, my joy was a little more restrained. Although I love that Alex wants to please Bella, we never discussed having a puppy, nor the work it would involve. He couldn't possibly have imagined the havoc one furry little body could cause, that it would turn the once-pristine kitchen into a war zone, with bits fenced off and dirty puppy pads dotted about. Not to mention chunks chewed out of the cabinetry.

Ignoring Figgy's pitiful whines, I climb back up onto my stool to rejoin Danny.

I dunk my biscuit into my coffee. 'She said she had proof.'

Danny eyes me. 'Didn't Alex say he would deal with it?'

'He did.'

'So?'

I spread my hands. 'I don't know if he's done anything.'

'Then ask him.'

'I don't want to bring it up again. At the very least, Keira needs help. At the worst ...' I don't want to think about the worst.

Danny shakes his head. 'You never change, Li.'

'What do you mean?'

'You can't let yourself be happy. There's always got to be a drama.'

'That's not fair.'

Danny just raises his tawny eyebrows. He catches my sombre expression and frowns.

'That's not it though, is it?' he says. 'Not all of it, anyway.'

I think about denying it, but he knows me too well.

'If you have something to get off your chest,' he prompts, 'just say it.'

'Alex loves Bella. Loves us both so much.' I hesitate. 'It's scary.'

He looks at me seriously for a beat, two beats, then bursts out laughing. 'You're sitting here in this gorgeous house, complaining that your handsome, supportive, rich new husband loves you too much?'

'I know that sounds mad.'

'You think so?' Danny's tone is incredulous.

It's impossible to explain to him what I mean. It's a feeling that's been creeping up on me gradually ever since the wedding. I don't deserve Alex. He thinks I'm upbeat, easy-going, effortlessly glamorous. But I'm not. Not naturally, anyway. The weight of being everything he expects me to be – everything he thinks I am – is starting to feel suffocating. I'm bound to disappoint him sooner or later. And then what?

'It just all feels too good to be true,' I say.

'What, Alex does?'

I frown. That wasn't what I meant, exactly.

'Listen to me, Li. Alex is one of life's good guys. I know

what I'm talking about. You need to get a grip, or you're going to sabotage it all, like you almost did with David.'

I recoil. That was below the belt. David and I had had a bit of a wobble the year before he died, but it hadn't been my fault. Not entirely, anyway.

Danny sees my expression. 'Sorry.' He grimaces. 'But you know what I'm talking about. People do have happy-ever-afters, you know. Just because it didn't happen with Mum and Dad, or you and David, doesn't mean it won't with you and Alex.'

Dad died when I was eleven and Danny was thirteen. Devastated, Mum never really got over it, retreating into a world of her own, accompanied by an increasingly present bottle of Famous Grouse. Danny effectively ended up being both mother and father to me. He made sure there was food in the house, and clean clothes to wear, and he made me do my homework. Mum died of liver disease two months after I started acting school.

I look at Danny over the counter. With his open, honest features and calm demeanour, it's easy to forget just how tough his life has been. More recently, the stabbing incident and the PTSD that meant he had to walk away from the job he loved. My eyes fill with tears.

He takes my hand. Squeezes it. 'You have to let yourself be happy, Li.'

The lights on the baby monitor flicker. Bella's woken from her nap. Danny jumps up and dusts biscuit crumbs off his sweatshirt. 'I have to go. But I'll give my favourite niece a kiss first.'

I DON'T KNOW whether it's guilt or a King Canute-like attempt to hold off the inevitable tides of reality, but when Danny has gone, I make even more of an effort to get the house – and myself – looking our best before Alex gets home. By the time I hear his car pull into the drive, there's a chicken casserole in the oven, Figgy has been taken into the garden, and while Bella has been occupied watching *Peppa Pig*, I've plucked and waxed myself to within an inch of my life.

'Ali!' Bella makes a beeline for him, hugs his knees. The puppy follows, falling over its own ears.

'Hello, gorgeous!' He scoops her up and kisses her, then pets the puppy. Together, they're a chocolate-box picture of domestic bliss. I watch them with a smile. Am I really going to let my own insecurities sabotage everything? That would be stupid. More than stupid. Tragic.

Bella runs off to play ball with Figgy.

'Hello, you.' He pulls me to him and nuzzles my neck. 'Mmmm, you smell delicious.'

'Thank you.'

He sniffs the air. 'And you're not the only thing.'

'Chicken chasseur.'

'You're spoiling me.' He reaches into his jacket pocket, then puts a small velvet box on the counter in front of me.

'What's this?'

'Just a little something to say thank you.'

'For?'

'For being you. For everything.'

I open the box. It's a stunning pair of emerald earrings, set in white metal. It could be silver, but, knowing Alex, I'm willing to bet it's platinum.

'I thought they matched your eyes,' he says. 'Aren't you going to put them on?'

I take out the plain gold hoops I usually wear, as I go to the mirror over the dresser. Alex watches as I thread the hooks through my ears.

'They're gorgeous.' I turn my head so the stones catch the light from the downlighters. 'A bit dressy for kitchen chores, though.'

'My Cinderella. They'll look stunning with your hair up.' He scoops up my hair and kisses the back of my neck. 'Oh!' He looks down at the floor. 'Jesus.'

I follow his gaze. I see he's trodden in a puppy turd, brown and sticky, that's now wrapped around his brogue. Figgy must have squeezed one out when I wasn't looking.

'Oh no.' I stifle a giggle.

Anger flashes over Alex's face. It's there and gone in a split second. I can't say I blame him, but his reaction only makes me want to laugh out loud.

'Take your shoe off,' I say, making an effort to smother my mirth. 'I'll clean it up.'

'Accidents happen, I suppose.' Alex scowls as he slips off his shoe. 'I'd forgotten puppies were so messy.'

'I hadn't. Who do you think has been cleaning up after it since it arrived? Just leave your shoe there. I'll sort it out.'

'Do I have time for a shower before dinner?'

'You have twenty minutes.'

'More than enough.' He stops at the door, then looks back at me. 'Unless ... you want to join me?'

I look meaningfully at the shoe, then at my four-year-old, who's playing with her puppy. 'I have my hands full at the moment.'

'I wish mine were. Full of you.' He gives me a lascivious grin and ducks out.

I can't stop grinning too. I can feel my beautiful new

earrings swinging against my jaw as I scrape puppy poo onto newspaper. Life is a mixed bag, full of contradictions. I'm sure that Alex and I will be able to steer our way through it together.

And Danny's right. People do have happy-ever-afters. I just need to give myself permission to be one of them.

CHAPTER FOUR

'And this is the quiet area.' Mrs Wilson, manager of the Pumpkin Patch nursery, shows us a padded corner furnished with beanbags and a bookcase. 'We encourage the children to come and sit in here whenever they feel things are too overwhelming, and to take their naps.'

One of the beanbags is occupied by a boy who has his jumper pulled up over his head; he is sprawled face-down like a starfish. I would worry he was suffocating if his snores weren't quite so loud.

'Very nice.' I nod. 'Isn't this nice, Bella?'

Bella says nothing. She's clinging to my jeans, staring at the boy, wide-eyed.

'Of course, our priority is education.' Mrs Wilson, a comfortable-looking woman in her forties, has to raise her voice to be heard over the noise coming from the open-plan area. 'We try to get the children used to a learning environment so it's not so much of a shock when they go up into the school proper.'

That's exactly why we're here. Bella will be starting

primary school in the summer. Alex and I discussed it and agreed it made sense to put her in the nursery now, for a few afternoons a week, so she can acclimatise and make friends before going up into school. I thought the preschool class would be fully subscribed, but they've managed to fit her in. I suspect Alex has pulled some strings. Once upon a time I might have balked at using that kind of influence, but when it comes to Bella, I'm happy to make an exception. All's fair in love, war and motherhood.

'We're all about to sit down for our lunch.' Mrs Wilson addresses Bella directly. 'It's lasagne today. You can have some lunch with us, if you like?'

Bella retreats further behind my legs.

I smile at the nursery teacher. 'Better not push our luck, Mrs Wilson. We'll see you on Monday.'

'See you then, Bella.'

I steer Bella out to the car. If I'm honest, I'm dreading Monday. I've resisted putting Bella into nursery so far, even though I could have afforded it after David died. I just wanted to keep her close. But now I know it's the right thing to do, for her sake. But it won't make it any easier. When we get back to the car, I check my phone and see I've missed a call from my agent. I wonder why she's calling me. It's been months since we spoke. I call her back.

'Dinah, how are you?'

'Great. You okay to talk for a minute?'

'Sure.' I check Bella in the rear-view mirror. Her eyes are closing even before I've started the car.

'I know you haven't been taking on any work, but something's just come across my desk I think you'd be perfect for.'

'Really?' My pulse quickens. I'd almost forgotten that feeling.

'It's a part in a police procedural. Not a lead, but a regular. She's spiky and three-dimensional. I think she's right up your street.'

'I don't know, Dinah, I—'

'Listen, I know you've been out of the saddle for a while. But this part is perfect for you. They'll be filming in London. And the EP still remembers you. Jerry Buckham ... remember Jerry? He says he loved your work on *Silent Witness*; he wants you to audition.'

An audition? I take a deep breath.

Dinah pre-empts me. 'Listen, don't say anything just now. Take a look at the material. I'll email it over to you. We'll speak again this afternoon.' She hangs up before I can protest.

My head is spinning as I drive home. I had resigned myself to never acting again, but maybe I was too hasty? Maybe now, with Bella starting nursery and about to start school, the timing might be right to take up my career again. What else am I going to do with myself, otherwise? I really can't see me becoming a full-time housewife, shopping and cooking and making sure everything's perfect for Alex coming home. Not that I think there's anything wrong with that, but I'm not great at being on my own. I'd be bored out of my skull within a couple of months. If there isn't much night-time filming ... if the schedule is flexible ... if we could get a part-time nanny to help ...

I realise I'm getting ahead of myself. The part might suck.

Dinah's email is waiting for me when I get home. I give Bella some lunch, then put her down for her afternoon nap and settle down to read the material. The pilot script is brilliant – sharp and darkly funny. As Dinah said, the part I'd be auditioning for isn't the lead – I couldn't expect that after being so long out of the spotlight – but she's the lead's sister, and she's in all the episodes. The filming is only scheduled for six weeks. Perhaps I could do it and see how it works out? The show might be given another series. Even if it isn't, I can see the part being the perfect springboard to bigger things if I wanted it to be. What will Alex think? Will he support me? I can't imagine he wouldn't.

My flight of fancy is disturbed by my phone ringing. I snatch it up, thinking it could be Dinah again, but the caller ID says it's Willow.

'Willow, hi! You'll never guess—'

'Oh, Lisa!' Willow wails. 'It's a disaster! We're only three weeks into the run and this happens! I can't believe it.'

'What? What's happened?'

'It's awful,' cries Willow. 'It's just my bloody luck!'

'Calm down and tell me what's going on.'

'I've broken my big toe! I stepped off one of these horrible steep kerbs in Bath and staved it. I have a bloody moonboot on! I can't go onstage.'

'So what are you going to do?'

'Greg's asked me to rehearse the understudy tomorrow. And then ...' She sniffs. 'Then I'll have to come home!'

'That is bad luck. I'm so, so sorry, sweetheart.'

Willow's properly sobbing now. 'I wish you were here, Li. I can't do anything with this bloody boot on. And I just feel so alone.'

I look at the clock on the kitchen wall. Two o'clock. How long would it take to get to Bath?

THE ANSWER IS two hours fifty-five minutes. I might have made it faster if I'd been on my own, but even though I had an overnight bag ready when Bella got up from her nap, she woke up grumpy, and after that, everything seemed to take twice as long as it should. I didn't get an answer on Alex's mobile, so I called his office. His PA, Tricia, said he was in a briefing with Bill Glover, so I left a message with her, explaining I was taking Bella to Bath overnight because of an emergency with Willow.

We catch a taxi to Twickenham station, change trains at Reading, then take a taxi from Bath Spa to Larkhall, finding ourselves on the doorstep of Willow's Airbnb at ten past five.

I ring the doorbell. Bella and I shiver as we wait for Willow to answer. People always imagine the West Country is warmer than London, but I've always found the opposite to be true. The early December wind cuts through our town clothes like a knife through butter. I ring the bell again, and eventually we hear shuffling on the other side of the door. It opens slowly.

'Lisa! Oh my God!' Willow gapes at us. She's wearing a huge black moonboot on her left foot, and her face is puffy and purple, bruised from her temple to her chin. I'm shocked at the state of her. It dispels any doubts I was having about whether we should have come.

'Auntie Willie!' Bella throws her arms around Willow, making her wince.

'Hello, poppet.' Willow kisses Bella's cheek, then grasps my hand. 'I know I said I needed you, Li, but I never thought you'd actually come.' She bursts into tears.

Bella looks at her in consternation. 'It's okay,' I soothe. 'Auntie Willow's just pleased to see us.'

'That's the understatement of the bloody century!'

Willow wipes her face with her hands, then gives me a fierce hug. 'Come in, come in.'

The flat is a tip. Willow isn't the most fastidious house-keeper at the best of times, and her accident clearly hasn't helped. Every surface is littered with empty take-away cartons, magazines and dirty glasses. She makes a half-hearted effort to tidy the sofa.

'Sit down, for heaven's sake.' I push her into an armchair. 'Put your foot up. We don't need you to run around looking after us. We're here to look after you, aren't we, Bella?'

Bella nods enthusiastically.

'Why didn't you tell me you'd hurt your face?' I ask. 'It must have been a hell of a fall.'

'It was. The doctor said I was lucky not to break anything else, or to fall under a car. I think I might have persuaded Greg to let me carry on if it had just been my toe. But looking like this ...'

She's so woeful, I give her another hug.

'What have you had to eat today?' I ask.

'Some cornflakes.' She looks guilty. 'And a croissant ... and a box of chocolates.'

'You must be starved.'

'Actually, I feel a bit sick. But some proper food would be good. We can order a take-away, if you like?'

I eye the empty cartons. 'I think it would be better to get something healthy inside you. What have you got in?'

It doesn't surprise me to discover there's nothing to eat in the fridge or cupboards, so I get directions to the nearest corner shop. It turns out to be a Waitrose, so I'm able to buy ingredients for a tasty tuna pasta.

Dinah calls me as I'm heading back to the flat through the dark streets.

'Have you read the script?' she asks. 'What do you think?'

I shiver and pull my coat more tightly around me. I've had a lot of time to think about it on the train, but still haven't reached a conclusion. 'I think it's a great part.'

'Will you audition?'

'I don't know. I need to think about it. Discuss it with Alex.'

'Okay, but don't take too long. Parts like this are like hen's teeth. I have at least two other actresses on my books who would kill for it. Let me know on Monday.'

When I get back to the flat, Willow has resorted to the TV to keep Bella occupied. They're both watching an old episode of *Bear in the Big Blue House*. Looking at them tucked under a blanket on the sofa, I don't know who looks more childlike, Bella or Willow.

After we've eaten, I put Bella down to sleep with Teddy Pea in the camp bed in Willow's room, and, afterwards, Willow and I watch some old episodes of *Friends*, bitching about the characters and how some of the actors have delivered their lines. I know there's going to be a battle later about who's going to sleep on the sofa, but I'm going to put my foot down. Willow can't do it in her condition, and she needs her sleep if she has to put her understudy through her paces tomorrow.

'The bugger of it is,' says Willow, when we're tired of kvetching and have switched off the TV, 'it was all going so well. We've had some great reviews.'

'I know.' I quote the *Bath Chronicle*. '*Schneider is the best Emilia since Anna Patrick*. But there'll be other parts. Try not to be too down about it.' I know that's easier said than done. Good parts really are hard to come by. I hesitate.

Should I ask her advice about the audition? It might seem insensitive under the circumstances, but the part's hardly in the bag yet. And she is my best friend. 'Talking about parts,' I say, 'Dinah got in touch yesterday. She has a—'

The doorbell rings, making us both jump.

Willow scowls. 'Who the bloody hell is that?'

I sigh and get up. 'You stay put. I'll see.'

When I see who's standing on the other side of the door, my mouth drops open.

CHAPTER FIVE

Alex's face is white, and he's almost trembling with the effort to control himself.

'What the holy FUCK, Lisa?'

'What?' My brain can't quite compute. Why is he so angry?

'What the hell were you thinking?'

I stare at him blankly.

'I got home and you'd gone. You'd both gone. There was no message on my phone. No message at home. Just an empty house.'

'But ...' I stutter, 'but I did leave a message. With Tricia.'

'Tricia?'

'Your PA?' I prompt. Surely to God he knows who his PA is?

He blinks. 'My meeting ran late. Tricia had gone home when I got out.'

'And she didn't tell you? Didn't pass on the message?'

'No.'

I feel myself relax a little. It's no wonder he's so worked up. But ...

'How did you know I was here?'

'I went onto your laptop. Saw you'd bought train tickets. When I saw they were to Bath, I knew you'd be with Willow. I rang the theatre company for her address.'

He went on my laptop? I had no idea he even knew my password.

'I've been calling you. Why the hell didn't you pick up?'

I check my phone. 'Shit. I must have accidentally knocked it onto mute.'

'Who is it?' Willow's voice comes from the sitting room.

'It's Alex,' I call through, not too loudly because I don't want to wake Bella. I open the door wider. 'Come in.'

'No.' He shakes his head. 'Just get Bella, please, and your things.'

'What?'

'The car's outside.'

I'm completely dumbfounded. 'You want me to come—'

'Home. Yes.'

I hear Willow hobble along the hallway. She appears in the doorway in her moonboot, her pink hair sticking up at all angles above her bruised face. Alex actually flinches when he sees her.

'Come in and close the door, Alex. You're letting all the heat out.'

He has no choice but to step inside.

'Willow broke her toe,' I explain. 'That's why I came in such a hurry.'

'I'm sorry to hear that,' he says stiffly, eyeing Willow's boot.

Willow's eyes flick from me to Alex's face and back again.

'I asked Lisa to come,' she says. 'I was in a bit of a state. I'm sorry.'

He doesn't respond.

I feel the need to defend him. 'Alex's PA didn't pass on my message,' I say to Willow. 'He didn't know where we'd gone.'

'Ah. No wonder you were worried. But all's well that ends well, eh? Why not come in for some cocoa?'

He shakes his head. 'We should get home.'

Willow's eyes widen. 'Surely you're not going to drive all the way back to Twickenham tonight?'

We stand staring at each other, like three gunslingers, each waiting for someone to draw a pistol first. I realise I don't fancy sharing a sofa with Alex. Not tonight. Perhaps it would be better if Bella and I went home with him, with as little fuss as possible.

'You should go,' says Willow, as if reading my mind. She sees my anguished expression. 'I'm feeling much better now. I only have tomorrow morning to get through; then I can go home too.'

I hesitate. I don't want to leave her.

'I'll be fine. Honestly.'

'If you're sure.'

'I am.'

Alex's expression is blank. Frozen.

'I'll go and get Bella,' I say. Willow clomps along the hall behind me in her moonboot.

We have to wake Bella to get her out of bed; she's so disoriented it's almost impossible to get her dressed.

'Just wrap her in that blanket,' says Willow. 'It's not

mine. The landlord will be getting a month's rent off me for nothing, so I think he can stretch to the cost of a blanket.' She watches as I bundle Bella up and hoist her in my arms. 'Are you okay?' she whispers.

I just nod. I'm not sure how I feel.

'I'll give you a ring when I get back to London,' she says.

'Promise?'

'Promise.'

WE DRIVE along the M4 in silence apart from Bella's gentle snores. In spite of the tension in the car, the hum of the engine and the sound of wheels on tarmac is soporific. My eyes drift shut. I guess I must have fallen asleep because, before I know it, we're pulling up at the house. Alex is out of the car as soon as we stop, taking Bella out of her car seat. I watch as he carries her into the house, then follow slowly with my bag.

I'm not sure what's happened tonight, but it feels as if a line has been crossed. Even though Tricia failed to pass on my message, Alex's behaviour is extreme. Indefensible, really. I'm too exhausted to be angry right now, but I know it will come. It will definitely come.

I put my bag on the kitchen counter and put the kettle on. I'm tired, but my nerves are too jangled to sleep.

Alex comes downstairs. 'She's fast asleep,' he says. 'I've tucked her in with Teddy Pea.'

I just look at him. What the hell does he expect me to say? Well done? Good job?

Neither of us speaks. Only the sound of the kettle fills the silence. Just the kettle. I look around.

'Where's Figgy?'

There's no sign of the puppy apart from the usual puddles of pee and a small, solitary turd on one of the puppy pads. He's not in his crate, and he's not in his pen. He doesn't seem to be anywhere else in the kitchen either. We search high and low, with a growing sense of dread. Eventually, I open the back door and find him huddled outside, almost stiff with cold. I hug the furry little body to me, trying to infuse it with some of my warmth.

'What the hell was he doing out there?'

Alex runs a hand through his hair. 'I let him out before I left.'

'That was hours ago. Didn't you think to check he was back in again?'

'I thought I had. Honestly.' He sees my accusing look. 'I … I wasn't thinking clearly.'

At last, the anger comes, hot and cleansing.

'How *dare* you?' I begin. 'How dare you come after me like that, tracking me down like some … criminal? How dare you insist on dragging us home? You don't own us, Alex.'

Alex sits, slumped on a kitchen stool. 'I'm sorry.'

But I'm just getting started. I pace the floor, hugging the shivering puppy to me like a furry talisman. 'Don't you have any idea what that looked like? How rude you were to Willow? She'll probably never talk to me again.' I know that's not true. But he doesn't. And I want to punish him. 'I can't believe you behaved so badly.'

He stares at me, bleak. 'You were gone,' he says. 'I thought you'd left me.'

'Left you? Why would I leave you?'

'Because everybody does.' To my horror, he bursts out crying.

I'm so shocked, I bump right down off my high horse. He

cries messily, shoulders shaking, struggling to control himself. The puppy wriggles, trying to get out of my arms, so I put him carefully in his crate and tuck him up in his blanket. I take my time doing it, giving Alex the chance to pull himself together. I find it hard to meet his eyes. I don't know what to do. I want to put my arms around him, to alleviate his distress, but honestly, I just feel too awkward.

He wipes his face with his hands. 'I owe you an explanation.'

My instinct is to tell him he doesn't, to make him feel better, but I swallow that down. Actually, he's right. He *does* owe me an explanation.

'You know I spent some time in care as a child, don't you?'

I do. It was one of the first significant things he told me about himself, although he didn't go into details. I nod; then I climb up onto the bar stool beside him.

'I never knew my father. He was out of the picture before I was even born, so it was just me, Mum and Georgia. Georgia's quite a bit older than me. She wasn't around much. Mostly it was just me – and Mum.' He takes a deep breath. 'Mum was a complicated woman. Too intelligent, really, to be stuck home alone with a kid. She was … frustrated. And often took that frustration out on me.' He falls silent.

'How?' I hardly dare ask.

He shrugs. 'Oh, the usual. She'd feed me when she felt like it, and let me go hungry if she didn't. Sometimes she'd thrash me if she thought I'd done something wrong. Sometimes just because I'd looked at her the wrong way. Growing up with her was like walking on eggshells all the time. But at least she was there.' He pauses. 'Until, one day, she wasn't.'

We both sit in silence for a long moment.

'I came home from school and let myself in. it wasn't unusual for Mum not to be around after school. So I did my homework, found something to eat. It got later and later, and … she just … never came home. I never saw her again.'

My heart swells with shock and pity. 'How old were you?'

'Twelve.'

'How awful. What did you do?'

'Oh, what any self-respecting twelve-year-old would have done. I tried to bluff it out, for a couple of weeks, living hand-to-mouth, until one of my teachers caught me stealing from another kid's lunchbox. She couldn't get in touch with Mum, so she called the police. When they realised Mum had done a runner, they got in touch with Georgia at college. She was only nineteen. She could hardly give up her studies to look after me, so I went into care.'

I frown and say nothing.

But Alex can read my mind. 'Don't judge her harshly, Lisa. She was still a kid herself. And, really, she didn't know me that well. I don't blame her at all.'

I'm struck by how similar our stories are. An absent father. A neglectful mother. But at least I've always had Danny's love. I feel so sad for Alex that he never had that kind of support.

'Tonight,' he says, 'when I came home and the house was in darkness … There was no note, no phone message. Nothing saying where you'd gone. And you weren't picking up your phone. I …' His voice catches. 'I felt like I was twelve again.'

I grasp his hand, imagining that poor little boy, alone in a house as it grew dark. 'Oh God, Alex, I'm so, so sorry.'

He shakes his head vehemently. 'It's not your fault.

Obviously. But I want you to know, to understand, why I overreacted. I'm sorry. So sorry.' He takes my other hand and grasps them both, hard. 'You have to know I'll do anything to make this marriage work. Anything at all. I love you, and I love Bella, and I'll adore any kids we might have together.' His eyes are dark pools, drawing me in. 'I promise you I'm going to be the best husband and father ever.'

CHAPTER SIX

'Isn't Figgy very well?' asks Bella.

'I'm sure he's fine, sweetheart,' says Alex. 'We just want the vet to give him a quick look over, that's all.'

The puppy isn't interested in his food this morning and seems a bit lethargic. Given his adventures outside last night, we've made an emergency appointment, just in case.

'Can I come?' asks Bella.

Alex's eyes meet mine. We had planned for me to look after Bella while Alex took the puppy to the vet. Figgy and Bella will be too much of a handful for Alex to manage on his own.

'We'll all go together, shall we?' I suggest.

Bella nods, enthusiastic. Alex looks relieved.

Luckily, it turns out there's nothing much wrong with Figgy. The vet takes some blood and gives him a vitamin injection. He's already looking much brighter by the time we get home.

Willow calls just as we arrive back home.

'How are you?' she asks. 'More to the point, how is *Alex*?'

'Fine.' My eyes slide to Alex, who's helping Bella take Figgy out of his carrier. 'How did your run-through go with the understudy?'

'Okay, I suppose. She's quite good. She should just stick a dagger in my heart and get it over with.'

I laugh.

'You sound surprisingly upbeat.'

'Yes.' Alex is watching me. I smile at him.

'Okay,' says Willow. 'You can't talk. I get it. Listen, I'm on the train home. I don't suppose you could pick me up from the station, could you? I don't fancy battling it out at the taxi rank with this bloody boot on.'

'What time are you due in?'

'Three thirty.'

'I'll be there.' I hang up.

'Willow?' asks Alex.

I nod. 'She's on the train. I've said I'll pick her up.'

He doesn't look too delighted about that. I suppose he must know we're going to talk about what happened yesterday.

'That isn't a problem, is it?' I ask.

'Of course not.' He picks Bella up and squeezes her. 'I'm sure we can find something to do together this afternoon, eh, sweetheart?'

WILLOW'S TRAIN IS LATE. I have to hang around at Paddington for more than twenty minutes, keeping constantly on the move to avoid getting a ticket. Eventually I see Willow waving from the concourse entrance. She has a young railway guard and a trolley in tow, piled with her luggage. She waves me into a disabled parking spot.

I wind the window down. 'I can't park here.'

'Don't be daft. I *am* disabled. We're only going to be here a minute, and Reece says it will be okay.'

I assume Reece is the guard she has with her. I didn't think railway staff were supposed to help passengers with their luggage these days, but I doubt the poor boy had much choice. He has a slightly dazed look, like a bird that's flown into a window.

I leave the car running as Willow manoeuvres her moon-boot into the passenger seat, and I help Reece heave the suitcases into the back of the car. Willow blows him a kiss as we drive off.

I grin. 'Still haven't lost your touch, even with a face like Tyson Fury.'

She sighs. 'God, that was a nightmare. I don't know how disabled people cope, honestly I don't.'

'They'd cope better if people didn't park in their spaces.'

Willow pulls a face. 'Thanks for coming to get me.'

'No problem.'

'What did Alex say? Was he cross?'

I give her a sideways look. 'Not now. I'm driving.'

THERE'S a huge black and white cat on her doorstep when we arrive at her flat. It jumps out of the way as I thump the suitcases down. I'm completely out of breath, having hauled both cases and the hold-all up the stairs myself.

'This is the one I was telling you about. The one who wants me to feed it all the time.' Willow bends to pet it. 'He's a monster, isn't he?'

I can't argue with that. He must be ten times the size of Figgy. We have to keep pushing him aside to get Willow's cases into the flat, and he still manages to squeeze in with us just before we close the door.

'Don't worry,' she says. 'I'll chuck him out later.' She gives me an accusing look as she picks the mail up off the mat. There is quite a lot of it.

'I haven't been in yet,' I say in my defence. 'You've only been away a couple of weeks.'

She sighs as she puts the armful of mail on the hall table. 'I'd kill for a cuppa. But I don't have any milk.'

'Ta-dah.' I produce a small carton from my bag. 'Your wish is my command.'

'SO,' she says at last, when we've sat down on the sofa bed with our mugs. The big cat pushes itself onto Willow's lap.

'So?' I knew this was coming, but I've been dreading it.

'Yesterday was a bit of a shocker, wasn't it?' she says. 'I can't believe Alex just turned up like that, to drag you home. 'Tis a monster / begot upon itself, born of itself.'

I recognise the quote from *Othello*, and I'm stung. 'Alex isn't jealous. He was worried. His PA didn't pass his message on. And my phone was on mute.'

Willow scratches the cat's chin. She doesn't need to say anything; her disapproval is written all over her face.

I'm torn. Yes, Alex behaved badly, but his reaction was understandable in light of what he explained about his mum's abandonment. I can't imagine how he must have felt coming home to a dark, empty house, with no idea where Bella and I had gone. It must have been awful for him. I can't tell Willow any of that, however. I'd be betraying his confidence.

I shrug. 'It was just a storm in a teacup.'

'No. It wasn't. It's a massive red flag.' Willow leans forward, cat forgotten. 'Come on, Li. Surely you can see that?'

'I can see how it looks to you. I can, really. But there are things you don't know about.'

'Like what?'

'Stuff I can't tell you. It wouldn't be fair.'

'Okay.' She's silent for a while. 'There was a time you could tell me anything. Anything at all.'

That's true. Ever since we were at drama school together, we've shared all our secrets, from the silliest to the darkest. When she had her affair with a very well-known, very married TV presenter, I knew about it from the start. When David and I had our wobble the year before he died, I told Willow everything. And then when David was given his diagnosis, she was the person whose shoulder I cried on. But somehow this feels different. It *would* feel like a betrayal.

'This isn't really about me, Willow.'

She raises her eyebrows.

Anger prickles. 'What do you want me to do? Do you want me to leave him? I've just got married. And I love him ... I love you too, and I don't want to have to pick sides.'

She softens. 'Of course you don't. And that's the last thing I want. I just want you to be careful, that's all.'

'I will.' I finish my tea and stand up. 'I should be getting back.'

I try not to see her wounded expression as I head for the door.

CHAPTER SEVEN

The jarring tones of Alex's phone pull me out of sleep. I hear him talk into it, then swing his legs out of bed. He hangs up.

'What's that?' I ask, rubbing the sleep from my eyes.

'I have to go in.'

'On Sunday?'

'It's an SS gone wrong. Sorry, love. There might be political fallout.' He kisses me on the forehead. 'Don't forget we have the gala tonight. I promise I'll be back in time.' He heads for the ensuite, and I hear him turn the shower on.

I snuggle back under the duvet. I have no idea what an SS might be, and frankly I don't care. I'm completely drained after the emotions of the last couple of days. Last night, after Bella had gone to sleep, Alex had taken me to bed too, where he had made love to me slowly, with a thoroughness that left me shaking. Now I just feel blissfully numb.

For once, there's no one clamouring for my attention. Bella and Figgy are both still asleep. My dash to Bath on Friday already feels like a dream, almost as if it happened to someone else. I feel a twinge of guilt when I think about

Willow. She wasn't happy with the way we left things yesterday. But what was I supposed to say to her? Yes, I know Alex behaved badly, but he's carrying the burden of an abusive childhood on his shoulders. I shouldn't have to justify his behaviour to her. She's a big girl. She'll get over it. I'll call her later today, or tomorrow, to see how she is.

In all the drama, I'd almost forgotten about my own audition. Dinah wants an answer tomorrow. I doubt I'll get the chance to mention it to Alex tonight because we're going to the annual police charity gala. We have a babysitter lined up – the daughter of one of our neighbours on the estate, who Alex has known for a while. She's a steady-looking girl, who's studying for her A levels. Usually Willow would be my go-to, but because we thought she'd be in Bath, we had to make other arrangements. It will be the first time we've been out together since before the wedding.

I stretch luxuriously. Until this evening, Bella and I have a whole day on our own. What shall we do with it?

AT ONE TIME, on any given Sunday morning, you'd have found Danny on some sports field or other – football, rugby or shinty – but since he's left the force, he's struggled to stay active. The yoga was my attempt to get him moving again, but since the wedding, he's dropped it. As far as I know, he hasn't replaced it with anything else.

He looks surprised and bleary when he opens the door to his Isleworth flat, dressed in boxers and a T-shirt.

I'm dismayed. 'Have we woken you? It's half eleven. I thought you'd be up by now.'

'Why didn't you call?'

'Bella wanted to surprise you.'

'Uncle Danny!' Bella throws her arms around his legs. He kisses her on the cheek.

'Morning, Bells. Okay, ladies, give me five minutes to get some clothes on.'

As we wait, I have a little nose around his flat. It is very much a bachelor pad, with chunky leather chairs and nothing on the walls. Clean but with few homely touches, not even cushions. I try to tell myself I'm not looking for anything in particular, but, really, I'm looking for bottles or glasses. For a few months after he left the force, Danny used alcohol to keep his anxiety at bay. That was a real worry, given what had happened to Mum. After I found him passed out one lunchtime, we had a heart-to-heart. He promised he would go to therapy and try to give up the booze. I'm pleased to see there's no sign of any in the flat today, not even a beer in the fridge.

'What are you doing in there?' Danny surprises me. 'Are you hungry? I have eggs if you want breakfast?'

'No.' I close the fridge door. 'We can get something while we're out.'

I see he's used his five minutes productively. Shaved, and dressed in jeans and a checked shirt, he looks much brighter now. More pulled together. 'Okay, ladies. All present and correct. What do you have in mind?'

'I thought we might go for a walk in Kew. Feed the ducks.'

'Ducks!' Bella claps her hands. 'Yay!'

Danny looks doubtful. 'I suppose I might have a couple of slices of bread.'

'Actually, frozen peas are better. Better for the ducks.' I pat my bag. 'I have some with me.'

He grins. 'Glad to see you've come equipped.'

'Always.' I hesitate. 'Actually, I just need the loo. Can you help Bella on with her coat again? I won't be a minute.'

I dash into the bathroom. As I pee, I note with approval how clean it is. The fittings are old-fashioned, with black and white tiles and a terrible turquoise suite, but everything sparkles. As I'm about to wash my hands, I hesitate. The sink isn't quite clean. There's a fine residue of something on the edge of the basin. It looks like some kind of powder. White powder.

I bend down to look at it. It's not a cleaning product. So what is it? Cocaine? Worse? No wonder he looked so much brighter. Has he snorted a quick pick-me-up?

I open the bathroom cabinet. Behind Danny's shaving gear and the usual meds – ibuprofen, throat lozenges, sticking plasters – I find a clear plastic bag of pills. They're white, shield-shaped and stamped with a thumbs-up motif. I turn them over in my hand. What the *fuck*? Whatever they are, they're clearly not prescription.

I put the pills back. I don't know what to do. I don't want to take Bella out with Danny if he's high on something.

Luckily, I have my phone with me.

'Okay.' I bustle back into the living room, where Danny and Bella are both waiting on the sofa with their coats on. 'Change of plan. Georgia's taking Bella to feed the ducks.'

'What?' Danny gapes at me.

I avoid meeting his eyes. 'I'm going to drop her off at Georgia's. You're going to stay here. I'll be back in half an hour.'

IT TAKES me longer than I hoped to get to Georgia's, and even longer to prise myself away from a tearful Bella.

'I want to feed the ducks with Uncle Danny.'

Georgia's expression is frosty. 'If she doesn't want to be here, I think it's unwise to leave her.' She has a surprisingly plummy accent – much posher than Alex's.

'Please. It's an emergency.' I find it hard to stomach Georgia's holier-than-thou attitude after Alex's revelations, but right now, I have no choice. Am I overreacting? I don't think so. I give Georgia the frozen peas from my bag. 'She'll be fine once you get to the river.'

DANNY IS WAITING for me when I get back to his flat.

'What the hell's going on, Li?' he asks.

'You tell me.' I push past him into the kitchen and turn to face him. 'What is it you're taking? Coke?'

He looks at me blankly.

'I saw it on your bathroom sink. You didn't clear it up properly.' I don't mention the pills with the thumbs-up sign. I don't want him to know I went through the cabinet. God knows why he didn't make more of an effort to hide them.

His shoulders sag. 'It's not coke. It's MDMA.'

I blink with shock.

'Normally, I take it in tablet form, but you caught me on the hop this morning, and I needed a quicker fix. So I crushed one and snorted it. You really shouldn't just turn up out of the blue like that.'

I glare at him. 'Don't try to put this on me!' I throw my hands up. 'To think I was worried that you might be drinking again! I wish you were.'

Danny turns on me, furious. 'You have no idea what I'm dealing with. The flashbacks. The nightmares. I'm constantly waiting, waiting for the next blade to come at me.

This thing's a beast, Li.' His anger fades as fast as it flared. He drops onto a kitchen chair and puts his head in his hands. 'It has me in its jaws, and it's shaking me to death.'

I'm shocked by his vehemence. His despair. I sit down opposite him. We're silent for a while.

'The MDMA helps?'

'It does.' He runs a hand over his face. 'In the US you can get it on prescription for PTSD, but it's really tough to get here. Virtually impossible. I've tried other meds, but they barely touch the sides. Without the pills, without the MDMA ... it's as if there's a wall between me and the rest of the world. I can shout, scream, lose my mind, and no one can hear me.'

That sounds awful. Like hell on earth. But ...' I reach for his hand. 'What about the risks, Danny? As an ex-copper, won't they throw the book at you if anyone finds out?'

'You don't need to worry about that.'

I frown. 'What do you mean?'

'I mean the police aren't likely to come after me.'

I stare at him. How could he possibly know that? Then it dawns. 'Oh, my God. Is one of your friends supplying you?'

He takes his hand from mine. 'If I tell you, you've got to promise not to say anything.'

'Okay, but—'

He sits in silence for a drawn-out beat, and I sense he's not going to tell me. Then: 'He says it's clean, untraceable.'

'*Who does?*'

'Alex,' he says, twisting his fingers one over the other. 'Li, Alex is getting me the stuff.'

CHAPTER EIGHT

I couldn't be more shocked if Danny had punched me.

He takes my hand again. 'Don't tell Alex you know. And please don't judge him. The day after his stag do, in Amsterdam, he was with me when I had a full-on panic attack. It was the booze, I guess. It takes the edge off for a while, while I'm drinking, but afterwards ... Luckily, there was just the two of us left by then. He went out and got me something, off the streets.'

Dear God.

'Since then, he's been looking after me. It isn't just the pills. He's found me a trauma-focused therapist who really seems to be helping, and he's paying for it off the books. He's my friend, Li. Probably the best friend I've ever had.'

'A friend who's supplying you with a Class A drug.' I still feel like I've been punched in the stomach. 'It's illegal, Danny.'

'I know it's a lot to take in.'

'You think?'

'He's not doing it for me, Li. He's doing it for you. Because he loves you.'

Right.

I PICK Bella up from Georgia's, and we spend the rest of the afternoon quietly in the house. Figgy is pleased to have company, and he and Bella play together in the kitchen and even outside in the garden for a little while. It's good to see the puppy back to normal after his freezing ordeal, and to see Bella so happy. But I am distracted.

Where is Alex getting the MDMA? I suppose it must be quite easy for a policeman to source drugs. He must encounter plenty of dealers. Perhaps he's come to an 'arrangement' with one of them? Somehow, I can't imagine Alex skulking around alleyways or putting himself at the mercy of someone like that. Perhaps he's taking the pills from police stores? From evidence rooms? Security would be tight, of course, but Alex is pretty senior. However he's managing to get the pills, I hope he's covering his tracks. He'll lose his job if anyone finds out. Worse. He'd likely go to prison. I can't believe he's willing to risk so much for Danny.

I can't quite get my head around the fact that the two men I love are breaking the law, are taking such terrible risks.

It has to stop. We have to get Danny the treatment he needs from a legitimate source. I need to have it out with Alex without letting on what I know. But when? We have the gala tonight.

He arrives home as I'm giving Bella an early supper.

'Hello, hello!' He kisses my cheek and is about to do the same with Bella at the table, but sees she's smeared in cheese and pesto and thinks better of it. 'That looks tasty,' he says to her instead.

She nods and grins at him, dropping pasta.

'Do you think we should grab something, too?' he asks me. 'I doubt we'll eat much before nine.'

'I think we have some sausage rolls in the fridge.'

'Perfect.'

I watch as he rummages in the fridge. He looks so hand-some, so relaxed and in control. Who would guess, from the way he behaves, that he's taking such huge risks every day? If it were me, I'd be a bag of nerves. It begs the question – just how well do I know this husband of mine?

'What time's the babysitter coming?' he asks, around a mouthful of pastry.

'I asked her to be here at six.'

'Will that give you enough time to get ready? The car's coming at six thirty.'

I glance at the clock. Half five. I hadn't realised it was so late.

He sees my panic. 'You go up. I'll look after her ladyship. It'll only take me ten minutes to get ready.'

I HAD INTENDED WASHING my hair, but I don't have time, so I wear a cap in the shower instead and style it as best I can with heated tongs afterwards. I'm particularly pleased with my dress, a simple sheath of sage green silk. It goes beautifully with my new emerald earrings and shagreen clutch bag. I dither before I put it on. Underwear, or no underwear? The dress is so clinging it will show anything I wear underneath it, even a thong. No underwear, it is.

Alex comes in as I'm applying my final coat of

mascara. His hair is damp, and he's already wearing his dinner suit and dress shirt; he's so handsome my heart flips. I realise he must have got ready in one of the other bedrooms. He goes to get some cufflinks from his bedside cabinet.

'Lianne's here.' He sees my blank look. 'The babysitter? She's getting Bella into her PJs.'

'Great. I'm nearly done.'

His eyes travel over me. 'You look lovely.' But he's frowning. 'I thought you were going to wear your hair up tonight?'

'Was I?' I don't remember saying that.

'You wanted to show off your new earrings?'

'Oh.' I push my hair behind my ears to admire them in the mirror. The emeralds sparkle in the light. They are very beautiful, but he's right – my hair will never stay behind my ears. No one will see them.

Alex steps behind me, so close I can feel the heat of him through the silk of my dress. He gently takes my hair in his hands and twists it up onto the top of my head. His eyes meet mine in the mirror, intense and passionate.

'Up, I think. Don't you?' He kisses my neck.

'Okay.' I'd still prefer to leave it down, but I don't have the emotional bandwidth to argue right now. 'Don't blame me if we're late.'

He blows me a kiss as he goes out. 'It'll be worth the wait.'

I sigh and settle myself at the dressing table. Putting my hair up is never an easy task. There's too much of it, and it never behaves the way I want it to. I realise I have to take my earrings off again first, or they'll get tangled and make it twice as hard. I slip the earrings out of my ears.

As I do, I fumble and drop one. It lands on the floor, skitters across the polished boards, then disappears under the bed.

Shit!

I jump up to retrieve it. What if it's damaged? What would Alex say? My heart thumps at the thought.

I don't want to get my dress dirty or rip it, so I have to hoist it over my thighs to kneel on the floor. I peer under the bed. I can't see the earring, just dust bunnies. I grab my phone from the dresser and use the torch. The light helps. I can see the earring glittering, right up at the top of the bed, beside the wall. I shuffle along, stretching in as far as I can, but my fingertips can't quite reach. They touch something else instead. I have another look with my phone. I can just see the corner of something pale pushed between the floorboard and the skirting board. I manage to get hold of it with my fingernails and pull it out. A folded sheet of paper. The earring isn't quite so easy to retrieve. It keeps sliding away from me, but I eventually manage to pin it against the skirting board long enough to get a proper grip.

I stand up, breathless, and look at the paper. What is it, and what was it doing wedged between the floorboards? I jump as I hear a car horn outside. The taxi.

Shit and double shit!

I smooth my dress down and check the earring. To my relief it looks fine, just a bit dusty. I blow on it to clean it, and – finally – sit down to put my hair up.

By the time I'm finished, I've used almost all my kirby grips and the taxi has been waiting twenty minutes. I grab my wrap and clutch bag and go out onto the landing. Someone has already put Bella to bed – Alex, probably. Her door is open just a little, the way she likes it. I peek in. She's already breathing deeply, fast asleep, tucked in beside Teddy Pea. I tiptoe in to kiss her soft cheek. She stirs, but doesn't open her eyes. My heart swells, brimming with love. Love ... and fear. She's so small, so fragile, and the world is so unpredictable. How can I keep her safe?

THE GALA at Guildhall is much more lavish than I thought it would be. It's a charity event, the great and the good of the Metropolitan Police all there to support former and serving officers and their children. I see a few famous faces being snapped by photographers in the plaza outside.

'Relax,' says Alex as he takes my arm to lead me into the main hall. 'You're as tense as a board.'

The vaulted ceiling of the fifteenth-century great hall is bathed in lilac and blue light, and the room is dotted with dozens of round tables, lit with candles. We look for our names on the table plan and find our seats. Alex knows some of our companions – someone he was in training with and his wife, and a couple of forensic scientists and their partners. Conversation flows easily, buoyed by the wine and an atmosphere of bonhomie.

The evening starts with an auction, which goes on for an hour and a half. It seems a bit silly to me, with people – mostly men – competing with inflated offers on things they could easily buy for less. An exercise in willy-waggling. But I try not to think too unkindly of it, as it's all in a good cause. Alex bids on a couple of things and eventually wins a three-night trip for two on the Orient Express. I applaud with everyone else. I've always wanted to go on the Orient Express, but I can't help wondering what we will do with Bella. I can't imagine leaving her with anyone for more than a couple of nights. Not even Willow. And certainly not Danny.

I hate not being able to trust Danny with Bella at the moment, but I can't. He isn't himself. As much as I love him and know he wouldn't do anything deliberately to hurt her, I just can't take that risk while he's using any kind of drug.

As for Willow ... I feel a twinge of guilt when I think about her. I still haven't spoken to her since our argument about Alex's behaviour. I don't want us to be at odds about it. I'll call her tomorrow.

When the auction is done, a few people make speeches, and then – finally – we eat. The food is plentiful, but largely tasteless. After the meal, the dance floor is cleared for music, and tables empty as people go in search of drinks.

'Champagne?' asks Alex.

'Yes, please.' I watch him weave his way towards the bar.

I'm not alone for long.

'Mind if I sit with you a minute?' Kathleen Glover is wearing a demure black gown with a sweetheart neckline. I can smell Coco Mademoiselle.

She leans in to me, confidential. 'I love your dress. Very chic. And very daring of you to wear it with no underwear.'

I flash her an alarmed look. Is it that obvious?

To my surprise, she winks at me. 'If I had your figure, my dear, I'd do the same.'

We can see Alex has been waylaid on the edge of the room by Bill. His height means that he stands out even in a room of tall men. Alex laughs at something Bill has just said, his head thrown back. I can't help but admire his strong neck and movie-star teeth.

'Bill thinks a lot of him, you know,' says Kathleen. 'He says he'll go far.'

I give her a tight smile. What would her husband say if he knew Alex was supplying drugs to my brother? The thought is jarring. Surreal. A million miles away from the glitz and camaraderie of the evening.

Kathleen misinterprets my expression. 'Sure, you'll get used to it. Being a policeman's wife. You have to build up your own resources.' She pats my hand. 'It helps that you have your little girl, and it'll be grand when you have more children. They'll be your life, just as the force is his.'

I try to keep my dismay off my face. I'm not sure I want to live like that. I love being a mother. Adore it, even. But if that's all there is? I'm not sure it's enough.

Kathleen's eyes widen as she looks over my shoulder. 'Oh, there's Patricia. Excuse me, my dear, I just have to have a word with her.'

She leaves me sitting alone at the table. People squeeze past, either heading to the dance floor or to the bar or to catch up with other people. Eventually, Alex makes his way back to me with two glasses of champagne.

'Cheers,' he says, handing one to me. His face is flushed with the wine from the meal.

'Cheers.' I clink my glass against his and take a sip.

'Are you enjoying yourself?'

'Of course,' I lie. In fact, the evening has been an ordeal, which is strange, because ordinarily I love the energy and extravagance of these kinds of events. But I can't stop thinking about Danny and the bloody MDMA.

'Want to dance?'

I nod and take his hand. They're playing 'Come on Eileen' by Dexys Midnight Runners. I can't imagine dancing to something so energetic in this dress, but I'm tired of sitting down, and besides, I want to take my mind off Danny. Luckily, as we reach the dance floor, the music changes to a slower number. Alex holds me against him, his lips close to my ear.

'You look sensational,' he murmurs as we dance. 'There's not a man here who can keep his eyes off you.'

I make a non-committal noise. I'm not sure that's as flattering as he thinks it is. It just makes me uncomfortable. Perhaps I should have worn underwear? Or something different altogether? Something more suitable for a married woman, anyway. For a Kathleen Glover-in-waiting. I swallow.

'I have something to ask you.' I hadn't planned on raising it now, but the words slip out.

'Sounds intriguing.' He smiles down at me, teeth glinting in the ultraviolet lighting.

'What would you say to my working again?'

'Acting?' I feel his body stiffen slightly. 'I thought you didn't want to do that anymore.'

'I hadn't decided definitely. And Dinah has a part I'm interested in.'

'Dinah?'

'My agent.' I'm sure I've mentioned her name before. 'Bella's starting nursery tomorrow, and she'll be at school properly in the summer. I'm going to have more time on my hands.'

'Yes, but' – he stops dancing and frowns down at me – 'will you have enough?'

'It might take a bit of juggling. We might need a child-minder to fill in the gaps. But ... it's a very good part. A great opportunity. I told Dinah I'd let her know tomorrow if I wanted to audition.'

He says nothing, but I can almost hear his mind whirring.

'What do you think?' I prompt.

'I understand you want to have a career. I love you and want you to do what makes you happy, but ...'

I guessed there would be a 'but'.

'I don't want you to spread yourself too thin. I'd hate to see you get exhausted and frustrated.' He squeezes my hand, then starts dancing again. 'Let's talk about it later. When we get home.'

I nod. We can talk about the MDMA when we get home, too. Even though Danny doesn't want me to mention it to Alex, I've decided that I really need to have it out with him. A married couple shouldn't keep such big secrets from each other.

We don't get back to Twickenham until the early hours, and by the time Alex has escorted a sleepy Lianne home and we're both undressed, I can hardly keep my eyes open. I feel him kiss my cheek and slide into bed beside me. Just as I'm dropping off, the thought occurs – did he know this would happen? Did he know we'd both be too exhausted to talk properly tonight?

CHAPTER NINE

Alex has already gone to work when I wake up. His side of the bed is rumpled but empty, and his car isn't in the driveway. I'm puzzled. He didn't say he had an early start this morning. Is he trying to avoid me?

I'm probably just being paranoid. If he's as hungover as I am, I should feel sorry for him, not irritated. My mouth is sour, and I have a headache – too much champagne on top of the red wine. I can hear Figgy scratching at the kitchen door downstairs, and stirrings of movement on the baby monitor from Bella's room. It's such a comfort to hear her as she wakes, even though she's more than capable of letting me know she's up and about.

Then I remember, my little girl starts nursery today!

It takes a mammoth effort to get us both ready in time. It doesn't help that she changes her mind three times about what she wants to wear, which means stripping her down and starting again. Ordinarily, I'd refuse to do it and insist on her sticking with her first choice, but I don't want to rock the boat this morning. I need her to be on her very best behaviour. On our way out, I see she has Teddy Pea in her hand.

'I think Teddy should stay here. What if you lose him?'

'I won't.'

'I'll keep him safe. He can keep Figgy company and will be here waiting for you when you get back.'

'No.' Bella shakes her head, stubborn. I don't have time to argue, so I capitulate.

Everything starts off smoothly at the nursery. Mrs Wilson helps Bella take her coat off, then shows her where to hang her coat and bag. Bella is delighted she has her own name label under the hook, with ladybirds on it. She's introduced to two other little girls, who are playing with Duplo bricks. I sidle towards the door, but before I make it, she catches my eye. My guilt must be written all over my face, because her face crumples. She starts to wail. I hesitate, torn, in the doorway.

'It's best just to go,' urges Mrs Wilson. 'She'll calm down as soon as she realises you're out of earshot. Honestly.' She practically pushes me out the door. 'We'll see you at three.'

I flee, leaving my heart in Bella's hands, with the brightly coloured Duplo.

When I get home, I expect to find the house empty, but Mrs T is there, wiping down the kitchen counters. I'm a little dismayed. I would have liked some time on my own to collect my thoughts. I have a lot to think about – Bella, Danny, how I'm going to broach the subject of the MDMA with Alex. And the audition. Dinah said she wanted an answer today.

'Can I make you a cup of coffee, Mrs McMahon?' Mrs T – it stands for Tunbridge – looks nothing like a stereotypical cleaner. In her fifties, whip-thin, with exquisite bone structure, she looks like a well-preserved movie star.

'Mrs McMahon?'

I realise I'd drifted off. 'Lisa, please.' It doesn't matter how many times I ask her to use my first name, she never does. 'No. No coffee, thanks.' I check on Figgy, who's snoring in his crate, then wander out of the kitchen. I don't know what to do with myself. I'm horribly on edge. Enervated.

I remember I haven't put away my clothes from last night, so I hurry upstairs to do it before Mrs T can get there.

The bedroom is a mess; it smells of stale booze. I open the curtains and windows to let some air in, and hang my dress in the wardrobe. I know it seems silly, but a room is easier to clean if it's tidy. It's also less embarrassing. I put my earrings away carefully in my jewellery box. As I do, something catches my eye on my dressing table. It takes a moment to remember what it is – the paper I found tucked between the floorboards last night when I was looking for my dropped earring.

Curiosity piqued, I unfold it and read.

I don't know who might be reading this, but whoever you are, please, please keep reading to the end.
My name is Polly McMahon.

What the fuck? I blink. Read on.

My husband – Alex – is keeping me prisoner in this room. I'm too weak to get away. I think he's poisoning me. I've tried not eating the food he's giving me, but hunger always gets the better of me. I have to eat. I know this note won't save me; it's too late for that. But I have to do something, so I'm writing this and hiding it here in the hope that someone – please God not Alex – will find it eventually. If you do find it, I will probably be dead. I have no idea how he's going to kill me, but I know he will.

Please go to the police and tell them it wasn't an accident.

I can hear him coming now, up the stairs. I have to go. Please do as I ask. Please.

Polly

I hear footsteps on the stairs. A tap on the bedroom door. I jump, crumpling the paper quickly in my hand as Mrs T sticks her head in.

'Is it okay if I do upstairs now?' she asks.

'Sure,' I answer mechanically.

She looks at me, forehead creased. 'Are you okay, Mrs McMahon? You look like you've seen a ghost.'

'Fine. I'm fine.' I force a smile. 'Just a bit hungover, that's all. I'll get out of your way.'

I go downstairs. Was the note actually written by Polly? There's no reason to think it wasn't. But ... why would she do such a thing? As a prank? Some kind of joke?

I can't imagine Alex – my Alex – poisoning anyone or keeping them prisoner or killing them. Polly died in a car crash. She wasn't murdered.

'He made it look like an accident. He's very clever.'

No, no, no. Keira has it wrong. Polly was drunk. Perhaps she was drunk when she wrote the note? Or struggling mentally, like Keira?

In the kitchen, I smooth the note out to read it again. It's so heartfelt, so distressed, it brings a tear to my eye. What kind of desperation would drive a woman to hide a note like this in her own bedroom?

'*It's a massive red flag, Li.*' I hear Willow's voice.

My head is spinning. I hate not knowing the truth. Perhaps I should show Alex the note tonight when he gets home? I'm sure he'll have an explanation.

'*I want you to be careful.*' Willow again.

She's right. I have to tread carefully. I can't just go rushing in like I usually do.

CHAPTER TEN

The puppy was a mistake. Not my first, nor my biggest – that was letting Keira Benson get anywhere near Lisa – but it was still a mistake. The damn thing makes such a mess and chews everything it comes into contact with. It's ruined the kitchen floor and cabinets. When I think how much that kitchen cost, it makes me wince. The puppy has to go. I'll just take it out and dump it somewhere. Say it ran off. Bella will get over it. I'll buy her a rabbit or a guinea pig. Something easier to manage.

'... and, as you can see, our fiscal position for the next quarter needs to be communicated carefully to the staff ...' Mike Wishart's voice drones on, but I doubt a single word of his earnest presentation is going to sink in. It serves him right for scheduling a meeting today, the day after the gala. We're all hungover to various degrees. Even Bill is a little green around the edges.

Lisa looked sensational last night in that dress of hers. I could see every inch of her under that silk, every curve, every dip. Everyone else could see it too. I suppose I might have been jealous, but I wasn't. I enjoyed the envy of the other men. I harden at the memory, shifting in my seat a little to readjust. Mike's second in command, Shireen Rahvani, catches my eye. I smile at her and wink. To my surprise, she blushes, the blood in her cheeks softening her usual businesslike expression. Nice enough, I suppose, if you like that sort of thing. But it's not for me.

I'm a married man, anyway. A happily married man.

I adore Lisa. From the minute Danny introduced us, I knew she was going to be my wife. It was laughable, really, when I didn't know the first thing about her – she could have been married or even gay, for all I knew – but I swore she was going to be mine. And now she is, and I couldn't be happier. We're the family I've always wanted, but never had. I love Bella like a daughter, and I'm looking after Danny like a brother. Lisa and I are going to have children of our own. Lots of them if I can get her over this nonsense about wanting to act again. Everything's going to be different this time, different to how it was with Polly.

I'm sometimes tempted to blame myself for that, but really I shouldn't. Polly seemed just as perfect as Lisa at first, easy-going and hot – so hot – in bed. But all the time she was pretending. I was shocked to the core when I found out what she was really like, that she was a murderous bitch ...

'... audit of the evidential stores in Bermondsey ...'

Mike's words cut through my daydream. Shake me out of it. Did he say audit? In Bermondsey? He did. I want to stop him, to ask why his department feels that's necessary, but I can't afford to draw attention to myself. I let him drone on, uninterrupted, and I sneak a glance at Bill. Bill is nodding. He seems to think it's a good idea.

An audit could be awkward. I look at Mike, assessing

him. He doesn't earn anywhere near as much as the rest of us in the room, the people he's presenting to. His shoes are slightly scuffed; they're middle-end high street, at best. His shirt is the same. Debenhams or Next, probably. I think I can manage him nicely if it comes to it. And if nice doesn't work, well ... there are alternatives. Whatever the problem, there's always a solution. You just have to look hard enough to find it, and then have the nerve to see it through.

Just like the puppy. I've made a mistake, I'll sort it. If Mike ends up being a problem, I'll sort him too.

My future is all planned out. I'm not going to let anyone fuck it up.

I'M LATER than usual getting home, thanks to a snafu in my diary caused by my new PA. Luckily, Bella is still up in her PJs, waiting for me.

'How did my best girl get on at nursery today?' I swing her up into my arms. 'Did you have a good time?'

Bella nods, but she's clutching Teddy Pea as if her life depends on it. I look at Lisa.

'Mrs Wilson said she settled well.' Her eyes slide away from mine to Bella. 'You're looking forward to going again tomorrow, aren't you, chick?'

Bella nods again. I tickle her until she squeals, and put her back on the floor.

'I'm glad it went well,' I say to Lisa. 'I've been thinking about her all day.'

'Me too.'

I kiss Lisa. 'What have you been doing with yourself today?'

'Nothing much. Mrs T was here. And I've made a bourguignon for supper.'

'Great!' I expect her to mention her agent and the part she told me about at the gala, but she doesn't. I don't raise it either. I'm happy to kick that particular ball down the road. My stomach growls, and I realise I haven't had much of anything to eat all day. Lisa isn't a great cook, but she is improving. I might buy her some lessons for Christmas. 'Do I have time to shower and change first?'

Bella falls asleep over her supper, and I help carry her to bed. I love the feel of her in my arms, so small and vulnerable. It makes me feel strong, protective. I can't wait for us to have more kids.

Lisa and I have a quiet night together. I do some paperwork while she watches TV. She still doesn't mention her acting. I suppose she's come to her senses and thought better of it. That's a relief.

I reach for Lisa in bed, but she catches my hand.

'Sorry,' she says. 'I still have a headache. I've had it all day.'

'Oh no.' My cock is throbbing – a biological imperative – and I struggle to sound sympathetic. 'Poor you. Why didn't you mention it?'

'It's just a hangover. My own fault. I'll be fine in the morning.'

I kiss her cheek and turn over. My cock is stiff in my pyjamas, but it's nothing I can't sort myself, just this once.

A marriage needs to be give and take, after all.

CHAPTER ELEVEN

I freeze when Alex reaches for me under the duvet, grabbing his hand before it can explore any further.

'Sorry,' I lie. 'I still have a headache. I've had it all day.'

'Oh no. Poor you. Why didn't you mention it?'

I suffer a twinge of guilt at his concern. 'It's just a hangover. My own fault. I'll be fine in the morning.'

I know that's not true. I won't be fine in the morning. I won't be fine until I learn the truth about Polly. To my relief, he just kisses my cheek and turns over.

I lie in the darkness, listening to the thudding of my own heart. This evening has been a strain, pretending there's nothing wrong, pretending I haven't found Polly's shocking note. It's probably a hoax. Or a figment of a disturbed imagination. But even so, it's a struggle lying next to Alex tonight. Let alone making love with him.

Poor Polly. I don't know much about her at all. Alex told me she taught at a sixth-form college, and they'd met at a garden party. They were married for eighteen months before she died. I didn't push him for any more details because I didn't want to intrude on his grief, but I have seen a photo of them together, which he keeps in his study – she was a vivacious-looking brunette, with a wide smile and a penchant for fifties-style clothes. I remember the night I came across him on the landing, with Polly's cardigan in his hands. He looked so lost, so heartbroken. I have to admit, I was jealous. And worried. How on earth was I going to compete with his memories of her? Surely his tears, his grief, can't have been an act? Why on earth would he kill her? Did his jealousy get the better of him? There's no denying Alex is a jealous man, and jealousy is dangerous. *'Tis a monster begot upon itself, born of itself.*

All these thoughts chase each other through my head as I lie beside my allegedly murderous husband.

After a little while, I feel him start to move rhythmically. He must think I'm asleep. After a minute he stifles a groan, then stops moving. Then he gets up to go to the bathroom.

I squeeze my eyes shut and pretend I'm asleep.

'I WAS WAITING for your call yesterday.' Dinah's voice is sharp over the phone. 'Why didn't you call me?'

'Sorry. I have been thinking about it.'

'And?'

'The timing isn't right just now, Dinah.' I can't imagine trying to work, or even auditioning, when I have so much else hanging over my head. Danny. Alex. Polly.

Dinah's silent, but not for long.

'In this business, if people stop seeing your face around, you might as well not exist. You do realise that?'

'I do. And I'm sorry. Honestly, I am. Perhaps one of your other clients would like to audition?'

'Okay. Now you're really worrying me. Since when did you concern yourself with my other clients?' Dinah's tone softens a little. 'Is that it, then? Have you thrown in the towel for good?'

'Honestly? I don't know.'

'You'd better make your mind up, Lisa. And do it fast. Or the decision will be made for you.'

'I understand that. I do. I promise I'll let you know soon.'

I hang up, stomach churning with disappointment. I *do* want to act again, and I'm gutted to lose the chance of trying for this part, but it really is the least of my worries right now. I turn to Bella, who is putting on her shoes on the kitchen floor, fastening and unfastening them. She's only just got the hang of Velcro, and it still delights her.

'Do you want cucumber or some tomatoes?'

'Cumber.'

'Please.'

'Please.'

I slice some batons of cucumber and push them in beside the sandwiches. Mrs Wilson said Bella didn't eat much lunch yesterday, so today I've made her a lunchbox. I know it's mollycoddling her, and know it will probably come back to bite me on the backside, but at the moment I don't have the capacity to take anything but the path of least resistance.

As I put the lunchbox into Bella's bag, I somehow drop the tea towel into the sink full of dishwater. Cursing under my breath, I open the drawer to find a clean one and instead find something else: Keira's red beanie. The piece of paper she gave me is still tucked inside it. It has a Dagenham address on it – not an area I know at all. In spite of Polly's bizarre note, I still don't believe Keira's accusations. Of course I don't.

But ... maybe it wouldn't hurt to return her hat? I don't have anything else I particularly need to do today.

After making sure Figgy has plenty of puppy pads in his enclosure, we head out. I know it's not fair to leave him on his own, but I do have a life, which is something Alex never took into consideration when he brought the puppy home.

All the same, I do hope Figgy will be okay. I have no idea exactly when I'll be back.

AFTER I'VE DROPPED Bella at the Pumpkin Patch, it's a real slog to get through the city and onto the A13 heading east. Luckily, I manage to find a parking spot close to the address in Dagenham. It's a ground-floor flat on the Becontree estate, just off the main road through the estate. There are no signs of life. The curtains are closed, and no one answers my ring or my knock.

'I don't think she's home, love.' A woman with a ponytail sticks her head out of the flat above. 'I haven't seen her for weeks.'

'Oh. Never mind. Thanks.'

She thumps her window closed again, but I can sense her there, still watching me. I dither, embarrassed, on the path. What should I do now? At the very least, I should return the hat. The glass in the front door is cracked, and it's boarded on the inside, but there is a letterbox. I take the red beanie from my pocket and start stuffing it through.

To my astonishment, the door swings open.

'Hello? Keira?' I call out. She must be in. She's not likely to have gone out and left the door unlocked. I tiptoe down the hall. 'Keira, are you here?' The flat is icy cold, and it smells musty, as if it hasn't been aired for a long time. There's another smell too. Something metallic, slightly sweet. I push the kitchen door open.

It is a state. Drawers have been pulled out, the contents dumped onto the floor. The fridge is open, and there's a carton of milk spilled on the counter. Has Keira been burgled? All my senses are tingling, as if there's an electric current passing through my body.

'Keira?'

The living room door is ajar. I go to it, push it open.

At first, I don't understand what I'm seeing. This room has been ransacked too, with cushions torn apart, stuffing everywhere, drawers tipped out. But that isn't what catches my attention. In the centre of the floor, where you might expect to find a rug, there's a large pool of black, congealed liquid. The edges are dark brown and clotted. I recognise the source of the metallic smell. My stomach lurches as I clutch my hand to my mouth. Dear God. What's happened? Where has all this blood come from? Is Keira's body somewhere here in the flat?

I flee.

When I get back to the car, I have to sit on my hands to stop them from shaking. I finally lose the fight against my body, and I open the car door to empty the contents of my stomach into the gutter. I close the door again and wipe my mouth. I need to *think*. Is Keira dead? There was so much blood, she must be.

Another thought pops into my head. The police might think *I* did it. I've definitely left my prints on the door handle and on the windowsill outside. I'm tempted to go back, to wipe everything down, but force myself to think logically. What if the police *do* find my prints? I don't have a police record, and they have no reason to think of me as a suspect.

But I can't just walk away from what I've found.

What if Keira *is* in there? If she is, how long has she been there?

I have to tell the police. I'll just have to do it anonymously.

I go on my phone, search 'public phone Dagenham' and see there are some new Wi-Fi phone boxes in Barking town centre. I'm surprised they're even installing new public phones these days, but I'm very glad they are.

I drive to Barking, parking as close to the town centre as I dare. There's bound to be CCTV on the streets, but there isn't a lot I can do about that. Or is there? I rummage around on the back seat for a bag of clothes I intended to drop off for charity, and find the oversized, ratty old hoodie I used to wear for gardening. There's a face mask in the glove box, left over from Covid times. My hair is probably my most distinctive feature, so I tie it back with my scarf, then hide it under the hood of my hoodie.

I walk into the town centre, adopting the stumbling gait of Sheena, the addict I played in *Casualty*. I must nail it, because no one looks at me twice. Actually, no one even looks at me once – not properly – they just give me a wide berth on the pavement. Eventually, I spot one of the sleek black phone boxes on the high street. It only occurs to me as I approach it that I'll probably have to use my bank card to make a call. My heart sinks. That's no good. No good at all. I peer into the box, on the verge of abandoning my plan, when I see a dedicated Emergency button. It's free. Of course it is. My head is so scrambled, I'm really not thinking straight at all.

'*Emergency services. Which service, please?*'

'Police.'

She puts me through to the police switchboard, and I use a newly downloaded app to disguise my voice as I give Keira's address. 'You have to come quickly. There's a dead body.'

I hang up again, heart pounding. Will that be enough? It should be.

After they've found the blood and the body – if there is one – the police will start an investigation. One that will lead to whoever has killed her.

To Alex?

I really don't want to think about that, but force myself to. I told Alex Keira had proof he'd killed Polly. That, combined with the desperate note Polly hid, is pretty convincing circumstantial evidence. My blood runs cold at the thought, but I can't deny it anymore.

My husband – my handsome, charming new husband – could be a killer.

TO MY SURPRISE, Alex's car is already in the drive when Bella and I arrive home a few hours later.

'Yay!' Bella claps her hands as I get her out of her car seat. 'Ali's here.'

She runs to the front door, but it's locked. She stands on her tiptoes to reach the bell.

'Don't do that, sweetheart; we can go round the back.'

My keys are in the bottom of my bag, but I can't be bothered to rummage for them. If the back door's locked, I can use the utility room key I keep under a plant pot on the patio in case I ever lock myself out. Alex doesn't know about it, of course. He's too security conscious for old tricks like that.

We go through the garden gate, then down the side of

the house. The lights are on in the kitchen. My hand is on the door handle, and I'm about to try the door when I freeze.

Alex is kneeling on the floor, with his hands in a bucket. I fight to get my head around what I'm seeing. Has Figgy made a mess again? Is Alex cleaning up? But no. Whatever he has in his hands is moving – struggling – as it's being pushed down into the water. Figgy! My heart jumps into my throat. What's even more shocking is Alex's expression. Or rather the lack of it – there is no emotion at all on his face as he tries to drown the dog.

I burst in through the door – thank God it isn't locked. 'What the hell are you doing?'

Alex pulls the puppy out of the water, his face betraying his surprise.

'I'm giving it a bath. What does it look like?'

I can't even begin to say what it looks like. I pull myself together.

'A bath? In cold water? With no soap?' I move to take the puppy from him, but he grabs my forearm, gripping it painfully hard. I gasp and look into his eyes. Usually they're dark brown, but now they're black, pupils dilated. With pleasure? He tightens his grip until I moan with pain. He's hurting me deliberately. And he's enjoying it.

Eventually, he remembers the role he's supposed to be playing. He smiles and releases his grip.

'I've never given a puppy a bath before,' he says casually.

I grab a towel from the rail and take Figgy from him. I clutch the shivering, soaking little body to my chest. I have to make light of this, as distressing as it is.

'A puppy needs warm water,' I say, ignoring the pain shooting up my arm. 'I'll show you how to do it. We can all give him his first bath together.'

'Can we do it now?' asks Bella eagerly.

'Tomorrow. It's your turn now. Come on, let's get you upstairs.'

I'm relieved to steer Bella and Figgy out of the kitchen, away from Alex. I lock us all in the bathroom, then turn on the bath taps.

'Why are you crying?' asks Bella.

'I stubbed my toe on the stairs.' I try to pull myself together. 'Come on, get your clothes off.'

I help her undress, then finish running the water.

'Can Figgy come in too?'

'No. The bubbles will hurt his eyes.'

I sit and watch Bella as she plays with the foam, but I don't really see her. I can hardly believe what's just happened. My forearm is red and swollen, already starting to bruise in the shape of Alex's fingers. It was alarming enough to see Alex's eerie lack of expression as he pushed Figgy into the bucket, but that wasn't nearly as traumatising as his physical assault on me. He knew he was hurting me, and he didn't care. Worse, I think he enjoyed it.

I knew, theoretically, that Alex might be capable of murder.

But none of this is theoretical.

I know now that Alex is dangerous. Really, really dangerous.

CHAPTER TWELVE

'Where did you get to today?' asks Alex casually as he pours himself a glass of wine.

'Nowhere in particular.' I pull my sleeve down to cover my bruises.

'You were out all day.'

I frown. How does he know that?

He nods towards the security camera high in the corner of the kitchen. 'I check in every now and then. Just to make sure you're okay.'

Of course. He did tell me that the cameras around the house, driveway and garden were connected to his phone. How had I forgotten that?

'I went to the gym. And got my hair done.' The second part is true. After I made it back from Dagenham, I had just enough time to grab a quick blow-dry before I picked Bella up from the nursery. I thought I might need an alibi, and I was right. All the same, his interrogation unnerves me. I can't quite believe we're having this conversation, as if he hasn't just tried to drown the dog, as if he hasn't just assaulted me. I should challenge him, bring everything out into the open, but Bella is here, and I can't risk him turning physical again.

'What kind of day have you had?' I ask, to deflect. 'Good, I hope?'

'Oh, you know. Same old, same old. Glad to get home to you and Bella.'

He takes his wine over to the French doors, where Bella is playing with Figgy. The puppy seems none the worse for his ordeal in the bucket.

Alex kneels on the floor beside them and strokes Bella's cheek.

All the hairs stand up on my arms and the back of my neck. I can't bear for him to touch her, but I'm determined not to show it. I've promised myself I won't do my usual thing of rushing in without thinking. Alex is dangerous. I need time, time to get my head around that shocking fact, time to formulate a plan. In the meantime, I need to act normally. I can't afford to overreact, do anything that might arouse his suspicions, or disagree with anything he says. I'm only just beginning to realise how hard that's going to be.

When he kisses Bella's forehead, I want to scream. Every cell in my body is telling me to grab her and run. Instead, I sit on the sofa beside them, letting an indulgent smile play on my lips.

He smiles back up at me. 'I'm so glad I found you. I can't imagine being without you both, now.'

I force myself to squeeze his shoulder. 'And we're glad we found you.'

'You'd never leave me, would you?' His tone is light, but his eyes are intense.

'Leave you? Why on earth would we leave you?'

He shrugs. 'I don't know. It's what people seem to do. Mum. Polly.'

I can't meet his eyes. 'Polly didn't leave you.'

'I know that. Not intentionally.'

No. Not intentionally. 'I'm not going to leave you,' I say.

'Glad to hear it. I don't know what I'd do if you did. Kill myself, probably.' He grins. 'Or you.' His smile doesn't reach his eyes.

I stare at him. How do I react to that? I decide to laugh, to make light. 'Well, that's nice, I must say. Thank you, Mr Bluebeard.' It's a terrible, shocking thing to say. Why is he saying it now? Is he picking up on something subconsciously? The worst thing is, I believe him, one hundred per cent.

He's laughing too, as if it weren't true. 'Oh, I nearly forgot.' He gets to his feet. 'I've bought you a present.'

'A present?'

He disappears into the hall and comes back carrying a box. It's exquisitely wrapped, with striped metallic paper and a frothy bow. Bella squeals with excitement when she sees it.

'Open it! Open it!'

He puts it on the kitchen counter, lifting Bella up so she can watch me unwrap it. It's the newest version of the iPhone.

'You shouldn't have,' I say, baffled. 'There's nothing wrong with my old one.'

'Don't be daft, it's ancient. Look, this one has a two-in-one camera and AI. I'll help you set it up tonight, if you like.'

So that's how we spend our evening after Bella has gone to bed. On reflection, I'm not so surprised by his extravagance. Alex always likes to have the latest, shiniest new gadget, so it's no surprise he likes his wife to have it too. If I'm honest, I'm glad he has something to distract him.

A couple of hours later, when everything's been transferred from my old phone, and the new one is working to Alex's satisfaction, I look at my watch and give an exaggerated yawn.

'You know what? I'm done in. I think I'll have an early night.'

'Mmm.' He slides his hand onto my thigh. 'Great idea.'

My heart plummets. I managed to avoid sex last night by saying I had a headache. I don't think I can use that excuse again. It's hard to believe that only a couple of days ago, he only had to look at me a certain way to get me in the mood. Now I'd rather sleep with a tankful of crocodiles. I put my hand over his to stop it sliding any further north.

'But,' I protest, 'it's very early. Isn't it too early for you?'

'Not at all. It's never too early to make love to my beautiful wife.'

I have no choice, not if I don't want him to suspect anything.

I give the performance of my life, sighing when I should be sighing, touching Alex where I should be touching him, and coming to a moaning, shuddering, entirely bogus climax.

Really, they should give me an Oscar.

I DON'T FEEL QUITE SO pleased with myself this morning. In fact, I feel disgusting. After Alex has left for work, I put Bella in front of a cartoon, while I stand under a long, scalding shower. But no matter how hard I scrub, I just can't feel clean. The bruises on my forearm are a nasty shade of green and black. I feel like I've been branded – 'Property of Alex McMahon'.

I go back downstairs in my joggers and sweatshirt, with my hair still wet. Bella isn't going into nursery today, so we can take our time this morning. I make us both some breakfast, eggs on toast. When it comes to it, I can only eat a few mouthfuls before my stomach rebels. I'm lucky to keep anything down.

I'm having second thoughts about my anonymous call. With hindsight, it seems a cowardly thing to do. Plus, it's killing me not knowing whether the police have responded. I scan the news online to see if there have been any discoveries in Dagenham, but there's nothing.

My mobile rings. Willow!

'Hi, Li,' she says, 'how's things? I thought I'd call and see if you're still talking to me.'

'Of course I am. I've been meaning to get in touch, but things have been a bit mad here lately.' Understatement of the century!

'Fancy some company? I could hobble over there to see you?'

'No. You're okay.' I glance up at the camera in the corner. 'How about if we come to you? Is it okay if the dog comes too?'

When I hang up, I dare to feel hopeful. Willow has no more power than I do, but at least she might be able to help me make sense of the whole thing.

If anyone's going to believe Alex is capable of murder, it's Willow.

WE FIND her standing in her bedsit, adrift in a sea of fabrics, feathers and fake fur.

'I've decided to have a clear-out,' she says, hands on hips. 'Now I have some time on my hands, I might as well do something useful with it.' She sees my expression and immediately sobers. 'What? What is it? Has somebody died?' She knows me too well.

'Help me get Bella settled, and I'll tell you.'

We make Bella a little nest with my laptop, putting my headphones on her so she can watch *In the Night Garden*.

'What is it?' urges Willow. 'Tell me now, for God's sake. The suspense is killing me.'

'Do you remember the woman who gate-crashed the wedding reception? The woman Tommy Becker escorted out?'

Willow nods. 'Alex said he was going to tell you who she was.'

'He didn't.' I shake my head. '*She* did. She came to the house.'

Willow frowns.

'She's Polly's sister. She wanted to warn me. You're not going to believe this, Willow, but she told me Alex murdered Polly.' I see Willow's blank expression. 'His first wife.'

'I know who *Polly* is.' Willow's tone is acerbic. 'What I'm struggling to get my head around is the bit before that ... the bit where you say Alex *murdered* her.'

'I think you'd better sit down,' I say. 'This could take a while.'

I tell her about Keira and her accusations, about Alex's reaction to them, my visit to Keira's flat, the blood I found there, and my anonymous call to the police.

'You think he's *killed* her?' Willow's eyes are huge with shock.

'Shhh.' I glance nervously at Bella. 'Keep your voice down. I think it's possible. If not him, then someone has.' I hesitate. 'There was so much blood.'

'Oh, my God.' Willow clutches poor Figgy to her chest in horror. Luckily, he doesn't seem to mind. 'What are you going to do?'

'I have no idea.' But I do feel calmer now. Better for having shared what I know. I can always count on Willow; I don't know how I could ever have considered falling out with her.

'I suppose you have to decide if you want to go to the police,' she says, 'and tell them everything.'

'I'm not sure Polly's note and Keira's warning is enough for them to take me seriously. They might say that Polly's note just sounds melodramatic. Hysterical, even. And what Keira claimed about it not being an accident is hearsay unless we find whatever proof she was talking about.'

'She's dead now. Surely that's too much of a coincidence?'

I shrug, feeling utterly hopeless. 'Unless the police find something in her flat that connects her with Alex, I can't see that her death is going to make any difference. He's a chief superintendent. He probably has the power to make it all go away. And then what? Will he tell everyone I'm mentally unstable? Lock me in the bedroom like Polly? What would happen to Bella?' I realise I still haven't told Willow everything. Not quite. 'And there's another reason I can't go to the police.'

'What?'

'Danny.'

Willow scowls. 'Danny?'

I take a deep breath. It's all so complicated. 'Alex is supplying him with MDMA to treat his PTSD.'

It takes a while for that to sink in. 'I had no idea it was so bad.'

'He doesn't say much about it, but he is suffering. Really, really suffering. The MDMA helps, apparently. If I tell the police *everything*, I'll have to tell them about the MDMA. And if I *don't* tell them about the MDMA, there's a fair chance Alex will. Or, at least, he'll tell them his version of the truth. I wouldn't put it past him to throw Danny under the bus if it means saving himself.'

'Bloody hell.' Willow rakes her fingers through her hair. 'That's awful. Do you think we should tell Danny what's going on? He needs to know that this could all blow up.'

'I don't know.' I'm torn. On the one hand, we probably should warn him. On the other ...

I can hear Danny's words in my head. *He's my friend, Li. Probably the best friend I've ever had.*

'I'm not sure Danny will believe me,' I say. 'He thinks the world of Alex.'

Willow frowns. 'But—'

'Danny's my brother, Willow, and I know he loves me, but I'm not sure he'd take my word over Alex's. I don't think we can risk it.'

We lapse into thoughtful silence.

Willow speaks first. 'We need something solid to take to the police. Proof. God knows where we're going to get it from.'

'Keira's flat was a mess. I think Alex must have searched it. Perhaps he found whatever it was she said she had.

Perhaps he has it now?' Even as I say that, I know I'm clutching at straws.

Willow gives me a look.

'No. You're right,' I say. 'Whatever it was, he'll have destroyed it.'

She sees my bleak expression. 'Let's not give up hope,' she says. 'In the worst-case scenario, he's killed two people. Stolen drugs. He has to have left some evidence somewhere. We just need to find the proof.'

'Easier said than done.'

'In the meantime, if he's as dangerous as this all makes him sound, we have to get you and Bella away from him.'

I nod, devastated.

'Do you think he'll let you take her away for a break somewhere? Just the two of you?'

'I doubt it. He's clearly so possessive. Look what happened in Bath.'

Willow nods at the memory. 'Good point. What about doing a runner?'

'I don't think we'd get very far. It might be different if it was just me on my own, but with Bella I couldn't move quite as fast. Plus, I'd be pretty easy to track down. He has a whole police force at his disposal.' I hesitate. '*And* ... he said if we leave him, he'd—'

'What?'

'He said he would either kill himself or us.'

Willow's eyebrows rise in horror. 'Was he joking?'

'He pretended he was, but I don't think so. He's definitely capable of it.' I shake my head, tears threatening as the situation overwhelms me. 'He tried to kill the dog yesterday.'

'He *what?*' I'd thought Willow's eyes couldn't get any rounder, but I was wrong.

'I know it sounds crazy, but I caught him trying to drown Figgy in a bucket. If we'd arrived home even a minute later ...' I can't finish that sentence. 'And ...' I push my sleeve up to show her my forearm. She stares at the ugly mass of yellow bruising.

'Oh my God. He did that to you? You can see his fucking *fingerprints,* Li. We have to get you away from him. We have to.'

'I can't believe I ever thought he was my knight in shining armour.' I can hear the self-pity in my voice. 'The worst of it is you tried to warn me, didn't you?'

Willow nods. 'I suppose I've always felt there was something not quite right about him. Something off ... But that wasn't it, not really. I think I was just shocked by how fast it all happened. And if I'm perfectly honest, I was jealous too.' She gives a sad, wry grin. *''Tis a monster / begot upon itself.'*

I squeeze her hand.

'You shouldn't blame yourself,' she says. Then she grins properly, her eyes sparkling. 'Okay, maybe you should, just a little bit. It'll make me feel better.'

I laugh and wipe my tears away. Her pixie features turn serious again.

'We need to buy some time. Some breathing space.' She looks confounded. 'You don't feel safe going to the police, you can't do a runner, and you really, really can't stay where you are. I don't see ...' She breaks off. Her eyes fly to mine.

'What?' I say.

'There *is* an answer.'

'Is there?'

She nods. 'It's staring us in the face.'

I carry on looking at her blankly.

'It won't be easy, but I think you can pull it off.'

My eyes widen, incredulous. 'You're not thinking what I think you're thinking?'

Willow nods, her expression brimming with the gravity of what she's suggesting, and ... can I detect just a trace of glee?

CHAPTER THIRTEEN

'So you're telling me she isn't dead?' In the squalid living room of Keira Benson's Dagenham flat, Detective Inspector Derek Mbala gives me a look of disbelief.

'Yes.'

He eyes the congealed pool on the floor. 'This is a hell of a lot of blood.'

'She'd cut her wrists. I found her just in time.'

'There's no record of an ambulance attending.'

I frown. He's done his homework on the address before attending the scene. Just my luck to get one of the plods who are halfway competent.

'There wouldn't be a record, Inspector. You know what response times are like round here. It was faster to take her to hospital myself.'

Mbala is silent for a moment, considering my revelation. 'When was this, sir?'

'Two weeks ago. The fourteenth.'

He returns my gaze steadily. I can almost hear his tiny mind whirring. I straighten the epaulette on my uniform – it can't hurt to give him a subtle reminder who it is he's talking to.

'Sir, I hope you don't mind if I verify what you've told me.'

Irritation flares, but I mask it. 'Of course not. You have to do your job. Check with Bellfield; they'll back up everything I've told you.'

'Bellfield? Bellfield Psychiatric Hospital?'

Now I let my irritation show. 'My sister-in-law suffers from severe borderline personality disorder. She'd just cut her wrists. I was hardly going to take her to sit on a plastic chair in bloody A&E. She needed to be somewhere she would be looked after properly. Protected from herself.'

'Yes, sir. Of course, sir.' Mbala frowns. 'It's quite a mess in here. It looks like it's been turned over.'

'I assume she must have done it herself. Before she cut her wrists.'

'What about clear-up?'

'I'll sort it.'

I look around the room, at the disembowelled cushions, the empty wine bottles, the cigarettes stubbed out into glasses, glossy interior magazines stacked incongruously beside black plastic binbags rammed with God knows what. The pathetic remnants of a pathetic life. It'll all end up either in a landfill or incinerated, which is fine by me. More than fine.

It had been a surprise when Keira turned up at the house, claiming to have proof I'd killed Polly. What kind of proof could she possibly have? Of course, I had to find out. She was shocked when she opened the door to this squalid place. Terrified, even, which was gratifying, but she still wouldn't tell me what her so-called proof was or where I could find it. I laced her wine with a couple of roofies and forced her to drink it, which gave me plenty of time to search the flat. Then I cut her wrists. In the end, though, I decided not to let her die. It wasn't necessary – she can't touch me where she is now. I'm not a monster.

I can feel Mbala's eyes on me through the window as I walk down the path and get into my car.

Fuck him. And fuck whoever it was tipped off the police. It was probably kids or a passing tweaker, looking for somewhere safe to score. Is it possible they found Keira's 'proof' before they made their anonymous call? Very, very unlikely, when I'd already given the place a going-over. It had probably never existed anyway. But even so, the possibility of someone else finding it – remote as it is – makes me twitchy. It's a loose end, and I hate loose ends. They always come unravelled.

I make a call.

'Superintendent, sir. How did it go?'

'It's a sad business, Tommy, very sad, but thanks for giving me the heads-up. I appreciate it.'

'Anytime, sir. Glad to help.'

'I want you to do me another favour. I want you to find out where the 999 call was made from, and get me a recording.'

'No problem, sir. I'll get onto it.'

CHAPTER FOURTEEN

'Wake up, sweetheart.'

As I struggle through the fog of sleep, I feel Alex's lips on mine. I jerk awake.

'Rise and shine, sleeping beauty,' he says. He smiles down at me proprietorially.

I push myself up on my pillow and rub my eyes. 'What time is it?'

'Almost ten.'

What the *fuck*?

'I just let you sleep,' he says. 'You seemed so exhausted.'

That's true. My revelations to Willow yesterday took a lot out of me, emotionally and physically. But I'd hoped I was hiding it better.

'Where's Bella?'

'I've taken her to nursery.'

'Why aren't you at work?'

'I have the day off, remember?'

Did he tell me he wasn't working today? I don't think he did. In fact, I'm certain he didn't. When he kisses me on the cheek, it takes all my willpower not to flinch away. His gaze drops lower, to the bruises on my forearm. They are completely black now, stark against the white of my skin and the sheet. I move my arm, intending to hide it under the covers, but to my astonishment, he catches hold of my wrist. He inspects the bruises, then gently kisses them.

'Come downstairs when you're dressed. I have a surprise.' He goes out.

I lie there, speechless. Every time I think I have the measure of Alex, he does something to surprise me. What was that kiss about? An apology? I don't think so. It felt more like a warning. And now he says he has another surprise? I don't think my nerves can stand it. I shower and dress as slowly as I can. The thought of spending a whole day with Alex is frankly terrifying.

The surprise is a breakfast of French toast and bacon with maple syrup. Slightly cold, but – I have to admit – delicious. Luckily, it stays down.

'What do you want to do today?' he asks, biting into a rasher of bacon. 'I thought we might go slumming it in the West End.'

'Actually, I have a doctor's appointment at twelve.'

'Oh?' His look of surprise morphs quickly into one of hope. His gaze drops to my stomach.

'No, it's not that.' I hurry to disabuse him. 'Sorry.'

He tries to mask his disappointment. 'Nothing serious, I hope?'

'I think I'm getting a UTI,' I lie. 'It's best to knock it on the head early doors.'

Something flashes across his face. Irritation? Distaste? Good. If it stops him from trying to have sex with me, even for a little while, that's a massive bonus.

'So it's just me and Figgy, then,' he says.

'Actually, I'm taking him with me. He's due his second lot of inoculations today, so we'll do that after I've been to the doctor's.'

'I can do it, if you like?'

'Don't be daft. The doctor is practically next door to the vet's.'

He lapses into silence for a while, pushing his French toast around his plate.

'You're going to leave me completely on my own? I'm not sure why I bothered taking the day off.'

Neither am I. I want to point out that if he'd told me he was doing that, I wouldn't have made the appointments with the doctor and the vet. But, of course, I bite my tongue and say nothing. No point rocking the boat. Instead, I kiss him.

'That was delicious! Thank you.' I stand up. 'If I don't go and dry my hair, I'll miss my appointment.'

'THANKS FOR FITTING me in at such short notice.'

'That's okay, Mrs McMahon. What can I do for you today?' My new GP, Dr Jennifer Fulton, a severe-looking woman in her fifties, examines me over the top of her specs.

'I don't know where to begin, really.' That's true. I twist my handkerchief in my hands. The doctor's silent, watching me. 'Lately ... I suppose lately, I've been feeling ... low. Very low.'

'In what way?'

I shrug. 'It's a struggle to get out of bed. A struggle to do anything, really. I feel like I've been going through the motions.'

'How are you sleeping?'

'Not great. I drop off pretty fast, but wake up again at one, two o'clock in the morning and can't go back to sleep. There's so much going on in my head.'

'Is there anything particularly on your mind? Anything troubling you?'

'Not particularly.' I give a hollow laugh. 'Unless you count the existential horror of being alive.'

She doesn't smile. 'When did you start feeling like this?'

'I don't know. Since just after Bella was born, I suppose. And it's gradually been getting worse. Yesterday, I realised I needed help. I don't think I can do this on my own.' I let a tear fall, wipe it away with my handkerchief.

'You say there's a lot going on in your head. What sort of thing?'

'I don't know ... thoughts. Dark thoughts. Why is everything so hard? What's the point of it all?'

'Do you think about suicide?' The doctor's expression is compassionate. 'I'm sorry to express it so baldly, but I have to ask.'

I'm not sure how to respond. I don't want to overdo it, but ...

'I suppose I do think about it, sometimes, but only in an abstract way.'

'Abstract? Not sure I'm following you.'

'It's hard to describe ... I find myself assessing things – bannisters, tree branches, that kind of thing – wondering if they might take my weight. And sometimes, when I'm walking on the pavement, I wonder what would happen if I just ... stepped out.' I hurry to reassure her. 'But it's not a serious thought. I would never do anything like that. Honestly. I couldn't leave my daughter.' A nice touch.

'Actually, these kinds of thoughts are quite common. It's

called passive suicide ideation. It can be alarming, but generally it's nothing to worry too much about. Most people have it at one time or another. Your insomnia and low mood are more concerning, but there might be a physical cause. We'll do some tests, blood and urine, to make sure everything is as it should be. After that, I can prescribe you medication to help you sleep and to help your mood generally. How is your appetite?'

'Not great. I'm finding it difficult to keep food down.' That, at least, is true.

'Is there any way you could be pregnant?'

'I don't think so.' Please God, no.

'Not to worry. We'll check at the same time as we do the other tests. When we get your results back, we can start you on some tablets I think will help. Mirtazapine. A low dose to begin with. I'm also going to put you on the waiting list for CBT. Cognitive behavioural therapy – talking therapy – can be very effective for anxiety and depression, but I'm afraid the waiting list is quite long.' Her gaze flicks to my clothes and takes in my diamond engagement ring. 'Of course, if you can afford it, you can go private, which means you'll be seen more quickly.' There's no sign of judgement on her face. 'I can make a referral, if you like.'

'That would be great. Thank you.'

She smiles at me. 'Don't worry. We can deal with this. I'll pass you over to the nurse, who'll take your blood and urine. As soon as we get the all clear from the tests, I'll write a prescription. In the meantime, if you find it all getting too much, please don't hesitate to make another appointment.'

And that's that. In and out in twenty minutes, including my visit to the nurse.

'It might be a few days until we get the results,' says the

receptionist as I leave. 'The lab has a backlog. Give us a ring in the middle of next week.'

I nod and head out to the car park, blinking back tears. Real tears, this time.

I feel terrible. Such a fraud, to be mimicking distress that so many people are suffering genuinely. I've been lucky. I've never really had depression. I've been down, of course I have. When David died, there were a few weeks when I didn't want to wake up, didn't want to get out of bed and deal with it all. But that was grief. I can't imagine what it must be like to feel that way all the time, to carry that kind of burden. I hate myself for faking it, but I have no choice. It's an essential part of the plan.

My mood lifts a little when I see Figgy waiting so patiently in his carrier in the back of the car. He wags his tail when he spots me. I take him into the vet's, make soothing noises, and ignore his look of utter betrayal as he's given his injections. This is his second lot of inoculations. He won't be able to go outside properly for another couple of weeks. But, of course, I won't be around then.

TO MY RELIEF, the house is empty when we get home. Alex has left a note.

Gone to the gym. Hope doctor's went well. Text me if you want me to bring you a coffee home. Skinny decaf latte? Love you, darling, Alex.

He's so considerate. Literally, too good to be true. I want to punch him.

I go on my laptop and do several searches – *fatal dose mirtazapine? what does drowning feel like?* After that, I do some research into tides on the south coast. I find the perfect spot – the coastal stretch between Pagenham and Selsey, where the powerful tides are most likely to carry anything out into the English Channel.

I know Alex will see all this. He has my password, so I'm pretty sure he'll check my search history after D-day. That's what I'm calling it in my head, but I'm not sure what it stands for. Death day? Drowning day? It feels so extreme. Surreal. But I really can't see an alternative that will buy me time and keep Bella safe.

After I've been online, I move to the sofa, which is directly under the CCTV camera. I know Alex can't see me there. I don't suppose he'll log in while he's at the gym, but it can't hurt to play it safe. I go through Autotrader on my phone, looking for a cheap run-around I can buy for cash. It has to be an automatic so Willow can drive it in her moon-boot. I highlight three possibilities, one in Hammersmith, one in Wimbledon and one in Chislehurst. I think we should try the one in Chislehurst first, as it's furthest away. Getting there is going to be a challenge. I'm determined not to use my car, just in case. It sticks out like a sore thumb. So very yellow.

I hear the front door open, and close down Autotrader, chucking my phone in my bag.

'Yoo-hoo!' calls Willow. 'It's me.'

Relief floods through me. 'In here!'

I get up to hug her. 'I wasn't expecting to see you today.'

She plops herself down beside me on the sofa. 'I thought, fuck it, and got an uber. I can't leave you high and dry in your hour of need.'

'I'm so glad you're here.' I squeeze her hand. 'We have to be careful, though. Alex could be home any minute. He's got the day off work.'

'Bugger.' She pulls a face. 'Did you manage to get an appointment with the doc?'

I nod. 'All done.'

'Great. I come bearing gifts.' She rummages in her bag, then pulls out a phone. 'My old one. I got you a new SIM card.'

'Brilliant. Thank you.'

'And I've been looking into setting up a fake bank account. Not easy ... Impossible, in fact, without a bogus driving licence and a utility bill, and I can't see how we're going to get you those.'

'I'm not sure it matters. I don't need to set up a permanent fake identity. I don't have to stay dead forever.'

'What you need is cash,' says Willow. 'Lots of it. I suppose you could just empty your accounts?'

'That's going to look suspicious. Alex is bound to go through my financials, and he'll wonder why I withdrew so much money.' Actually, now I think about it, it would have looked suspicious transferring funds out of my account too. A fake bank account was never going to work anyway. Suddenly, I remember something.

'I have a savings account Alex doesn't know about. My rainy-day fund.' I had made a point of putting something away every month when I was working on the soap, knowing it might be a while before I had another regular income. I didn't need to worry about that when I was married to David, and haven't given it much thought lately. I haven't deliberately kept it a secret from Alex; there's just never been a reason to mention it.

'How much do you have in it?'

'About seven grand, I think. The car's going to take most of that.' I pull a face. 'How do I get my hands on the money? Even though Alex doesn't know about the account, it could be risky withdrawing so much cash from an account that's in my name.'

'Transfer it to me. I'll withdraw the cash. No one's going to come poking into my business. Not anytime soon, at least.'

We get to work. Luckily, my rainy-day savings aren't with my day-to-day bank. I download the savings app onto the phone Willow gave me, and transfer everything in my savings account to Willow's account. Then I delete the savings app from the phone Alex bought me. As I'm doing that, I wonder whether he might have noticed exactly which apps were on it when he was setting my phone up. I don't think so. There were so many of them.

'I have some cash you can have too,' says Willow. 'A few hundred. It's not much, but it'll help.'

We both freeze as we hear the front door open. I push my illicit phone into my bag and hurry to the counter. Willow grabs a magazine and lounges artfully on the sofa with her moonboot.

'You didn't text me, but I brought you a latte just in case —' Alex spots her as he comes through the door. 'Willow. How are you? How's your foot?' He smiles, but it doesn't reach his eyes. He really struggles to hide how much he dislikes her.

'Much better, thanks.' Willow is insouciant. 'How are you, Alex?' She hides her dislike better, but not completely. That would be suspicious. I silently applaud her acting skills.

'Fine, thanks,' says Alex.

This is painful. I take the coffee off him and kiss his cheek.

'Thanks, darling.' His face is flushed from his exercise, his hair still damp. Even knowing everything I know about him – knowing he killed Polly and probably Keira too – I still have to admit he's attractive. How can someone so wicked look so damned good? It isn't fair.

'Actually,' I say, 'I'm just about to run Willow home.'

Willow nods. 'It's just a flying visit.' She pushes herself off the sofa.

I grab my bag. 'I'll pick Bella up on my way back,' I say before he can volunteer to do it. It's a relief not to have to spend the rest of the afternoon with him, but I don't want him to be on his own with Bella if I can help it.

'Great.' He dumps his sports bag on the floor. 'I'm so glad I bothered to take today off.' He simmers with passive aggression. 'I suppose I'll take Figgy out for a walk, then.'

'We can't do that yet. The vet said he can't go out for another couple of weeks.'

My eyes slide to the puppy chewing on a ball in his pen. I don't want to leave him with Alex either. 'You know what, I might take him with me in the car. Bella will be so pleased to see him when I pick her up.'

Alex looks mutinous, but softens when I put my arms around him.

'I'll grab something special for dinner on my way home, if you like,' I say. 'How about lobster? We haven't had that for ages.'

I need to keep him sweet. It won't be for much longer.

Willow averts her eyes as he kisses me. The kiss is deep. Unnecessarily lengthy. Is he making a point to Willow? Marking his territory? As good as he looks, the intimate contact makes my skin crawl, but I steel myself and lean into it.

'Lobster sounds great,' he says when he eventually releases me. 'Hurry home.'

My hands are shaking as I let myself out of the house with Willow and Figgy. Alex is a dangerous man. A powerful man. I know he won't hesitate to do whatever it takes to cover his tracks. But Willow and I aren't completely defenceless. He has no idea we're onto him, and that's a huge advantage. We have our wits, our acting skills, and each other.

I just hope that will be enough.

CHAPTER FIFTEEN

I stare at the sky through my window. I'm finding it hard to concentrate on anything today, struggling to get back in the swing of things after my day off yesterday. What a waste of time that was! I thought Lisa would be delighted to spend time with me, imagined we would have a romantic day together, but it didn't turn out that way. She hardly spent five minutes at home, and her bloody best friend was there for most of that. Still, that's what you get for choosing women who don't bore you to death. They have minds of their own. That has its charms, but in the long run it can get wearing.

She'll learn, though, she'll learn. It's a bit like training a dog. Praise them when they do something good, ignore or punish them when they do something you disapprove of. The message sinks in over time. It might take a few months, but I know I can bring Lisa to heel eventually. It would help if I could get her pregnant. That would make her more malleable.

The phone rings on my desk, and I answer it.

'It's Becker, sir. I have that recording you asked me to get. And some CCTV footage too.'

'Good man, Tommy. Email them over, would you?'

'They're pretty big files, sir. It might be better if I upload them onto the server for you.'

I get myself a coffee while I'm waiting. Ordinarily, I would ask my PA to do it, but my new one seems to be struggling with her workload. It's a pity I had to get rid of Tricia, but I couldn't risk her talking to Lisa after that ridiculous business in Bath. I probably shouldn't have gone haring after Lisa and Bella like that. It was hasty. Undignified. But when Tricia gave me Lisa's message, I couldn't believe she'd just take off to see Willow without thinking about me at all.

Naturally, I saw red.

Luckily, there was no harm done. I managed to smooth things over with Lisa afterwards with my sob story about my mum. Not that it was invented – it was all true, every word. It still surprises me how people react when I tell them about my mum's abandonment. I suppose when you give them the bare facts, it does sound shocking, like something out of Grimms' fairy tales. Personally, though, I've never thought of my childhood as a disadvantage. On the contrary, it's often come in useful. I haven't gone round blabbing about it indiscriminately, of course, but I have dropped my sorry tale into a few selective ears. News spreads quickly in the force, both good and bad, and juicy personal details spread fastest of all. Now everyone knows I'm a neglected care-home boy made good, who has managed to claw his way up through the ranks. It's been a useful mythology. In fact, I think it's one of the main reasons Bill Glover has taken a particular interest in my career. Every cloud has a silver lining.

As ill-advised as my dash to Bath might have been, my

tears and sorry story of abandonment won Lisa back over to my side.

The same can't be said for Willow. I suspect I've made an enemy there. Not to worry. I'll work on Lisa to sideline her, gradually freeze her out. It shouldn't be too difficult. In fact, I'm going to enjoy it.

I see Becker has uploaded the files to the server, and I open them.

I listen to the audio recording of the emergency call about the blood in Keira's flat. To my disappointment, I don't get much from it. Whoever the caller is, they clearly used voice-altering technology, making it impossible to tell if they were even a man or a woman. That's very strange. Why would someone who had just stumbled into Keira's flat by accident feel the need to disguise their voice? I suppose it could be someone with previous, but even so ... it doesn't seem to make much sense.

The CCTV footage from Dagenham isn't much better. It's grainy and indistinct, but it does at least solve one mystery – the caller was a woman. Of sorts. I watch her, again and again, as she shambles in and out of the phone box. I can't see her face properly at any point, thanks to the hood and face mask she's wearing. Which is a pity. I could have asked some of the drugs lads if they know her. As it is, she could be any one of the hundreds of similarly pathetic men and women haunting our cities. If I had my way, I'd just clear them off the streets. Dispose of them. It would solve a lot of problems. Save a lot of money.

I close the files. I'm probably worrying about nothing. Whoever the woman was who made the anonymous call, she had no idea what she was blundering into when she went into Keira's flat. And she'll be long gone by now. The clean-up company I hired called this morning to let me know Keira's flat has been cleared. Everything she owned has been taken to the dump. So that's that. I can safely forget about her.

There's a knock at the door. Bill Glover sticks his head in.

'Alex, just checking you've got your ducks in a row for the conference on Friday?'

'Of course.' Actually, truth is, I'd forgotten about it. Quite why he's sending me to the back of beyond – Birmingham, for God's sake – is a mystery. But I play the game. 'I'm looking forward to it.'

'It's really important to make friends with our peers in the regional forces. Solidarity and all that.'

Does he think I'm fucking dense? 'Of course, Bill. I've already sent Phil Smith an email thanking him for his hospitality.' I haven't. But I will.

'Great stuff.' Bill nods and ducks out again.

I suppose this visit to Birmingham could be good for my career, but it's really not what I need right now. I don't want to leave Lisa and Bella on their own. Lisa's been acting a bit odd. Distracted. Is it because of the bruises I gave her when she stopped me drowning the dog? I don't think so. I barely touched her, and we had sex just after that, which always keeps her sweet. But lately, whenever I kiss her, it's as if she's somewhere else in her head. We've barely had sex at all. Perhaps it's the UTI? I hope the antibiotics will do the trick. She said the doctor told her to keep warm, drink lots of fluid and take it easy. She needs to be doing that; I need things to be getting back to normal on the intimacy front.

I open the home security app on my phone to check in on her. The kitchen is empty apart from the damn dog, and there's no sign of Lisa anywhere else in the house. Her car isn't in the driveway. She's not home. Again. Irritation prickles. So much for taking it easy! I open the app for the tracker I put on her phone. It takes a moment or two for me to log in and then to decipher the unfamiliar geography of her location. Sidcup? No, Chislehurst.

What the hell is my wife doing in Chislehurst?

CHAPTER SIXTEEN

Luckily, the owner of the Jeep Renegade I've come to look at doesn't live too far from Chislehurst station. Mr Williams is a man in his late fifties, with a combover and a crushing hand-shake. He has quite a few other cars pulled onto the hard standing in front of his house, which means he probably buys and sells cars either as his main income or as a sideline. That's not ideal. I'd rather buy from a private seller. But I'm here now, so I might as well make the best of it.

I look the car over. I don't care about the mileage, the colour or the general condition. I just have to be sure it's reliable. I do the usual checks – tyres, electrics, fluid levels – and take it for a quick test drive. It seems to drive well for its age and mileage. I haggle on the price a little, but not too much. I just need to get this done.

Mr Williams is a little surprised when I take the four thousand cash from my bag and ask if I can drive the car away, but we shake hands on the deal, and he gives me the necessary paperwork. Before I know it, I'm on my way to Willow's in my new Jeep.

'HERE YOU GO.' I give her the keys.

'It was okay, then?' Willow's just washed her hair. It's sticking up in soft pink peaks above her anxious face.

'It's no Rolls-Royce, but it'll do the job. I've put some petrol in it.'

'What about insurance?'

'I think driving uninsured is the least of our worries, don't you?' I drop wearily onto her sofa bed. 'We're going to have to do this soon, before I lose my nerve.'

'I agree.' Willow sits cross-legged beside me. 'But it's not something we can do in broad daylight. *Come, thick night ...*'

'*... and pall thee in the dunnest smoke of hell.*' I finish her quote. 'We have to choose a time when Alex is out in the evening. God knows when that will be. He's sticking to me and Bella like glue at the moment.'

'If we get everything ready to go,' says Willow, 'we can do it at a moment's notice if we need to. We have the car' – she checks off our list of essentials on her fingers – 'we have the cash, and we've chosen the place. Do you have your meds from the doc yet?'

'Not yet.' I shake my head. 'I'm still waiting for the test results.'

'Let's hope you get them soon. Prescribed meds will lead straight to your GP, who can confirm she was treating you for depression. If we don't get them in time, we'll just have to use paracetamol. I suppose the police or the coroner will get to your GP eventually.' She pulls an apologetic face. 'There's one more thing we need you to do.'

I know what she's talking about, but I really, really don't want to do that now.

She sees my mutinous expression. 'Don't wait until you

have to do it in a rush,' she begs. 'It'll be so much harder, and you might fuck up.'

I know she's right.

The first note is to Alex. I don't know where to start. I stare at the paper and pen Willow has given me, hoping that inspiration will strike. The temptation is to dash off something apologetic and half-hearted, but I know I can't afford to do that. I have to sell it to him. He has to truly believe I'm at such a terribly low point that I can't see I have any alternative but to end my life. And – even more horrifyingly – Bella's.

Alex, my love,

If you're reading this, I will be dead, and so will our darling Bella. I can hardly begin to tell you how sorry I am, or know how to explain the terrible thing I have done. I have a shadow over me that's been there for a long, long time. When I met you and fell in love, I hoped my love for you would drive it away. But it hasn't. It's always there, in me and around me, swallowing up all my pleasure, all my joy. I just can't live with it anymore.

I'm taking Bella with me, where she'll be safe. This world is too hard a place, too unpredictable and savage. I can't leave her in a world so dangerous, even with you in it. I know I'm asking a lot – too much, probably – but I hope you will someday come to understand, even a little, why I've done what I've done. And maybe even to forgive me, just a little bit.

Your Lisa x

When I'm finished, Willow reads it.
'That'll do,' she says sombrely.
The second note is to Danny. This one is even harder. He knows me so much better than Alex does. I take a deep breath; then I sink down, deep inside, dredging my psyche for my suicidal self.

Danny boy,

My twin, my other half.

I've done a terrible thing. You once told me I needed to give myself permission to be happy. I guess in the end I just couldn't do that.

But I'm hoping that you, more than anyone else, will be able to understand it. Ever since David died, I haven't been able to see any sense in this world. I know that you can't either.

I don't want to leave you. I hope we'll meet again, somewhere, somehow. In another life, maybe. Or a better, more forgiving world.

In the meantime, please try to get better. Try to find the joy. Just because I couldn't doesn't mean it isn't there. Keep looking.

And forgive me, please, if you can.

Li xx

WHEN I'M FINISHED, tears are streaming down my face.

'I can't do this. How can I do this to him?'

'You have to. As long as Alex is supplying him with MDMA, his life isn't his own.'

'Yes, but how is that going to change? If we do find evidence against Alex, how do we know he won't throw Danny under the bus, just out of spite? We haven't thought this through properly.' I'm sobbing now. The reality of the situation has hit me hard, and it's overwhelming. It's all too horrifying, all too much. 'Where are we even going to start looking for evidence? We haven't thought it through, Willow. I can't do it.'

She takes me in her arms. 'What's the alternative? How do you know Alex won't simply decide to kill you? Or Bella? Tonight? Tomorrow? We have to get you both somewhere safe, and then we can think about our next steps.'

I wipe my face.

Willow reaches for my hand. 'I don't know how we're going to bring him down, Li, but we will. I promise.'

She looks into my eyes and sees how full of doubt they are.

'I promise,' she assures me.

'Okay.' I give her a watery smile. 'Can you put the kettle on? I'm dying for a cup of tea.'

She grins. 'I'll make you one. But you haven't finished yet. What about *my* note? Wouldn't you write one to me?'

'AREN'T YOU HUNGRY?' Alex eyes the lamb chop I'm pushing around my plate.

'Not really.' That's true. My stomach is in knots.

'You're not feeling well?'

'No, I'm fine.' I give him a tired smile.

I'm having to tread a very fine line. I'm supposed to be depressed, but can't overdo it. I don't want Alex to think my feelings towards him have changed, for him to wonder why that might be, for him to get suspicious. It's really bloody hard. Writing the notes today, combined with the constant vigilance and role-playing, is taking a toll on my nerves.

Alex cuts up his own chop. It's slightly bloody on his fork. 'You really should be taking it easy, with that infection of yours.'

His tone is critical. Does he know I was out today? Those bloody security cameras.

He pauses with his fork raised halfway to his mouth, waiting for me to tell him where I was. There's something about the way he's looking at me, an almost wolfish watchfulness, that puts me on my guard. He can't possibly know where I've been, can he? It's best to play it safe.

'I was in Chislehurst.' I don't look at him as I say it, taking a bite of my meat and chewing it carefully.

'What on earth were you doing there?'

I take my time, chewing and thinking. 'I can't tell you.'

His eyebrows rise. 'Why not?'

'I just can't.'

He scowls.

I put my hand over his. 'A woman has to have some secrets, you know.'

'I don't see why. We're husband and wife. Tell me.'

'Okay.' I squeeze his hand. 'It's your birthday next month. Let's just say it has something to do with that.'

I watch as emotions chase each other over his face. It's

hard to say what they are. Relief? Pleasure? And something else – disappointment? Was he actually *wanting* an argument?

Finally, he puts his food in his mouth and chews. 'I've been meaning to tell you. I'll be away on Friday.'

'Away? Overnight?'

He nods. 'A conference in Birmingham. A pain in the backside, if I'm honest, but Bill's asked me to go. He was invited to speak, but can't make it. He suggested me instead.'

'That's flattering.'

'I hate leaving you and Bella.'

'We'll miss you.'

'I can try to get out of it if you want?'

'Don't be daft. It'll be good for your career. Raise your profile.'

He looks pleased. 'That's what I thought.' He finishes his meal, puts his knife and fork down. 'But I do have to prep for the conference. Is it okay if I leave you to clear up?'

'Just this once,' I joke, kissing him softly on the cheek.

I wait until I've heard him go into his study and close the door, then sneak my secret phone out of my bag to text Willow.

WE'RE ON. FRIDAY IS D-DAY.

CHAPTER SEVENTEEN

The next day – Wednesday – I finally find something in the online edition of the *Barking and Dagenham Post* about Keira.

> *Emergency services were sent to an address on the Becontree estate at around 7 p.m. on Saturday 11 December after an anonymous tip. A statement issued by the Metropolitan Police reads, 'The presence of police and medics has caused some people to be worried about what has happened and others to speculate online.' The statement added: 'Please be reassured that there were no suspicious or illegal circumstances involved. Local officers are in the area to provide a reassuring presence and to speak to anyone with worries or concerns. Please feel free to speak with us if you see us on our patrols. Thank you.'*

That's it. Nothing about blood. Nothing about a body. What the hell? Where is Keira?

I call Willow.

'I don't understand,' I say. 'How can they say there's no suspicious circumstances? Surely they would have reported Keira's body if it was there? Do you think he got rid of it?'

'I don't know,' she replies. 'But this shows we're doing the right thing. We can't go to the police. Alex is a powerful man, Lisa.'

THAT AFTERNOON I go shopping with Willow's credit card. I buy a small rucksack, toiletries, a little suitcase on wheels for Bella, and warm new jackets and shoes for us both. When I get home, I hide everything in the laundry room, where I can be sure Alex won't find it.

The rest of Wednesday and Thursday pass in a blur. Part of me wants Friday to arrive quickly so Bella and I can finally get away from Alex, but part of me is dreading it. I know our lives will never be the same again.

When Friday – D-day – finally arrives, I help Alex pack his overnight bag for Birmingham.

'Will you need anything nice for this evening?'

'Not particularly, I shouldn't think,' he calls back from the ensuite. 'Just some chinos and a sweater.' He comes out wearing only a towel around his hips. His skin is flushed from his shower, his hair wet.

I avert my eyes as I put his grey chinos and a sweater into the bag. I'm disconcerted by my physical reaction to him. Knowing what he is, I should be utterly revolted, yet my pulse quickens, and I can feel heat rising in my face and body. Is it residual, instinctive sexual attraction? Or is it the adrenaline of a fight-or-flight response? I'd never have guessed they could feel so similar. 'What time's your train?' I ask.

'Eleven.'

'Text me and let me know when you get to your hotel.'

'Will do.'

I try not to stiffen as he pulls me towards him.

'Do you think those antibiotics will have done the trick by the time I get home?' he asks.

'I should think so.'

'I hope so. I've missed you.' He nuzzles my neck and runs his hand over my buttocks under my jeans.

'I've missed you too.'

He takes my hand and guides it to his cock under his towel. It's hot, damp and hard.

'You'll be late,' I say. Every cell in my body is fizzing with tension. I feel I might explode. I can't risk annoying him or arousing his suspicion, not when I'm so close to getting away.

'We have plenty of time.' He kisses my neck.

It's too much. I can't do it. Not this morning. I withdraw my hand.

'Bella?' I say, turning my head sharply towards the door. I turn back to him. 'I thought I heard Bella call.'

'Really?' Alex scowls, frustrated. 'I didn't hear anything.'

'Sorry.' I kiss him on the cheek. 'I'd better go and see.'

Bella is playing happily in her room with Teddy Pea. I kneel beside her. Poor little thing. She has no idea her whole life is about to be turned upside down.

'Is she okay?' Alex appears in the doorway.

'Seems to be.' I stroke her hair. 'You're fine, aren't you, sweetheart?' I smile up at Alex. 'I'll make you some breakfast. We don't want you going up to Birmingham on an empty stomach.'

When he leaves at last, I heave an inward sigh of relief. Now my day can begin.

I take Bella into nursery as usual. I had considered keeping her off, but then realised Alex might spot her on the CCTV and wonder what was going on. I don't want to give him any excuse to come home. I'll be a bag of nerves until eleven, when he's safely on the train.

Being careful to keep out of sight of any of the cameras, I get everything ready for our escape.

First of all, I pack my new rucksack. It's tricky because I can't take anything Alex might notice is missing. Although, to be honest, I'm not sure how much Alex notices my clothes apart from a few overtly sexy dresses. I choose my most boring underwear, a couple of pairs of jeans and some of my most unremarkable tops and sweaters; then I pack them into the rucksack with the toiletries I've bought. I'll have to leave all my make-up, toiletries and jewellery here, together with the rest of my personal stuff. Lastly, I pack the cash Willow has withdrawn from her bank – my rainy-day fund – splitting it between the rucksack and my jacket pockets. I never imagined my rainy day would be so dramatic, or so dangerous.

Packing Bella's suitcase is a little trickier. Alex takes an interest in what she wears, wanting her always to look smart and pretty. He's spent quite a lot of money on designer clothes for her. A waste of money, in my opinion – at Bella's age clothes get dirty so easily, and she'll grow out of them quickly. Of course, I've never said as much to Alex. The consequence is, though, that all her newer clothes are ones he might notice are missing. I search in the back of her chest of drawers and find some older ones she hasn't worn in a while. I hope they'll still fit her.

While I'm packing Bella's suitcase, Teddy Pea watches from his vantage point on Bella's pillow, his single beady eye unblinking. He is a problem. If we take him with us, Alex is bound to realise he's not here. But if we don't take him, Bella won't settle at all. I decide to take him, and hope Alex will think we've taken him on our final journey. That wouldn't be too much of a stretch to imagine.

When I've packed both bags, I smuggle them down past the cameras on the stairs into the utility room, disguised as baskets of washing. Alex texts me at two thirty, to say he's arrived at the conference, and I relax a little, knowing he's more than a hundred miles away.

It's already dark when I pick Bella up from the nursery at four. I leave my car on the road rather than parking it on the driveway in view of the CCTV camera. I make myself a sandwich and Bella her favourite macaroni and cheese. I leave the dishes in the sink.

We can't leave until six. Our journey is timed so the tide will just be starting to go out when we get to Selsey. I check Figgy is okay, with plenty of water and food in his enclosure to last him until tomorrow. I hate to leave him, but really don't have any choice. He'll be too much of a liability to take with us.

'You'll be okay, won't you, boy?' I hug him to me, and he licks my face. Willow has promised to take him home when she gets here. Will Alex look after him in the meantime? I hope so. I give him one last squeeze, and I wipe away a tear. 'We'll be back soon,' I whisper. 'I promise.'

I steer Bella into the utility room.

'Come on,' I say. 'Let's play a game.'

'A game?' Her eyes widen.

'We both need to get changed first.'

I help her strip off the clothes she's wearing – a pink Kenzo Paris dress that Alex bought her – and get her into her old comfy hoodie and leggings. I'm relieved they still fit. Then I help her put on her new jacket and boots. After I've also changed, I put everything we've both been wearing all day into a carrier bag.

'Ready for an adventure?' I ask.

She nods, enthusiastic. 'Can Teddy come too?'

I produce Teddy Pea from the rucksack.

'Yes!' squeals Bella.

I shoulder the rucksack, and, letting Bella wheel her new suitcase, we make our escape out the utility room door.

CHAPTER EIGHTEEN

We make it to my car through the shrubbery so we don't get picked up by the camera on the drive. It seems like a lot of effort to go to, but I can't risk Alex going through the footage later and wondering why we're wearing different clothes and carrying luggage.

'Where are we going?' asks Bella as I strap her into the car seat.

'The seaside!'

'Yay!'

We set off. It's less than thirty miles to Guildford, but the roads are busy, and it takes longer than I expect. By the time we hit the Guildford bypass, Bella is fast asleep, soothed by the sound of the engine and passing headlights. From Guildford, I head to Chichester on the A286, then eventually head east just after RSPB Pagenham Harbour.

It's quite a contrast here to the buzz of the main roads. The lane to the little village of Church Norton zigzags through open fields and woodland, growing narrower and narrower until the headlights are guiding me through a tunnel of trees. It's much wilder here than I expected. Am I going the right way? I don't want to end up in someone's driveway. The next minute, I see I have no need to worry, as the lane unexpectedly broadens, and I spot my destination – St Wilfrid's chapel. It stands alone in the darkness, surrounded by gravestones. I park in the small car park and turn the engine off.

Silence rushes in. I wind the window down and take a deep breath of chilly air.

This is it. The point of no return

So far, I haven't really been thinking about the magnitude of what I'm about to do. I've just been carrying out my plan mechanically, one step after another. But now I have to make my final decision.

Am I really going through with this?

I could just turn around now and drive back to Twickenham. Alex will be none the wiser. He'll come home from Birmingham tomorrow, and everything will be the same as it was when he left. But what then? Can I really carry on with my marriage, knowing he's capable of physical violence, suspecting he killed Polly and probably Keira too? Of course I can't. I would have to leave him, walk out, like any normal, disillusioned wife would do. But I know, beyond a shadow of a doubt, that he would come after me. And then who knows what he might do? Danny would be collateral damage. And I can't bear to think what might happen to Bella.

I can hardly believe all the plans that Willow and I have made have brought me here, to this quiet, moonlit graveyard in the middle of nowhere. I'm tempted to call Willow now. She's driving, but I know she'd pick up. She'd give me the backbone I need to go through with this.

But no. This is a decision I have to make on my own.

I sit, listening to Bella's gentle breathing, to the sounds of the night outside the car – the trill of a curlew and a low, distant susurration. The sea. The clock on the dashboard says it's just after nine. The tide is high, but it's on the turn, starting to head out again. It's now or never. I grip the steering wheel, strung out with nerves. Even in the moonlight, the bruises on my arm are still faintly visible, smudges on the snow of my skin. If I go back, who's to say it wouldn't be my face next time? Or a broken bone? Or – God forbid – Bella? And when would that stop? It wouldn't. Not until one or both of us are dead. Like Polly.

I am doing this. I don't have any choice.

My test results and the doctor's prescription for mirtazapine didn't come through in time, so I have to use paracetamol. I put an empty plastic bottle in the glove compartment with the almost empty half-bottle of vodka that's already there, and drop a single paracetamol tablet into the footwell, for good measure. Then I put the notes I've written to Danny, Alex and Willow on the passenger seat.

I get out of the car, put my coat on, and stretch. Bella is fast asleep. It would be easier to leave her sleeping while I do what I have to do, but I can't risk it. I can't leave her on her own out here. She grumbles when I wake her, resisting my attempts to get her out of her car seat.

'We're here, sweetheart. We're at the seaside.'

She blinks, then lets me unclip her from the seat. She climbs out of the car and looks around. It must seem so strange to her, to be going on a trip in the middle of the night.

'Do you want to bring Teddy Pea?' I suggest, wanting to comfort her. She clutches the bear tightly as I retrieve the carrier bag of clothes from the back seat.

I leave my iPhone in the car. Ever since Alex's interrogation about Chislehurst, I've suspected he's been tracking me. I think he knew exactly where I'd been the day I bought the car, so he was hoping to catch me in a lie. It was naïve of me to let him set up the phone, with all my apps and passwords.

I wonder what he's doing now, in Birmingham. Has he checked the cameras at the house? Does he know we're not there? Is he tracking my phone right now? If so, he must be wondering what the hell I'm doing all the way down here. But what could he do about it?

Bella and I set off down the track, hand in hand in the moonlight. I can sense her apprehension. She's hanging back, ever so slightly. She senses this isn't any kind of usual adventure.

'It's okay, sweetheart. We're nearly there.' I've memorised the way, past the Norman earthworks, to the edge of the Pagenham nature reserve. We turn right at the harbour edge, then continue to the main beach, over wooden sleepers set into the ground. Our feet crunch on the gravel path and then on pebbles as we emerge onto the main beach.

I stop. I don't want to go too far from the harbour entrance, which has a notoriously dangerous tidal inflow and outflow. The deserted beach stretches out on either side of us, a broad expanse of shingle. Ahead, the silvery sea is punctuated here and there with groynes. The night is silent apart from the shushing sound of waves on pebbles.

'Can I go for a paddle?' asks Bella.

'No, love. It's too dark to paddle just now.'

She pouts. 'I want to paddle.'

I kneel down and hug her. 'I just thought you'd like to see the sea by moonlight. It's pretty, isn't it?'

She nods, unconvinced.

I empty the bag of clothes and shoes we wore earlier in

the day onto the pebbles, folding the clothes on top of our shoes. Luckily, Bella is too mesmerised by the moonlight on the sea to notice what I'm doing. If she spotted her Kenzo dress, I'm pretty sure she'd protest fiercely at leaving it. I feel the same way about the wallet I've left in the pocket of my jeans. A credit card would come in *very* handy in the next few weeks, but I know it would be stupid to keep it. The police could trace me if I were to use it. I hesitate. Have I thought of everything? The two little piles of clothes look so ordinary on the pebbles. I have an idea.

I pick up Bella's shoes.

'Shall we go and have a closer look at the sea?'

She nods.

We trudge over the beach, right up to the water's edge. The retreating waves leave a tracery of foam on the pebbles, white in the moonlight. Before Bella can see what I'm doing, I throw her shoes as far as I can out into the sea. I have no idea whether they'll be carried out by the tide or washed back in again, but I hope someone will find at least one of them. If they do, it'll be taken as proof we went into the water.

'What's that?' asks Bella. 'What did you throw?'

'Food, for the fishes.' I lie easily, which is just as well. Lying is going to be my way of life for the next few weeks.

WILLOW IS WAITING for us when we get back to the car park. She gets out of the Jeep when she sees us coming towards her, moving awkwardly with her boot. Bella spots her in the moonlight.

'Auntie Willie!' she cries, delighted, running over to her.

'Bella!' Willow picks her up and squeezes her tight. 'How's my poppet?'

'We've been feeding the fishes,' volunteers Bella.

'Have you?' Willow gives me an amused look. 'Everything go okay?'

'Like clockwork.' Now it's done, I'm anxious to get away.

Willow straps Bella into the new car seat in the Jeep while I retrieve the rucksack and Bella's suitcase from the boot. My poor old car has done me proud. I hope Alex doesn't do anything drastic like selling it while I'm gone. As I'm putting the rucksack and suitcase in the Jeep, Willow and I both freeze. We hear a car, and we can see headlights on the lane, coming towards us.

'Bugger,' says Willow.

It would be a disaster to be spotted by anyone now. They would definitely remember seeing us here. We're the only cars in an otherwise empty car park. We watch, holding our breath as the headlights get closer and closer. Then the car turns off the lane about fifty yards before the entrance to the car park. There must be a driveway there that leads to one of the neighbouring houses.

'Phew,' says Willow. 'That was close.'

'Come on,' I gasp, my heart thumping harder than it's ever done before. 'Let's get out of here.'

I drive along the lane slowly, without headlights, sending up a silent prayer of thanks that the moonlight is so bright tonight. Luckily, we don't meet anyone coming the other way. It's only when we get back to the A286 that Willow and I put the headlights back on, and we breathe a sigh of relief as I relax into the driver's seat.

Two and a half hours later, I pull up to the kerb by

Willow's bedsit. Bella is fast asleep again, and Willow's eyes are closed too.

'We're here,' I say.

Willow jerks awake. 'Did I nod off? Sorry.'

I grin. 'You were snoring most of the way.'

'I was not.'

We get out of the car.

'Well, this is it,' I say.

Willow hugs me tight. 'You've got the phone I gave you? Stay in touch. I'll let you know how things are doing here, and I'll come and see you as soon as I can. There's a hamper in the back seat, with enough food to last you both for the trip.'

'Thank you. I don't know what we'd have done without you.'

We hug again, and Willow dashes a tear away with her hand.

'You and Bella are safe now.' She sniffs. 'You're definitely doing the right thing.'

'I hope so.' We both hesitate, not knowing what else to say, not wanting to say goodbye.

'Go on,' she sobs, at last. 'Bugger off before I start messy crying.'

I kiss her cheek, then get back in the Jeep.

I catch a final glimpse of her in the rear-view mirror, standing on the pavement in that ridiculous moonboot, hugging her arms around herself. I hope it's not too long before I see her again.

I pull out of the street, turning my thoughts to what lies ahead.

I head north.

CHAPTER NINETEEN

'Are you sure I can't tempt you to another?' Phil Smith, assistant chief constable of West Midlands Police, nods at my now-empty tumbler of Bowmore. Smith is a real grassroots copper, blunt and coarse featured, with no conversation beyond the job, but when he offered dinner after the conference, I was happy to accept. It never hurts to make friends in high places.

'I'm sure, thanks. I have an early train in the morning.'

He nods and gets to his feet. 'In that case, I'll say good night. Well done today. I hope we'll see more of you.'

We shake hands.

'I'm sure you will, sir.'

I'm glad to get back to my hotel room. It's hardly luxurious – Met expenses won't stretch to anything more than a Premier Inn, even for someone of my rank – but it's clean and comfortable. And I'm knackered. The travelling, then presenting, then being on point all evening have taken their toll.

I strip for bed and check my phone. Nothing from Lisa.

That's odd. But she's probably asleep. I text her a goodnight message, get into bed and put the light off. But even though I'm tired, I find it hard to get to sleep. I lie in the darkened room and stare at the ceiling. Lisa's lack of communication is preying on my mind. She usually stays in touch whenever we're apart. I sit up and reach for my phone again.

For my own peace of mind, I check into the security system. The house is in darkness. We don't have cameras upstairs, so I assume Lisa and Bella are safely asleep in bed. But something feels off. I don't know what it is. I check the cameras again. Everything looks normal. The dog is in the kitchen, the house is tidy, peaceful. I check the driveway camera. Lisa's car isn't there.

What the *fuck*?

Where is she? Has she done another flit to Willow? She didn't say she was going to. Anger bubbles as I log into the phone tracker. Why the hell can't the woman stay where she's supposed to be? To my surprise, I see her phone is – where, exactly? Somewhere on the south coast? Selsey. What the fuck is she doing down there? I sit up and put the light on, wide awake now.

Why would she take off like this, without a word to me? I call her. Her phone rings out ... and out. Eventually it goes through to voicemail. I don't leave a message. I can't trust my voice not to betray my anger. I hang up instead. Does she have friends on the coast? If so, she's never mentioned them to me.

I force myself to switch off the light and lie down again. I'll speak to her tomorrow. I'll *more* than speak to her tomorrow. In the meantime, I need my sleep.

THE NEXT MORNING, Lisa's phone is still on voicemail. I'm astonished. Incensed. She must know I'll be trying to get in touch with her. Is she deliberately avoiding me? I let my anger build as I grab breakfast and head for the station.

My train leaves on time. I settle myself at my table, open my laptop and log into the Wi-Fi. All the time my mind is working overtime – where has Lisa gone, and why? I assume she has Bella with her. I zoom into the location of Lisa's phone on Google Maps. It seems to be literally in the middle of nowhere. A car park surrounded by trees. St Winifred's Chapel. What the hell is she doing there? I just don't get it.

I CALL WILLOW. If anyone knows what Lisa is up to, it'll be Willow.

'Hullo?' She sounds sleepy when she picks up.

'Hi,' I say. 'It's Alex. I'm trying to get in touch with Lisa. Do you have any idea where she is?'

'Lisa? Isn't she at home?'

'Would I be calling you if she was?' I take a breath, try to inject a little more casualness into my tone. 'I'm on my way back from Birmingham, but Lisa's not picking up her phone. She mentioned she might take Bella on a trip to the south coast. Do you know if she did?'

'The south coast?'

I bite my tongue. Her parroting is really getting on my nerves.

'Are you sure that's what she said?' she asks.

'It doesn't matter. She'll probably be home when I get there. Thanks anyway.'

I hang up before she can say anything else, then dial another number.

Becker answers after a couple of rings.

'Chief?'

'Tommy, I want you to do something for me. I have a car – my wife's car – at a location on the south coast, a village called Church Norton, near Selsey. Can you get a couple of the local coppers to do a check, and get back to me asap?'

'What exactly are we looking for, sir?'

'See if there's any sign of the driver. Any houses nearby. Knock on doors if we have to.'

'No problem.'

He doesn't ask if the driver is my wife, or if the car has been stolen. That's why I use him for jobs like this. He doesn't ask unnecessary questions.

'Send me the details,' he says, 'and I'll get someone on it.'

I hang up. Why would Lisa take off like that, without telling me? And why go to such a remote location? Has she been carjacked? Is she safe? Is Bella safe?

My anger is laced with something darker now. Apprehension.

THAT APPREHENSION BUILDS on the two-hour journey back to London. I ring into the office and tell my new PA I'm going home before coming in. I want to search the house. There may be clues there.

When I get home, I can hear the puppy yowling through the front door. The kitchen stinks. The dog's enclosure is dotted with turds, puddled with urine. The wretched thing is happy to see me, yelping and leaping up and down. I ignore it and search the house.

There's no sign of my wife or of Bella downstairs, other than a few dirty dishes in the sink. I run upstairs to check

Lisa's wardrobe. All her clothes are still there. All her jewellery. She hasn't left me, then. Why would she do that anyway? We're idyllically happy, aren't we?

What the hell is going on?

My phone rings as I'm heading back down the stairs.

'Chief.'

'Any news, Becker?'

'I'm afraid so, sir.' His tone is grave, troubled. 'You might want to sit down.'

'I DON'T GET IT.' Danny looks bruised, disoriented, as if someone has mugged him. 'Why would she do that? Did she say she was depressed? Did she look like she was struggling?'

I shake my head. This has come completely out of the blue. Or has it? I think back to the last couple of weeks. If I'm honest, Lisa has seemed distracted. Not quite herself. I'd assumed it was the UTI, but maybe it was something more?

Danny turns to Willow. 'Didn't she say anything to you?'

'Not a thing.' Willow shakes her head. She looks hollow, drained of her usual animation. 'But if Lisa was trying to put a good face on it, I wouldn't have known. She's an *actress*. A bloody good one.'

We're all together in the kitchen, waiting for news from the coastguard. I called Danny as soon as Becker told me what they'd found on the beach, and Danny called Willow. If it were up to me, I wouldn't have her here. I know she doesn't like me, and it's an irritation.

I did consider going down to Selsey myself, but sent Becker instead. I couldn't bear to be the centre of speculation and gossip from the local force – *there's Chief Super McMahon. His wife has just topped herself. And their little girl.*

Bella. Dear God.

'She never said anything,' says Willow, stroking the puppy on her knee, 'but she's not been completely right since David died. She loved him so much.'

'Really?' I snap. I don't want to hear that. She met *me*. She married *me*, for God's sake. Wasn't I enough for her?

Willow picks up on my tone. 'I'm just saying. There must be an explanation.'

'Not necessarily. Not an obvious one.' Danny looks totally forlorn. 'Sometimes these things aren't logical. I just wished she'd talked to someone about what was going on in her head. I can't believe she never mentioned anything to me. Never talked to me.'

I go to the coffee machine on the counter, to hide my irritation. If Lisa was going to confide in anyone, it would have been me, wouldn't it? I'm her husband, for God's sake. Or was. 'Anyone want another cup?'

Danny shakes his head.

'Not for me,' mutters Willow. She throws me a poisonous look. I don't know why she's looking at me like that. None of this is my fault.

The doorbell rings, sending the puppy into a frenzy of barking.

'Can't you shut that thing up?' I snap at Willow as I go to answer the door.

'Sir.' It's Tommy Becker. He looks tired and deeply uncomfortable standing on the doorstep.

'Come in,' I say, 'come on through.'

'Tommy!' Danny stands up when he sees who it is. 'Any news?'

'The coastguard is still looking. Hampshire has a forensic

team looking at the car and the stuff on the beach. But,' he hesitates, 'I thought I should bring you these.'

He takes three envelopes from his coat pocket. 'There's one addressed to you, sir.'

He gives it to me. I recognise Lisa's handwriting. 'And there's one for you, Danny. And Willow.'

'That's me.' She grabs the envelope off him, puts the puppy back into his enclosure to read it.

I look at Becker. By rights these should be with the forensics team, or at least in evidence bags. He's looking at me anxiously. I nod my thanks and see his relief.

We all read our notes.

Any doubts I had that Lisa intended to commit suicide are swept away. I'm numb with shock. Danny drops heavily onto the sofa.

Willow folds in on herself as if someone has punched her in the stomach. Then she howls, the sound ripped out of her, her face ugly with grief. Danny watches, white-faced and stricken.

Tommy Becker stands in the middle of this circus like an awkward ringmaster.

I clench my note in my fist. 'Thank you, Tommy. Are you going back down there?'

'Yes, sir. If you want me to.'

'If you don't mind. Let me know if there are any developments.'

'Will do, sir.' I'm gratified by the look on his face. Pity and admiration.

But my hands are shaking as I let him out. How could Lisa do this to me? How dare she take Bella away? When I go back into the kitchen, I'm pleased to see Willow is more in control of herself. She's sitting on the sofa beside Danny, red-eyed and sullen. I don't like the way she's looking at me.

The three of us stare at each other in silence.

Willow gets to her feet, wipes her face. 'I'm going home,' she says, abrupt. She gives Danny an awkward hug. 'Call me if you hear anything.'

Danny doesn't respond to her. He's somewhere else.

'I'll let you know if we do,' I say. She gives me a sour look, then marches to the enclosure to scoop up the puppy.

'I'm taking the dog,' she says. 'He's filthy and needs feeding.'

My instinct is to stop her, to show her whose damn dog it is, but instead I shrug.

'If you want,' I say. In fact, that suits me very well. It'll save me from having to take it out and dump it somewhere. 'I'll give you a hand into your car with its things if you like.'

When Willow and the dog have gone, the silence in the kitchen is profound. Danny still hasn't said anything since he read his note.

'How are you, Danny?' I ask. I'm not sure I care that much, actually, but the silence is shredding my nerves.

He shakes his head. 'I'm a terrible brother. Why didn't I know?'

'I had no idea, either,' I say. 'If you're a terrible brother, that makes me a terrible husband, and you don't think that, do you?'

I expect him to shake his head, but he doesn't. He doesn't do anything. It's as if someone's unplugged him at the wall. I swallow my irritation. If Lisa really is dead, Danny isn't family anymore. He'll be a weight around my neck if I don't find some way of distancing myself from him.

But I can think about that another day.

For now, I just have to take one step at a time.

CHAPTER TWENTY

The drive north takes forever. Aware of how exhausted I am, I take a nap in a layby near Peterborough for a couple of hours. Bella sleeps through until York, but after that is a complete pain, moaning and grumbling. It's still dark when we stop at some services near Durham to use the toilets and eat the food Willow has packed for us. The food is delicious – sandwiches, croissants and jam, hot coffee in a Thermos, and Bella's favourite, chocolate milk. It puts her in a better mood, but it's still another two and a half hours' drive to Edinburgh.

Sod's law, we arrive on the eastern outskirts of the city bang on rush hour, about an hour after sunrise, when it also starts to rain. As we fight our way into the city with the commuter traffic, I get the occasional glimpses of Arthur's Seat and – once – the castle, bleak and grey on its outcrop of rock. Mostly, though, I have to concentrate, navigating the warren of unfamiliar buildings and one-way systems, trying to find our way to the address Willow has given me.

Eventually, however, we find our way south, where the

city's tenements and office buildings start to thin out, giving way to grand houses. I find the address on a leafy, tree-lined street and drive past it a few times. It's a rambling, gabled Victorian house, set back from the road. The gates are closed. All the parking on the street seems to be permit only. I drive round, looking for a spot that isn't.

'I want a wee, Mummy.'

'You can have one in a minute, sweetheart. We're almost there.'

I eventually find a parking place that doesn't seem to have any restrictions, but it's quite a long way back to the house. I collect our bags from the boot, and Bella, and we start to head back through the rain.

'I'm going to wee now. It's coming out.'

'Hold it, please, just for a minute.' I look around, desperate, for somewhere to take her. There is nowhere unless she squats in the gutter or goes in someone's garden, and I don't think I have the brass neck to do that.

'Oh no! I've done it.' Bella's face crumples into tears.

Her legs and feet are sopping, almost as wet as the rest of her.

'I'm sorry, Mummy.'

'Don't worry, sweetheart. I know you couldn't help it.' I wipe her tears away. 'We'll get you cleaned up soon.'

'My feet feel nasty. They're all wet.'

'I know, sweetheart. Not long now, I promise.'

Finally, we make it back to the big Victorian house. I check the address again, just to be sure. This is definitely it. The gate is locked, but there's a buzzer and an intercom. I press the buzzer. As we stand there, I'm conscious of the rain dripping down my neck, soaking into my entirely inadequate coat. Bella's jacket isn't much better. She's soaked to the skin. She smells quite strongly of urine too.

'Yes?' A woman's voice.

'Is this the refuge?'

A hesitant beat. 'Who is this, please?'

'I need help. Please. I'm desperate. *We're* desperate.' Silence. 'Please.'

The intercom buzzes, and the gate swings open. I pick up our bags and hustle Bella through it. We squelch up the drive. We're almost at the big double doors when they're opened by a woman in a tweed skirt and cardigan.

She looks at us both with a mixture of alarm and compassion.

I burst into tears.

'HOW'S DANNY?' I hardly dare ask.

'You don't want to know.' Willow's voice over the phone is weary.

'I feel terrible. Beyond terrible. I think we've made a mistake.'

'It's too late to change your mind now,' says Willow.

'How did Alex take it?'

'Hard to say. He was shocked, but played his cards pretty close to his chest.'

'How did *you* take it?

'Magnificently. *These external manners of laments / Are merely shadows to the unseen grief / That swells with silence in my tortured soul.*'

'I'm glad you've still got your sense of humour.'

'It's the rock I cling to. What time did you get there?'

'About nine.'

'What's it like?'

'Fine, I think. I haven't had the chance to look round yet. I'm just relieved they took us in. I don't know how long they'll let us stay, though. I still have to talk to them properly.'

'I'll let you go. Stay in touch, yeah? We'll talk about our next move.'

'Look after Danny, will you?'

'I'll do my best.'

When she's gone, I'm bereft. Willow is my only link – the umbilical cord – to my old life. This new one is very different. Our room is in the attic; it has a sink in the corner, a single bed and bunk beds. The bedding is worn but clean, and there's a colourful rag rug on the painted floorboards. I'm immensely grateful for it, but it's still very different to what we're used to.

'Can I watch telly?' asks Bella. She's clean and dry again, looking at the only picture book I could risk bringing with us. It isn't one of her favourites.

'Sorry, sweetheart. I don't have my laptop.' I had to leave it at home. Home. For all its amenities, all its luxury, the house in Twickenham never did feel like home. It was Alex's house. And Polly's. I'm swept by a sudden, overwhelming nostalgia for the ramshackle flat we shared with David. He was very different from Alex, with a slightly sideways sense of humour and an open, optimistic way of looking at the world. He was honest – brutally honest, at times – but was always there when I needed him. Right to the end.

I try to blink back the tears, but they're falling too fast. I have to turn away to hide them from Bella. I just can't stop crying. In the end I have to splash my face with cold water to stop the flow. When I finally have myself under control, I dry my face on one of the towels the refuge has provided.

'Come on,' I say to Bella. 'Let's go and make some new friends.'

We go downstairs. The landings and staircase smell of disinfectant and cooking. The paintwork is chipped, but there are colourful children's paintings pinned on the walls.

The office is on the ground floor, and the door is open. I knock.

'Hello!' A woman with a lined face, cropped silver hair and CND earrings looks up from her computer screen. 'You must be Debbie.' She gets up and gives me her hand. I shake it.

'I'm the manager, Roo McKellan.' Her voice is deep, with a Scottish burr. 'Sorry I wasn't here when you arrived this morning. Come in.' She clears some paperwork off a chair beside her desk. 'Have a seat.'

There's another woman in the office. I recognise her as the tweedy one who took me in this morning. She gives me a friendly nod and spots Bella. 'Hello again, hen. What's your name?'

Bella pouts. 'I'm not a hen.'

'Sorry,' I say, mortified. 'Her name is Bella.'

The woman laughs. 'Shall we have a little look in the playroom, Bella? We have princesses and castles.'

Bella looks at me, doubtful. I nod my encouragement. Bella lets the woman steer her out.

'It's okay,' says Roo. 'She'll be fine with Mhairi. She has five of her own. Can I get you some tea?'

'Please.' I hadn't realised until she asked, but actually, I could kill for a cup of tea.

As Roo busies herself in the kitchenette in the corner of

the room, I take the opportunity to look around. Above a big, old-fashioned photocopier there's a forties-style poster of a strong-armed woman in a polka-dot headscarf – WE CAN DO IT! The noticeboard is stuffed with thank-you cards and press cuttings: *50 shades of anger. 88 women killed by their partners in a year. Pregnant Callie knifed 20 times by boyfriend.*

'Milk?'

It's hard to tear my eyes from those horrifying headlines. 'Yes, please.'

Roo sloshes milk into both mugs and gives one to me.

'We don't usually take people in off the street,' she says. 'But Mhairi thought you were both too distressed to send away.'

We *were* distressed. Exhausted, soaked to the skin and smelling of urine, from Bella's toilet accident.

'Thank you so much for letting us stay. I don't know what I'd do if ...' I tail off, my eyes prickling with more tears. They're still swollen from my last bout.

Roo sips her tea. 'Can I ask how you heard about us? We try to keep our location here a secret, for obvious reasons.'

'I have a friend who knows someone who stayed here a couple of years ago. She's living in London now.'

'Safe?'

'I believe so.' Willow's friend is now in a lesbian relationship.

'That's good to hear. You're from London yourself, are you?'

Shit. 'York.'

'And Debbie's your real name?'

That takes me by surprise.

Roo smiles, a genuine smile that crinkles her eyes.

'Sorry for the interrogation. I understand why you might not want to tell us everything, but you are safe here. And we can't help you properly without knowing who you really are.'

I still don't want to tell her my real name, but don't want to give her another false one, either. I've a feeling she'll see right through it.

'Okay,' she soothes. 'Let's not worry about it for now. What's brought you here? Can you tell me what's happened?'

I'm not sure where to start. I want to tell her as much of the truth as I dare, but I know I can't afford to tell her everything, in case Alex comes after us.

She can see I need another prompt. 'You're running away from your partner? Your husband?'

'My husband.'

'Bella's father?'

I nod. Not true, but close enough. I don't want to go into details.

'Has he ever hurt you or Bella?'

'Yes.' I find it hard to meet her eyes.

'Look at me, please.' Her voice is gentle.

I do.

'The shame isn't yours,' she says with quiet fury. 'It's his. Never forget that.'

I nod. 'He's got me second-guessing everything. What I say, what I wear, what I eat. If I put a single foot wrong ... honestly ... I think he might kill me. God knows what he'll do when he realises we're gone.'

'Is this the first time you've left him?'

'Yes. I don't know why, but I ... something snapped. I realised I had to go. Not just for me, but for Bella. I suppose I panicked. I wanted to put as much distance between us as possible.'

'Which is why you've come all the way from York. Do you have any substance issues at all? Alcohol, drugs?'

Again, she's taken me by surprise. I shake my head.

'How are you fixed financially?' Her gaze drops, discreetly, to my clothes and brand-new boots. 'You're not on benefits.' That's a statement, not a question.

'No. I have some cash that I borrowed from a friend. But not much.'

'Okay. We can give you legal advice, if you need it, and support from social services, but I'm afraid we can't let you stay for long. We're getting dozens of referrals every day for women in Edinburgh and the Lothians, and our funding's been cut to the bone.' She sees my dismay. 'But we can give you a few days, a week maybe, to let you catch your breath and decide what you want to do next.'

I nod. It's not as long as I'd hoped, but longer than I have any right to expect. A thought occurs to me. 'I need to move my car.'

'Your car?'

'I have to put it in long-term parking somewhere.'

From her expression, I realise that isn't a problem she often has to deal with. But, to her credit, she nods anyway.

'I'll ask Mhairi to look into it, and you can sort it out this afternoon. Let's go and find Bella, shall we, and see what she's up to?'

We find Bella playing with Mhairi and a little boy in the playroom. The room is stacked with storage boxes full of toys, paints and picture books. Bella and her new friend are crayoning at a small plastic table.

'Gently now, Rory,' chides the boy's mother. 'Let the

lassie have a go.' She smiles at me. She has deep shadows under her eyes, and a bruise stretching from her temple to her jaw. God knows what she's been through. I feel a fraud.

I notice there are little notes pinned around the walls. They have messages on them, written in childish hands –

'I want my mum to be happy.'

'It's good to be here. I feel calm, and my mum is happy.'

'I like being here because no ones out to get me, and my mum will always be by my side.'

I blink back more tears. I feel I've stumbled into a parallel universe I had no idea existed. Every city in the country has shelters like this, full of women whose worlds have been shattered. I'm humbled, and ashamed at having always been so very oblivious to it.

CHAPTER TWENTY-ONE

'I have to wait seven years, is that right?' I ask.

'That is the usual protocol if a person is missing, but, given the suicide notes and the evidence on the beach, you can apply for a Declaration of Presumed Death.' Diana Wilson-Howe, the solicitor recommended by Bill Glover, gives me a reassuring smile. She's a brunette, with striking features and a capable manner. In any other circumstances I might find it fun to flirt with her, but I have to remember I am a grieving husband and father.

'The police also found one of your daughter's shoes on the beach at Bognor, is that right?' Her brown eyes are full of sympathy.

I nod and swallow, as if overcome by emotion. 'It was washed in by the tide. We're pretty certain they both went into the water.'

'I'm sorry to hear that. But it does make your case for a declaration stronger.'

'How long do you think it would take?'

'If we make the application today, probably around five to six weeks. Of course, if you have strings you could pull, it could be quicker.'

I almost smile at her. A woman after my own heart. I notice she isn't wearing a wedding ring. I'd say she was … what? Mid- to late thirties? If she's unattached, her biological clock will be ticking. Perhaps when the dust has settled on this business, I might ask her out. For now, though, I have to get this over with.

'If we could make the application, that would be great.' I let emotion break through my voice. 'Thank you so much.'

Her face softens with sympathy. 'This must be very difficult for you, Mr McMahon.'

'Alex, please.' I summon a weak smile.

'I'm sorry for your loss, Alex.'

I nod and get to my feet. 'Please let me know when you've made the application. And stay in touch to let me know how it's progressing.'

'I certainly will.'

I look deep into her eyes as we shake hands. I see sympathy there and something else … interest. She finds me attractive. Good to know. She's just my type.

I think about her, and Lisa, as I drive home. I loved Lisa – no one could say I didn't – but I don't think I'll ever forgive her for killing herself and Bella, for taking my family away from me. It was a terrible, selfish thing to do. Not the act of a loving wife and mother. Who could blame me for wanting to move on?

As I pull up onto the drive, I realise that might be easier said than done. Danny's car is here. Again. Ever since Lisa went into the water four days ago, I haven't been able to get rid of him. I wish she hadn't given him a key.

He's waiting for me in the kitchen, sitting on one of the stools at the counter with a coffee, like he owns the place.

'Alex,' he says, 'you're late.'

What is he, my bloody wife? I didn't realise I'd married him as well as his sister. 'I had a meeting with the solicitor.'

'What does he say?'

'*She* says we can apply for a Declaration of Presumed Death.'

'So soon?'

'Is that a problem?'

'I don't know.' He rubs his face. 'It just makes it feel so ... real, somehow. We haven't even had a memorial service yet.'

'It is real, Danny. She left suicide notes. We found Bella's shoes in the water. Lisa's GP has confirmed she was prescribing her antidepressants. How much more real does it need to be before we make it official?'

Danny says nothing, but his eyes fill with tears.

His weakness nettles me. 'What are you doing here? Have you just come for a chat, or ...' I let it dangle, knowing he will bite.

'I need some more pills.'

'No can do.'

'It's not urgent. I can last for another couple of days.'

'I said no.'

He just looks at me.

'My supply has dried up. I can't get any more.' That's kind of true. If Mike Wishart is going to do the audit in Bermondsey, I have to be careful. It's not worth the risk. Not for this loser.

Danny looks as if I've punched him. 'What? You can't get any more, ever?'

I shake my head, then: 'Sorry ... oh ...' I pretend I'm

remembering something. 'Can I have the keys Lisa gave you? I have some workmen coming in tomorrow, and I don't have any spare ones to give them.'

He fumbles in his trouser pocket, then hands over his keys.

'What am I going to do?' he says. 'Without the MDMA?'

I just shrug and go to the coffee machine.

That's not my problem. Not anymore.

THE NEXT DAY I detour to Dagenham on my way to work. Keira's landlord is waiting for me in her flat. The clean-up company I hired has done a good job. There's no sign of my sister-in-law – all her furniture has been cleared, and her belongings have gone to the landfill, along with any so-called 'proof' she might have had. The only sign she was ever here is the bloodstain on the living room floor.

'I can't return the deposit.' The landlord, a fat man in his fifties, huffs and crosses his arms. 'Not with this floor in such a state.'

He's expecting an argument, but I couldn't care less.

'That's fine,' I say, and give him the keys.

I head for the front door. To my irritation, he follows me down the hall.

'If you arrange to have the floor sanded, I might be able to return the rest of your deposit.'

'I don't have time to do that. Keep the deposit.'

'Really? That is an awful lot of money.'

'Look.' I swing round to face him. 'I've said I don't want the fucking deposit back. I. Don't. Want. It. Got that?'

He nods, wide-eyed. I turn to open the door, then freeze. The letterbox has something stuffed into it. Something red.

Keira's hat.

The last time I saw it was in my kitchen. How the hell did it get here? I tug it out of the letterbox's grip and stuff it into my pocket.

'Oi!' A woman on the other side of the fence stops me as I walk down the path, a woman in leggings and a scraped-back ponytail. I recognise the upstairs neighbour – I saw her looking out the window when I arrived. I shouldn't have worn my uniform. It pisses me off, being accosted like any old plod on the beat.

'Can I help you?' I force a polite smile. No point agitating the natives.

'What's going on?'

'Nothing. Nothing to be concerned about.'

'What happened to Keira? I liked her. We got on. But nobody can tell me where she's got to. I saw you lot crawling all over the place. She's not dead, is she?'

'No.' Even if she were, I wouldn't tell her. Nosy bitch. But then a thought occurs.

'I don't suppose you saw anyone here the day the emergency services arrived? Any one poking about?'

The woman looks thoughtful. 'There was someone, yeah. Some bird, asking for Keira.'

'Can you describe her?'

'Nah, not really. She was quite posh. And she was a ginger.'

'A ginger?'

'A redhead. A bit of a looker too.'

I jolt, as if an electric current has gone through me. I find my phone and scroll through my photos.

'Is this her?' I hold out the phone.

'Dunno.' The woman squints at it, and I watch closely as her face clears. 'Yeah. Yeah, it might be.'

I stare at the photo of Lisa, her red curls tumbling round her face. What the *fuck*?

CHAPTER TWENTY-TWO

'Where the fuck are my pies?' Jenna, stick-skinny with fiercely dyed ink-black hair, glares at everyone in the communal cooking area. 'I had two Fray Bentos pies in here, and they're both gone.'

'Perhaps you ate them and forgot?' suggests Kelly, who's feeding her baby on her lap. Her tone suggests she doubts the existence of the pies in the first place.

Jenna glares at her. 'Aye, right, as if I'd forget that.' Her eyes narrow. 'Are you calling me a liar?'

Kelly deflects with a placatory comment while I concentrate on my food. I want to object to Jenna's language in front of the children, but it's not worth the inevitable aggravation. Bella and I have tended to eat most of our meals in our room for precisely this reason. This, and the barrage of questions I'm subjected to every time I show my face in the kitchen or other communal areas.

'What did your man do to you, then?'

'Where are you from? English, are you?'

'*How long will you stay?*'

All innocent enough questions, but not ones I want to answer.

'What the fuck are we supposed to eat now?' Jenna sits down and puts her head in her hands. Like Kelly, I doubt the pies ever existed in the first place. Jenna's twitchy paranoia suggests her benefits have been spent elsewhere. Her son, Logan, sits at the table with hungry eyes.

'I have some tuna pasta in the fridge if you want it,' I volunteer. I was going to use it for lunch tomorrow, but I can buy something else.

Jenna eyes me as if I've just offered her a dog turd, but she goes to look in the fridge all the same.

'This it?' She takes the tub with my name on it – Debbie – out of the fridge.

I nod.

She sniffs it.

I catch Kelly's eye. She raises an eyebrow. Kelly is the woman with the bruised face I met in the playroom our first day here, mother to five-year-old Rory and baby Tamsin. Rory is sitting at the table beside Bella. They're both eating, taking no notice of what the adults are doing.

'What's in it?' asks Jenna suspiciously.

'Tuna, pasta, cucumber and mayonnaise. Good with a baked potato.'

'Nah, you're alright.' She puts the tub back in the fridge. 'Logan would never eat that. We'll just get a Maccy D's. Come on, Logan.' She marches out, trailing Logan after her.

I go to the fridge to put the lid back on the tuna properly.

'You don't need to do that,' says Kelly. 'You don't need to give your food away. Jenna's a survivor – a taker – she'll always manage.'

'And Logan?'

'I don't want to sound hard, but he will too.' She finishes spooning baby food and wipes little Tamsin's mouth with the bib. 'He's used to it.'

'I guess,' I say. 'I wish she wouldn't swear so much in front of the kids.'

Kelly shrugs. 'What's a few bad words? We try to cut each other some slack in here. It's hard enough, being on your own, without having to watch your Ps and Qs.'

I snort. 'It's harder *not* being on your own.'

Kelly grins. 'You got that right.' She sits her baby in the playpen. 'Want some tea?'

I hesitate, then nod. Bella and I have spent most of our time in our room since we got here. The streets of Edinburgh are too cold at this time of year to spend much time wandering about. I'm going a little stir-crazy. Luckily, Willow is coming up on the train tomorrow. I can't wait to see her. We have so much to talk about. To plan.

As Kelly pours two mugs of tea from the urn, Rory drops his knife and fork with a clatter.

'Finished! Can I go and watch telly, now?'

Bella looks at me, eyes eager. 'Can I go, too?'

I hesitate. She's finished her dinner, so I don't have an excuse not to let her.

Kelly senses my reluctance. 'Go on,' she urges. 'Let the lass have a bit of fun. They usually have cartoons on in the TV room about now. You'll look after Bella, won't you, Rory?'

He nods, then gallantly helps Bella off her chair. I watch them scamper out.

Kelly eyes me over her tea. 'It's weird, but ever since I first saw you, I've a feeling I know you from somewhere.'

Alarm bells ring in my head. 'I doubt that. I haven't been in Scotland long.' Perhaps she's seen me on TV? That wouldn't be too much of a stretch.

'Where are you from, again?' she asks.

'York.' I'm keen to deflect her questions. 'What about you?'

She laughs. 'Leith, born and bred. I live two streets away from the house I was born in. A terrible lack of imagination, that's my trouble. Probably why I'm still with Colin. We've been together since we were at school.'

I look at her, trying to work out how old she is. It isn't easy, with her bruised face and world-weary manner. She could be anything from twenty-five to forty.

She sees my struggle and takes pity on me. 'I'm twenty-six now.'

'Why did you stay with him so long?' I genuinely want to know.

Kelly shrugs. 'Who knows. I suppose it's like what they say about boiling a frog, isn't it? When you get in, the water's cold, but then it gets hotter and hotter, a wee bit at a time, and before you know it, you're boiling your arse off and you don't know how to get out.'

I want to say something to show her I understand, to comfort her, but I can't. My experience has been very different – cold one second, scalding the next. He might have bruised me, but Alex never used his fists. Would he ever have resorted to it? I suspect he might have done, eventually. If he hadn't killed me first.

Kelly looks into her mug. 'This isn't the first time I've left him. It probably won't be the last. He'll turn up at my mum's, full of tears and apologies, and I'll take him back.'

'Why would you do that?'

'I don't know. Maybe it's because I remember him the way he used to be. Maybe it's just what I'm used to. Easier.' She turns her eyes to me. 'What about you? Do you think you'll ever go back?'

'No. Definitely not.'

'Good for you.'

Roo sticks her head in the door, earrings swinging. 'Debbie, could I have a word?'

I'm relieved at the interruption. 'See you later,' I say to Kelly as I get up. She nods.

In the office, Roo gets straight to the point.

'I have a family of five coming in on Monday. I'm afraid I'm going to have to ask you to move on.'

I nod. I've been expecting this.

'You've been here almost a week. Have you managed to get anything lined up?'

'Yes,' I lie. I'm not sure what we'll do. Drive north and find a guesthouse, probably. I still have some money, but I have to buy food and other necessities. It's dwindling every day. Willow might have some ideas tomorrow.

'I'm sorry.' Roo's eyes are full of sympathy. 'If I could keep you here, I would.'

'It's okay, honestly. When do you want us out?'

'Monday morning will be fine.'

I go into the TV room, a large room decorated with a fresh blue and yellow scheme and worn leather sofas. Some of the women look at me as I come in, nod, then go back to chatting as the little ones watch cartoons. I find a chair to perch on. Rory and Bella are sitting close together, his arm protectively around her shoulders. A lump rises in my throat.

I swallow it down. I would have liked Bella to have a brother or a sister one day, but that seems impossibly out of reach now. A fairy tale.

This new story I'm living in is a different kind of story altogether. But it still has a big bad wolf in it.

CHAPTER TWENTY-THREE

I let myself into the house. It's quiet – so quiet – without Lisa and Bella. The fresh flowers on the hall table tell me Mrs T has been in today. In the kitchen, all signs of the dog have gone, and the floor is pristine again. Everything smells of lemons.

I sit on one of the kitchen stools and let the silence of the house soak into me. My head has been fried – stuck on a loop – ever since my trip to Dagenham this morning.

Has Keira's neighbour identified Lisa correctly? Or is it just a bizarre coincidence that the woman who was asking for Keira on the day of the anonymous call looks like her? As a copper, I'm sceptical of coincidence. And what about the hat? How did Keira's hat get from my kitchen to Dagenham? It couldn't have walked there on its own. Lisa had to have brought it.

I've spent the afternoon playing and replaying the CCTV footage of the phone box in Barking, but still can't tell if the caller shambling in and out of the box could be her. It *might* be. If so, she's a better actress than I realised. But if it is her, then that would explain why she felt she had to disguise her voice.

Surely she didn't go all the way to Dagenham just to return the hat?

Perhaps she believed Keira's accusations, or some part of them? Why? I've treated her and Bella like queens. There was that episode in Bath, but I don't think that was totally unreasonable.

And there is the dog. I don't know what made me suddenly decide to drown the bloody thing, not when I knew Lisa would be home any minute. I was just fed up with its whining and mess. The bucket was there. I knew it would only take a moment or two. I ran the water without really thinking about it, then pushed it in. I couldn't have been more shocked when Lisa turned up. Talk about bad timing. I probably shouldn't have grabbed Lisa's arm when she tried to take the dog from me – that was a mistake. Pure instinct. But surely, Lisa couldn't suspect I'm a murderer because of *that*? That would be so unfair.

But … I can't think why else she would have gone to see Keira. If she thought I might have killed Polly, then stumbled across the blood and mess in Keira's flat, she would naturally think I'd killed Keira too. The obvious thing to do then would be to go to the police.

But she wouldn't do that. Not unless she was stupid, and I know she isn't stupid.

So what *would* she do?

Kill herself and Bella? I don't think so. That makes no sense.

No sense at all.

I have no idea what's going on. But I know someone who might.

I WAKE up early and leave a message for my PA that I won't be in until this afternoon, giving her some bullshit about attending a court hearing. By six thirty I'm in the car, heading into town.

Willow answers the door almost as soon as I ring the bell. She has her coat on and a packed holdall at her feet. The expression of shock on her face is almost comical.

'Alex.'

'Willow, are you off somewhere?'

'I ... I ...' she stammers, but recovers quickly. 'I am, actually. I'm going to Bath, to see how things are going with the play.'

She's lying, but I don't pick her up on it.

'Can I have a word?' I say instead.

'It'll have to be quick. The taxi's due any minute.'

She shows me into her cramped little bedsit. I've only ever been in the hallway, and I'm shocked by the main room. It's littered with mismatched crockery and gaudy clothing. It looks like an explosion in a charity shop. She lives exactly as I imagined – chaotic and dirty.

'What's this about, Alex?' She doesn't ask me to sit down.

'Sorry to bother you. But you were close to Lisa. And I'm really struggling.' I add a tremor to my voice. 'I just don't understand how she could do such a terrible thing. I've read her note again and again, but can make no sense of it. I was wondering ... could I look at yours?'

'Mine?'

'Your note. The one Lisa left you?'

'Sure, I guess.' She looks around, opens a drawer or two, then finally finds the suicide note under a glass on the coffee table. A strange, careless place to put her best friend's final farewell.

'Here.'

My dearest darling Willow ... blah ... blah ... hope you understand ... blah ... blah.

I make a show of reading the letter, but I'm really reading her. Watching her surreptitiously. Her face looks calm enough, but her left hand is clenching and unclenching at her side. I almost smile. I didn't get where I am without learning how to read body language. For all her acting skills, there are some things she finds hard when she hasn't had time to rehearse.

The entry phone buzzes behind me.

'That'll be the taxi.' Willow's expression is carefully neutral, but her treacherous hand is still twitching.

I'm standing between her and the door.

'I'm sorry, Alex, but I really have to go. I'll miss my train.'

I smile at her. 'Which train, exactly?'

She opens her mouth, but I cut in before she can speak.

'Please don't tell me to Bath. We both know that's not true.'

She stares at me, eyes wide. I can see the pulse in her jaw.

Adrenaline spikes in my veins – familiar and heady. 'Do you have something you want to tell me, Willow?'

CHAPTER TWENTY-FOUR

'More cake!'

'More cake, *please.*'

'Please.'

'You've eaten all yours. I suppose you want some of mine, do you?'

Bella nods, gleeful. I put what's left of my chocolate muffin on her plate. I'm too queasy to eat the rest anyway. I'm so excited to be seeing Willow again. Bella and I arrived at Waverley station far too early, almost an hour ago, and we've been killing time in one of the nearby cafés, a bland chain that could be anywhere in the world. It's only the view from the rain-spattered window – pedestrians and tourists dodging traffic on Princes Street – that betrays where we are. That, and the faint sound of bagpipes from a busker somewhere. He must be wet and cold, but I imagine he's used to it.

As impersonal as the café is, it's still better than the refuge. I've been finding it increasingly claustrophobic, increasingly oppressive. I'm not sure why. Maybe it's the air of quiet desperation that saturates everything, as pervasive as the cooking smells. Or maybe it's because we'll soon be leaving, and I'm mentally already on my way. It doesn't help that Jenna has taken against me for some reason. I overheard her talking to another woman on the stairs last night about how I shouldn't be there because I'm English and rich. I pushed past them without saying anything, but they must have known I'd heard. In fact, I wouldn't be surprised if Jenna only said it because she knew I was in earshot.

I wouldn't argue with her, even if I didn't mind aggravation, because she's right. I don't belong there. There are other women who need the space at the refuge much more than I do. Local women with fewer resources and even fewer choices than I have.

As Bella tucks into my muffin, smearing chocolate, I try calling Willow again. I've been trying all morning to reach her. The phone signal on the train is likely to be patchy, but it's odd that it's been out of action for the whole journey. I asked her to text me when she was on the train, but she hasn't done that either. As I listen to her phone ringing out, a dark feeling of foreboding creeps over me … and something else. Something more urgent.

I grab a protesting Bella and make a dash for the loo.

We only just make it in time for me to heave everything I've eaten into one of the toilet bowls. Bile, mostly, and muffin. It takes a few minutes of deep breathing for my stomach to settle again. I splash my face with cold water. This is the second time I've been sick this week, but perhaps it isn't so surprising. Perhaps I've caught food poisoning from the shared fridge, or a bug from one of the many coughing and sneezing women and children in the refuge.

I look at my flushed reflection in the mirror, brushing the

hair out of my eyes. I peer more closely. There's a new softness to my face, along my jawline and behind my eyes. A
softness I recognise.

Dear God, no.

'I want a wee.' Bella has somehow managed to smear
chocolate all down the front of her sweatshirt. She starts
tugging down her leggings and pants before I have the
chance to get her back into one of the cubicles.

'Not here. Hang on. Hang on a minute.' I lift her onto
the seat. 'There.'

She sits for a moment, frowning with concentration. 'No.
It's gone now.'

I don't have the heart to scold her. My thoughts are
elsewhere.

THERE'S a chemist on the station concourse, but no
pregnancy tests on display. I have to ask the pharmacist for
one from behind the counter. I push it into my bag and
hustle Bella back outside.

The arrivals board says that Willow's train has just
arrived on platform 11. I steer Bella in that direction,
dodging through the crowd on autopilot.

When was my last period? I can't remember. I had to
leave Twickenham before the results of my tests came
through. Could I be pregnant? It would hardly be an immac-
ulate conception. Until last week, Alex and I were at it like
rabbits, and – at his request – never used protection. I didn't
think it was a particularly big deal because it had taken me
eighteen months to get pregnant with Bella. It wasn't a
conscious decision to start a family with Alex, but I wouldn't

have been unhappy if it had happened. In fact, I probably would have been delighted.

But that was then. Everything is different now.

Platform 11 is bustling with people who've just got off the train from Kings Cross, bumping bodies and suitcases in their hurry to get wherever they're going. They stream through the barriers towards us.

'Up!' demands Bella.

I pick her up, and we scan the crowd of bobbing heads.

'Can you see Auntie Willow?'

Bella shakes her head, then squeaks. 'There!'

My heart soars as she points, but bumps back to earth when I see it's not her. It's a much younger woman – a teenager – with pink hair.

'That's not Auntie Willow,' I say. 'Keep looking.'

The crowd starts to thin until there's only a trickle of people coming through from the platform. The trickle slows to a dribble, then stops altogether. The platform is completely empty.

I stare at the space where the crowd once was.

Where is Willow? Why didn't she call to let me know she wasn't coming? I put Bella down, feeling nausea creep up on me again.

'Where's Auntie Willie?' asks Bella.

'I don't know. Perhaps she just stopped off somewhere.' That's not as unlikely as it sounds. She might have stepped off the train at a station on the way to get something, and didn't manage to get back on it. It wouldn't be the first time she's missed a train. Or even a plane. But why didn't she call me?

I'm about to ask one of the station guards whether there might be another train from Kings Cross, one we don't know about, when I realise we have to make a run for it again. I don't make it. I spew the contents of my stomach right in front of the entrance to the public toilets. There isn't a lot of it, but it burns my throat. Other travellers pushing their way in and out of the toilets look at me, then quickly look away again. They probably think I'm pissed. I lean back against the wall to try to steady my pounding pulse.

'Are you okay, Mummy?' Bella looks up at me, brow furrowed with concern.

'Yes, I'm fine, sweetheart.'

But I'm not. Not even a little bit.

'YOU ALL ON YOUR OWN?' Kelly comes in to the TV room to find me watching the six o'clock news with the sound turned down. Bella's asleep on the sofa beside me with Teddy Pea. Kelly has her coat on, cheeks ruddy from being outdoors. I can hear Rory's feet thumping up the stairs to their room. 'Where is everyone?'

I shrug. 'Dunno.' It is unusually quiet for this time of the evening.

'I hear you're off tomorrow.'

I nod. Our bags are packed and ready, but now the time has come, I wish we weren't leaving.

'Where will you go?'

I shrug. I don't have the energy for conversation, or the heart for it. I have no idea what Bella and I will do next. I've tried calling Willow again, at least half a dozen times, but she still isn't picking up. I feel completely alone in the world.

Kelly frowns at me, concerned. 'Perhaps you could try another refuge?'

As she's speaking, the light in the room changes to a

cooler hue. Blue light strobes through the thin material of the curtains. Kelly goes to the window to peer out, scowls.

'Police,' she says. 'Trouble for someone.'

We hear a stir at the front door, booted feet in the hall. The intrusion of masculine energy changes the atmosphere of the place immediately, like stones thrown into a pond. Kelly and I both creep to the door to listen.

'Yes, I got your message.' Roo's voice, from the office, is impatient. 'But we don't have anyone staying here of that name.'

'What about the description I gave you?'

All the blood in my veins turns to ice. I know that voice. It's Danny's friend Tommy, Tommy Becker, the man who threw Keira out of the wedding. At Alex's instigation. My eyes flash to Kelly's.

'My husband,' I whisper. Not strictly true, but true enough. All the moisture has gone from my mouth.

Her eyes go round with horror. 'He's police?'

I nod.

'Fucking hell.' She frowns. 'We'd better get you out of here.' She dashes to the sofa and scoops up Bella and Teddy Pea as I grab my bag.

'But how?' I ask. 'How will we get past them?'

'We don't have to. There's a back door.'

We peer out into the hall. Tommy and the other officers – I don't know how many there are – are still in the office with Roo. The door is open, only metres away, but they're out of sight.

'Now!' says Kelly.

We make a break for it, through the hallway and down the rear passage, through a laundry room to a door I didn't know was there. Bella stirs in Kelly's arms, but she doesn't wake. Kelly passes her to me, then takes off her coat and the jumper she's wearing underneath.

'Take these. It's freezing out there.'

I want to argue, to protest at her generosity, but I don't. She's right. We'd freeze to death in what we're wearing. I wrap Bella in the jumper and put the coat on.

'Your bag.' Kelly picks it off the floor and thrusts it at me. Our eyes meet. She hugs me fiercely. 'Good luck.'

Booted feet clomp in the hallway and up the stairs.

'Go on.' Kelly pushes me towards the door, her eyes suspiciously bright. 'Fuck off!'

I plunge out into the night with Bella in my arms.

The garden is too dark to see where I'm going. I bump into a wheelie bin and trip over something else – God knows what – before I find the gate. It opens into an alleyway that runs beside the house. I flee down it, away from the flashing blue light at the front of the house.

Bella stirs in my arms. 'Mummy?'

'Shhh. It's okay. Go back to sleep.' I could wake her up and make her walk, but I know I can move faster carrying her even though she's a dead weight in my arms. I don't think about the direction I'm going in, just try to put as much distance between us and the hostel as I can. I stick to the inside of the pavements, ignoring the other pedestrians. There are quite a lot of people about, hurrying home from work, and students heading back to their shared houses. Even though we attract a few curious glances, I'm grateful for the anonymity of a crowd. We walk until the street leads out into a wide-open space. I realise we're on the Meadows, the big park just to the south of the city centre. Paths criss-cross away in all directions. I could take any of them. Head in any direction. Then I remember – I have my car keys in my bag! I could nearly cry with relief. We set off to the east, towards the supermarket where I've left the car.

It takes forever to get there. I keep having to stop and perch on random walls just to take the weight of Bella off my arms for a moment. All the time I'm expecting to hear sirens or see a police car turn the corner. When we finally get to the car park, my legs are like jelly and my nerves are completely shredded. I strap Bella into her car seat, tucking her in with Teddy Pea and the sweater. After I've taken the tickets off the windscreen – we've outstayed our allotted time – I get in the car and switch on the ignition. I turn the heater on full to blast some warmth into the interior and get rid of the frost on the windows.

What now?

We're safe from Alex for the time being. He has no idea what car I'm driving.

Or does he?

I force my weary brain to try to put the pieces together. How did Alex know he could find us in the refuge? There's only one person who knew, only one person who could possibly have told him. Willow. But there's no way she'd do that, not unless he … Is Willow okay?

I take out my phone to try her number again. Still no answer. I don't want to think about the implications of that.

Not knowing what else to do, I head out of the city in a panic.

I drive on autopilot for almost an hour before I come to my senses and realise we're on the A1, heading south. Really, it would have been better to head north, but I suppose it can't be helped now. I'm bone tired – too tired to drive – and I know we need to find somewhere to stay the night. But where? Wherever we go, we're going to arouse suspicion. A hotel would probably want to take a credit card when we check in, and we're going to stick out in a smaller guest house. We have no luggage, nothing more than the clothes we're dressed in. People are going to take one look at us and recognise us for what we are – fugitives. If they call the police, we're done for.

I squint against the headlights of the oncoming traffic and see the next sign marks a turnoff to somewhere called Haddington. I take it, relieved to get off the main road.

Haddington turns out to be a little market town, lined with Georgian shops, festooned with Christmas lights. It's not even eight o'clock, but everywhere seems to be closed except the pubs. I drive around for a while, but don't see a single hotel or a guest house.

A light flashes on the dashboard, signalling I'm almost out of petrol. Great. I haven't seen a filling station anywhere, and I don't want to risk driving round randomly trying to find one. I turn off the high street, down a cobbled side street, and park up. The houses that line the street show no signs of life except the lights behind their curtains. I turn the engine off. At the end of the street is a surprising sight – a huge, illuminated church, surrounded by a graveyard. I have a flash of déjà vu. It's only a week since we were at the chapel at Church Norton, but it seems like years ago. Another lifetime.

I realise we can't stay in the car without the engine running. We'd freeze to death before morning. Perhaps the church is open? Perhaps it will be warm?

I winkle Bella out of her car seat and carry her down the path towards the church. There's a river running silently beside the path, dark except for lights reflected from the pub on the opposite bank. Music and laughter drift across the water, but they don't comfort me. They make me feel more alone than ever. We go through the iron gates into the churchyard. The gravestones are centuries old, leaning against each other, but the church itself is magnificent, much bigger than you would expect in a small market town.

The lights are on inside, turning the huge stained-glass windows into jewels. I spot a side door and try the door knob, but it's locked. The main door at the end of the church is actually two doors, side by side. Luckily, one of them is open.

The warmth hits us as soon as we step into the vestibule. There are benches, flowers, a fitted carpet. I'm tempted to snuggle down in a corner here, but know we would be spotted too easily. I carry Bella into the body of the church, where we find a bench at the back of the nave, tucked away behind one of the massive columns that soar up to the vaulted ceiling. I don't know how old this church is, but it smells of antiquity. I can sense the centuries of worship that have taken place here. It's oddly comforting.

My parents weren't religious, but I was taught in a Church of England school, where we sang hymns and said prayers in assembly every morning and went to church for annual carol services and harvest festivals. I haven't been in a church much since, apart from a few weddings and christenings. David and I didn't have Bella christened. It seemed hypocritical, when neither of us were active Christians. It's not that I don't believe in God, it just isn't something I've given much thought to. Perhaps I should.

The soothing silence of the big church, after the bustle of the refuge, followed by our frantic escape, is balm to the soul. I hug Bella to me and let the tears come. What's going to happen to us now? How can I keep my beautiful girl safe?

Kelly's sweater smells of soap and fried food. It just makes me sob all the louder.

'Mummy?' Bella stirs, looks around.

I hastily wipe my tears. 'It's okay, sweetheart.'

Bewildered and disoriented, she sees my wet face. Her lip trembles, and she starts to cry too.

'I want to go home.'

'Shush, sweetheart. Everything is okay. We're okay.' I don't know who I'm trying to convince, Bella or myself.

'Hello?'

I jump with fright.

A tall man in a grey T-shirt and black cardigan has appeared from behind one of the columns. He looks down at us, brows drawn with concern. I make an effort to pull myself together.

'We were just ... taking a look at your beautiful church.'

'It is beautiful, isn't it? Fourteenth century. Some of it, anyway.' But he's still frowning. I'm very conscious of my tear-stained face.

I gather Bella up with my bag and struggle to my feet. 'We'll be on our way.'

'Are you sure?' he says. 'Would you like a cup of tea first?'

CHAPTER TWENTY-FIVE

'Okay, Tommy, thanks for letting me know.' I hang up. *Fuck, fuck, fuck.* He had her, and he let her slip through his fingers. What the hell is she doing? And why is she doing it to *me*?

The situation is getting out of hand. I should have gone to Scotland myself – I would never have let her get away – but I had a loose end to tie up here. It wasn't easy to explain to Becker why my wife and child are running round Scotland like lunatics when they're supposed to be floating somewhere in the English Channel. In the end, I just told him the truth – that my wife has lost her mind, staged her own suicide for reasons known only to herself, then gone on the run with our daughter. He's promised to keep it on the down-low until we find them. It's only a matter of time before we do.

I called in a favour from one of my tech contacts, who was able to get Lisa's new number from Willow's phone. As soon as she switches her phone on again, I'll have her.

Of course, my contact doesn't know who Willow's phone belongs to. I'm going to have to keep as much blue sky between these two investigations – the private and the public – as possible. It's getting really bloody messy.

'Is everything okay, sir?' asks DI Mbala. 'Can we go in now?'

'Yes, carry on, Inspector.'

The two uniformed officers have to move a huge black and white cat away from the door to use their Enforcer. It only takes one thump and they're in – not surprising because it's only locked once, with the key I found at home, on the hook where Lisa left it.

The uniforms step aside for Mbala to go in first. I follow.

Willow is in plain sight, on the floor where I left her. Stark and frozen.

I gasp. 'Oh my God.'

Mbala kneels beside the body and spots the hypodermic syringe on the carpet. I push past him, pick it up.

'Sir!' Mbala barks at me.

I drop the hypodermic. 'Sorry, I wasn't thinking.' My face crumples with grief. I imagine it's pretty convincing. I've had plenty of practice lately.

'Step away from the body, please, sir, if you don't mind.'

I don't mind at all. My job here is done. Any DNA that belongs to me they now find in the flat, they'll have to dismiss because I've contaminated the scene.

Mbala's already on the phone. 'Yeah ... we have a DB. An overdose, it looks like.' His eyes slide to me. 'Yeah ... the chief super's here too. He knows the victim.'

Victim? Hardly a victim if she's overdosed.

I don't know what Mbala's doing here. I requested the entry because I was concerned about my wife's friend, who's been depressed since her death. I arranged to meet a team here, but wasn't expecting a senior officer to come with them.

I certainly wasn't expecting Mbala. He's off his patch. Why is that?

I watch him as he speaks on the phone. I know very little about him, really, other than what I've heard on the grapevine. He's well thought of. Good at his job. Which is unlucky. He's bound to be suspicious. First there was the blood at Keira's flat, then Lisa's death, now this. It's almost as if death is stalking me. Of course, if he's followed up with the Keira situation, he'll know that what I told him was true – she's not dead at all, but locked up safely at Bellfield. As for Lisa ... well, I suppose he'll find out soon enough that she isn't dead, either. Which only leaves Willow.

But even so, the whole situation is turning into a shit-show. And it's all Lisa's fault. I push down the hot rage I can feel rising in me. There'll be time for that later.

'Forensics are on their way,' says Mbala, when he's hung up the phone, 'with the ambulance.' He scans the room. 'I wonder what happened to her dog?' He's spotted a couple of tins of dog food on the counter of the kitchenette in the corner. 'Did she have a dog?'

I nod. 'A puppy.' I don't feel the need to elaborate; he doesn't need to know it's actually *my* dog. I unpacked Willow's holdall after I'd killed her. It would have looked suspicious for her to be packed for a trip. But I'd forgotten about the damn dog. She must have left it with someone. Did she tell them she was going away?

'We'll have to get the place taped off,' says Mbala. 'Go through it properly.'

'Of course.' I nod my agreement. 'Although it looks pretty cut and dried to me.'

He looks at me, his gaze challenging. 'It does, doesn't it?'

Fuck. 'I'll let you get on, then, Inspector.'

He calls me back as I get to the door. 'Sir?'

I turn.

'That's a nasty scratch you have on your neck there.'

I put my hand to my neck instinctively, to the place where Willow raked me with her fingernails during our last desperate struggle. I'd thought it wasn't noticeable under my collar.

'A new razor,' I say. 'You know what they're like.'

'I do, sir.' Mbala tilts his head at me. 'Nothing worse.'

CHAPTER TWENTY-SIX

I wake with a start. There is a figure looming over the bed. His face is twisted with rage, all traces of the handsome man I married erased by hatred.

'Alex ...' I try to speak, but his name sticks in my throat. It only comes out as a whisper.

'You stupid, stupid bitch.' He leans down to hiss at me through clenched teeth, fury rising off him in invisible waves, like heat from a hot road. 'Look what you made me do.' He thrusts his hands towards me. They're covered in blood.

I try to twist away from him, but I can't move. My body is heavy, pinned to the bed. He bends closer until his nose is almost touching mine, and I can see the flecks of amber in his eyes, feel the heat coming off his skin. His hands go round my throat, tightening. I try to push him off me, but my body doesn't respond. There's nothing I can do. I can smell blood, feel it wet on my neck under his throttling hands. I can't breathe.

Willow!

I wake with a gasp, heart pounding.

It takes a while for the shock to subside, for me to realise where I am. Pale light filters in through the curtained window, revealing a wardrobe, pretty floral wallpaper and a sink in the corner. I'm at St Mary's rectory, in Haddington. I'm with Bella, and we're safe. I swing my legs out of bed, grope for the phone in my bag. Hands still trembling from my nightmare, I switch it on and dial Willow's number. It just rings out, like I knew it would.

Where are you, Willow? Are you safe?

'Mummy?' Bella's eyes are open.

'I'm here, chick.'

She sits up, rubbing her eyes, and I kiss her.

'Where are we?

'With one of mummy's friends.' I don't think it's too much of a stretch to call the Reverend McAllister a friend. I honestly think he saved our lives last night. 'Let's go down and say hello, shall we?'

We freshen up as best we can at the sink and get dressed. Our clothes are crumpled, and Bella's sweatshirt is still covered in chocolate from the café at the station.

'Teddy Pea!' Bella runs back to the bed to get him.

My nose twitches at the delicious smell of bacon as we go down the Georgian staircase. I didn't really get a chance to look at the house last night in the dark, but now the sunlight is shining through the big arched window on the staircase, I can see it's handsome rather than pretty. Foursquare and solid. We find the reverend cooking in the kitchen, an airy but rather bleak room with doors into the garden.

'Perfect timing,' he says. 'I'm just making breakfast.'

This is the first time I've had a proper look at him, too. I'd say he was in his late forties or early fifties, but boyish, with rumpled hair and warm brown eyes behind his glasses. Today he's wearing a floral apron.

'I have bacon and porridge, and I can do eggs any way you like.' He addresses Bella. 'What would you like?'

'Scrambled egg!' She grins. 'Please!'

'Scrambled egg it is. Coming right up.' He turns to me. 'And for mum?'

'I'll have some too, if that's okay, please? And some bacon.' The smell of the bacon is making my stomach growl. We haven't had anything to eat since the ill-fated croissant at Waverley, and most of that ended up in the toilet. Which reminds me – the pregnancy test is still in my bag. But I can't face doing that just now. Or even thinking about it.

'Can I give you a hand?' I ask.

'You can set the table, if you like. The cutlery's in the drawer. There's tea in the pot if you want it.'

I help myself to tea from the old-fashioned brown teapot.

I lay the table, sipping my tea as the reverend beats egg and adds it to the pan.

'How are you feeling this morning?' he asks. His eyes behind his glasses are warm with sympathy.

'Much better, thanks.'

'Everything always looks better in the morning.'

'It does if you've slept in a bed.' I smile at him. 'Thank you.'

He nods. 'You're welcome. If you want toast, you can stick some bread in the toaster.'

Bella and I eat breakfast like we haven't seen food for days. Afterwards, the reverend gives Bella some books he keeps for the local mother and toddler group. She settles down to look at them in a corner while he pours me another cup of tea. I prepare myself for the questions I know are coming.

'What's your story, Lisa? Do you feel able to tell me?'

I shouldn't have told him my real name last night, but I was too tired, too distressed to invent a fiction. I don't want to lie to this lovely, trusting man, but I can't tell him the truth. Not all of it, anyway.

'My husband is trying to kill me.'

His eyes widen.

'I know that sounds extreme, but it's true. We only just managed to get away. I'm not even sure how we got here. I just drove.'

'Couldn't you have gone to family? To friends?'

I shake my head. Tears prickle my eyes. I can't tell him I think Alex has killed Willow; he'll think I'm completely mad.

The reverend scratches his chin and pulls a regretful face. 'I would like to extend my hospitality, but I'm afraid I can't. You can't stay here. I'm not really equipped for it.'

I nod.

'Perhaps we can try to find you a place in a women's refuge?'

I don't want to tell him I've already tried that, so I have to improvise.

'My husband works with social services. He would find us in a refuge. I need to get somewhere as far as possible from the city.'

'Do you have money?'

'Some. Not a lot, but enough for now. Really, I could do with a job.' That hadn't been part of our plan when Willow and I were plotting my escape. We thought we just needed time – a few weeks at most – to find some proof against Alex.

That feels like a fantasy now. I don't know what the hell we were thinking.

The reverend looks thoughtful. 'I might have a solution. Don't get your hopes up just yet. I'm going to make some calls.'

'Please don't tell anyone my name when you talk to them.'

'I won't.' He gets to his feet.

'Bella and I have to go shopping. We need clothes. Cheap clothes.'

He smiles. 'You've come to the right town for that.'

IT TURNS out that Haddington has more than its share of charity shops. I trail Bella round every one of them. We find a warm jacket for her in Save the Children, to replace Kelly's jumper, and a selection of little hoodies and trousers in Cancer Research. In Oxfam I find her some pyjamas, a pair of jeans for myself, and a couple of T-shirts and jumpers. Finally, I grab us both some underwear in Tesco. All in all, I spend less than a hundred pounds. Bella's delighted with our haul. She seems just as happy shopping for clothes in charity shops as she was in Harrods with Alex splurging on Kenzo dresses. What was I thinking, letting him spend so much money? I shove the thought to the back of my mind. That hardly matters now.

After we've shopped, I treat Bella to a hot chocolate in one of the little independent cafés. I watch her queasily as she slurps cream off the top. The scrambled eggs are sitting heavily in my stomach, and the pregnancy test is burning a hole in my bag. I know I need to use it, but I'm not sure I can face the consequences. I give myself a mental shake. Surely, it's better to know, one way or the other, and deal with it.

I catch the eye of a girl in a Cath Kidston apron who's wiping down a nearby table.

'Can I use your loo?'

'Sure. It's just through the back there, to the right.'

'Would you mind watching my daughter for a minute?'

The girl beams at Bella. 'No problem. You'll be okay with me, won't you?'

Bella is too occupied scooping marshmallows from her hot chocolate to answer.

I hurry through to the bathroom with my bag. There's only one cubicle, with a sink and mirror. I pee on the test, put the test on the cistern, and wash my hands to wait for the results. The instructions say to wait three to five minutes. The numbers on my phone creep at a snail's pace. One minute. One and a half. Two. Two and a half. I can't stand it any longer, and I can't leave Bella much longer either. I peer at the test. I look at it, then look again, just to be sure.

Two pink lines in the window. Clear and unambiguous.

I'm pregnant.

My stomach roils. Luckily, I'm already standing beside the toilet.

When I get back to the table, Bella hasn't even noticed I'm not there. She's licking cream off her fingers and chatting to the girl in the apron.

'They're blue and yellow and have a dog on them.' I realise she's telling her about the pair of pyjamas we've just bought.

'Sounds lovely.'

'Let her see, Mummy.'

Too preoccupied to argue, I fish the pyjamas from the charity bag to show them to Bella's new friend.

'Very nice. Do you like dogs?'

Bella nods, enthusiastic. 'I have one at home. A puppy.' Her brow furrows. 'I miss Figgy, Mummy.'

'How's that hot chocolate?' I try to deflect. I really can't deal with tears just now. 'Is it tasty?'

Bella nods.

'Thanks so much for keeping an eye on her,' I say to the girl.

'A pleasure.' She winks at Bella and goes back to the counter.

I watch Bella as she finishes the very last drop of her drink, but I'm not really seeing her. I'm not thinking about anything either – my mind has gone into freefall. Eventually she declares her mug is empty. We leave a tip on our way out, even though I can't really spare it.

When we get back to the rectory, I spot the reverend looking out one of the windows, waiting for us. He hurries to open the door.

'How did it go?' he asks as he ushers us inside. 'Did you get everything you need?'

'We did.' I hold up the charity-shop bags as evidence.

'That's great.' He's not his usual calm self; he looks distracted. Excited, even. 'I have some good news.'

CHAPTER TWENTY-SEVEN

'I have some good news.' Andy Barker, my contact in technical support, sounds very pleased with himself. 'Your perp used their phone this morning. I have their new location.'

'Can you send it to me?'

'No problem.'

'Keep tracking it, Andy, will you?'

'I can do better than that. I'm going to transfer it to your phone so you can track it yourself.'

Perfect. 'I'm on my way down.'

I cancel the meeting I was supposed to be going into, and hurry down to the basement, where we keep our geeks and freaks. In his felt-lined cubicle, pinned with photos and quotes from obscure movies, Andy adds the tracking info to my phone.

'Thanks.'

'Any time, sir.'

'I don't need to say, do I, that this is between the two of us?'

He makes a zipping motion across his mouth. I know he won't say anything, anyway. His girlfriend was arrested for shoplifting last year. High-end beauty products from Harvey Nicks. Knowing it can never hurt to have a tech expert in my pocket, I managed to have the charges dismissed. He owes me.

The tracking shows Lisa's phone is in a town called Haddington, just off the A1, south of Edinburgh. Google says it will take seven hours to get there. I reckon I can do it in six or less, using the good ol' blue lights. I clear my diary, change into my civvies, then set off for Edinburgh.

This time I'm doing it myself. This time I'll get her.

I'M HALFWAY up the A1, driving through the flat countryside of the Vale of York, when my phone rings. I answer it on hands-free.

'McMahon.'

'Hello. This is Dr Jennifer Fulton, from the Meadows Medical Practice in Twickenham. Your colleague Tommy Becker gave me this number to call. Do you have a moment to talk just now?'

'Yes, that's fine.'

'First of all, I'm very sorry for your loss. I had no idea, when your wife came to see me, just how desperate she was.'

'None of us did, Dr Fulton. You shouldn't blame your-self.' Get to the fucking point.

'When Lisa came to see me, we did some tests. They included a pregnancy test.'

My hands grip the wheel more tightly.

'I wanted to let you know, before you see any coroner's report, that the test results were positive.'

I don't believe it. I don't know what to say.

The doctor misinterprets my silence. 'I'm really very, very sorry.'

'Thank you.' I try to make my voice as flat as possible, to squeeze all the exultation out of it.

'Are you okay?' Her voice is ripe with concern.

'I'm fine.' More than fine. 'Thank you for letting me know.'

I hang up, punching the air. Yes! All that fucking did the trick. I'm going to be a father! A proper father, like the one I never had. After all this time, I'm finally going to get what I wanted. But ... it does complicate things. When I find Lisa, I'm going to have to handle her carefully. Very, very carefully.

'SORRY, no, I haven't seen her.' The old woman shakes her head at the photo on my phone. 'She's a bonny-looking lass, though. I hope you find her.'

I swallow my irritation. Does she think I'm here looking for a date?

'Thanks anyway,' I say, trying not to snap.

She closes the door. Andy's tracker isn't accurate enough to tell me exactly which house Lisa is in, although it has narrowed it down to three possibilities. One is an art supplies shop, already closed for the night, shuttered and in darkness. That just leaves one more residential address to try – a big house, set back from the road with its own drive. This has to be it. I certainly hope so, because I'm out of patience and energy. My eyes are gritty, and my whole body aches from sitting in the car so long.

The sign on the gate says St Mary's Rectory. As I crunch

down the driveway, my senses start to tingle. This is it. Lisa's here; I can feel it. The curtains are all drawn, but there is a light in one of the downstairs rooms. I know I have to tread carefully. I don't want her sneaking out the back way like she did in Edinburgh. I hesitate before ringing the doorbell. I don't want to alert her, but I don't see any way around it.

A thin, rather nondescript man in glasses opens the door. He's shocked to see me. Perhaps I shouldn't have changed back into my uniform. I had reservations about whether I should – I'm pretty certain it was Tommy's unsubtle invasion of the refuge that sent Lisa scurrying off last time. But in the end I decided I might need the extra clout – the moral and actual authority – the uniform gives me.

'Evening, sir.' I keep my voice low. 'Would you mind stepping outside a moment?'

'What?'

'I need to have a word with you. A private word.'

'Then you can come in.' He opens the door wide for me to enter. 'There's no one else here.'

Not what I wanted to hear. 'You're alone in the house, sir?'

'I am.'

The tracker says Lisa's here, but perhaps she's gone out and left her phone? If so, I need to get inside, out of sight. I step into the hall.

'I'm the Reverend McAllister.' He closes the door and shakes my hand. 'What's this about, officer?' His gaze slides to the insignia on my epaulettes.

'We're looking for a woman who's on the run, with her little girl. We have reason to believe she might be here.'

'What's she supposed to have done?'

'Fraud. Grievous bodily harm.' I throw in the last for good measure. His eyes widen, but he keeps his composure.

'Do you mind if I see your ID?' he asks.

Cheeky fucker. I flash the badge from my pocket and also show him the lanyard around my neck, which has my photo ID on it.

'Chief Superintendent? This seems a little above your pay grade, if you don't mind me saying so.'

I do mind, but try not to show it. 'Lisa McMahon is a dangerous woman.' Why is he being so cagey? Is she here? I take out my phone and show him her photo.

'Have you seen her?' I know he has. He couldn't hide his flash of recognition.

Luckily, he doesn't try to deny it. 'She was here. Her and her little girl. They've gone.'

'Gone where?' I'm not sure I believe him. I know Lisa's phone is still here.

'I don't know.'

I definitely don't believe that. He isn't making eye contact. The Reverend McAllister is a bad liar, but I suppose he hasn't had a lot of practice.

'We know that her phone is here.' I talk as levelly, as calmly as I can, to hide my impatience, when what I *really* want to do is shake the truth out of him. 'Would you mind if I take a look around, see if I can find it?'

'Do you have a warrant?'

'I'm afraid not.' Of course I don't have a fucking warrant. I struggle to keep my temper. 'Could you please take a look for me, then, sir? See if you can find the phone?'

He goes upstairs.

I wonder if I've made a mistake letting him do that. What if Lisa is still here? What if he's helping her hide? Or escape? I realise that's pretty unlikely, with Bella in tow. What are they going to do? Toss her out a first-floor window?

He returns after a couple of minutes, a mobile phone in his hand. He gives it to me.

'She must have forgotten it.'

Or realised I'd be able to trace it using Willow's phone.

'Are you sure you don't know where she might be now?' I ask again. I still suspect she's upstairs.

He shakes his head. 'Quite sure.' But, again, he doesn't meet my eyes. It's telling, too, that he shook his head rather than nodding in answer to my question. There's a disconnect between what he's saying and what the rest of his body is telling me.

'That's a pity.' I can see I need to pull out the big guns. I scroll through my phone. 'I'm sorry to have to show you this, sir, but I need you to realise how serious the situation is. We believe Mrs McMahon is involved in something much worse than GBH.'

I show him a photograph of the scene at Willow's flat. Of her lifeless body sprawled on the floor.

He recoils. 'Christ!'

I almost smile. Wasn't there something about taking the Lord's name in vain?

I continue, enjoying the violence of his reaction. 'This is Lisa McMahon's best friend. We believed she killed her in a fight over drugs.' In for a penny, in for a pound. 'I don't know what lies she might have spun you, but she's a dangerous, desperate woman. Anyone helping her to escape would be considered an accessory after the fact.'

I let that sink in. The man seems to have aged years in just a few seconds. I almost feel sorry for him.

'She told me she was on the run from an abusive

husband.' He takes off his spectacles to rub his face. 'She seemed so—'

'Plausible? She is, sir. She's a practised con artist. It's to your credit that you helped her, like a good Christian, but you can't help her now. We need to know where she is.'

He nods; I've broken him. 'I'll get you the address.'

CHAPTER TWENTY-EIGHT

The West Highland Hotel stands on the brow of a hill in Perthshire, overlooking the valley and the Tay below. The Victorian building sprawls in all directions, with multiple turrets, and bay windows reflecting the light of the setting sun. The car park is large, empty apart from one other car. I park up and prise a still-grumbling Bella from her seat. It's hardly surprising she's in such a stinking mood, being bundled about from one place to another. Hopefully this will be our last move for a while.

The big double doors to the hotel are closed. I pull on the old-fashioned bell and hear it ring inside the building. After a few moments, there's movement inside, and the door is opened by a middle-aged woman wearing a waxed Barbour jacket, a jaunty knitted hat and a broad smile.

'You must be Lisa.' She shakes my hand, then bends to Bella. 'And what's your name?'

'Bella.' Bella pouts and clutches Teddy Pea, unwilling to be coaxed from her sulk.

'I'm Rachel McAllister. Come in, come in, both of you, and get out of the cold.'

It isn't much warmer inside. The hall of the building – an echoing space with panelling and a fireplace – has no furniture or floor covering. There's a stack of Victorian radiators lined up like dominos against the wall, and a small cement mixer in the corner. A huge oak staircase, also devoid of carpet, stretches heavenward.

'Come through to the housekeeper's quarters; the heating's on in there.'

Rachel bustles through a green door behind the reception desk, which leads into a maze of corridors.

'Don't worry about getting lost. Everyone does at first. It just takes a bit of time to get your bearings. These are the staff quarters – the kitchen is that way, but it's a building site at the moment. You don't need to worry about that. Down there to the left is the delivery entrance, and to the right is the back stair to the spa.'

We go down a flight of narrow stairs to the basement.

'Here we are.'

She pushes open a door marked 'Housekeeper' and ushers us inside. We find ourselves in a small, comfortable sitting room, with overstuffed floral armchairs and a kitchenette in an alcove. There's a fire burning in the grate.

'This is where you'll be staying. There's a bedroom through the back, which I've made up for you both. I would have put you in one of the suites, but the heating's off everywhere but here. It's the heating we're having overhauled, you see. Messy job, but it was installed in the thirties, so it desperately needs doing. Kettle's just boiled; would you like tea or coffee?'

'Tea, please.' I'm a little overwhelmed by her chattiness,

but relieved. I was expecting an interview, but she seems to be taking it for granted that Bella and I will be staying.

'Milk for the little one?' Rachel goes to the small under-counter fridge.

'That would be lovely.'

'I can't tell you what a relief it is that you're here. I mentioned to Peter a few weeks ago I was having trouble finding someone to stay on site while the work was being done. And now here you are. An angel sent from heaven. He tells me you haven't been in Scotland long?'

'Just a couple of weeks.' I'm keen to shut down her enquiry. 'But we love it here.'

'Eden, isn't it? Apart from the weather, but you get used to it. Layers. The secret is to dress in layers. Sugar?'

'No, thanks.' I take the tea from her. 'It's very good of you to consider me, but I don't know anything about construction. I hope I'm not expected to make any decisions?'

'Nothing like that. Just be here to take deliveries and keep an eye on things. Last time we had builders here, extending the pool, they cut through an underground pipe before they left for the weekend. We didn't know anything about it until the Monday morning, when we found the ground floor under water.' She laughs. 'Extend the pool? The whole hotel was a swimming pool!'

I smile. Her good humour is so infectious it even seems to be cheering Bella up. Or maybe that's the milk and biscuits Rachel has given her.

'Now ... down to business.' Rachel sits opposite me at the table. I notice her eyes are the same warm brown as her brother, the reverend's. 'I'll pay you three hundred and fifty pounds a week. Bed and bills are included, obviously. I've stocked the cupboards and the fridge, so you won't have to go shopping straight away.'

I nod my thanks. 'What exactly do you need me to do?'

'I'll go through all that when I give you the tour, but I've written everything down in here.' She taps a ring binder on the table. 'The builders will be back in the morning. Just ignore them if you can. They're a good bunch, but not the quietest. I'll be popping in every now and again, of course, and my number's in the binder if you need it.' She looks at me. 'So what do you say? Do we have a deal? Are you staying?'

'Yes, please.' As if I could turn down an offer like this. It's a miracle.

Rachel beams. 'Excellent. Finish your tea, and I'll show you round.'

We start in the attics, which are mostly empty apart from stored furniture, then work our way down. All the bedrooms and suites on the first floor are locked.

'If the boys need access to any of the rooms, the keys are hanging in reception. There are spares in the filing cabinet in the office, but you shouldn't need them.'

Other rooms on the first floor include a small sitting room and a library, with bookshelves stuffed with a mish-mash of titles from *Five Go Down to the Sea* to *Fifty Shades of Grey*.

Rachel picks up the copy of *Fifty Shades* lying on a chair and slots it back into the bookcase.

'We keep these on the top shelves,' she says, with a wink, 'so the little ones can't reach them.' Her phone rings. She takes it out to check the caller ID.

'Peter,' she says. 'Wanting to make sure you've found your way here, I imagine.' She pushes the phone back into her voluminous pocket. 'I'll call him later. Come on down and see the ground floor.'

We follow her down the echoing staircase.

Downstairs, there's a restaurant, bar, billiard room, office, crèche, spa and a swimming pool that leaks a faint whiff of chlorine into the corridors nearby. The corridors themselves are tricky to negotiate, littered with tools, uncoupled radiators and pipework, both new and old. We pass a huge conservatory, devoid of plants but stacked with white wrought-iron tables and chairs.

'You should see this place in the summer,' says Rachel wistfully. 'We fill the place with rented greenery, keep the French doors open and serve high tea on the terrace. It really is wonderful.'

'I can imagine.'

I realise we're back at reception. I keep one eye on Bella as she goes off to investigate the cement mixer.

Rachel hands me her bunch of keys. 'They're all labelled. All you need to do is a quick tour in the mornings, to open everything up before the builders start at eight. Then lock up after they've gone.'

'That's it? You don't need me to do any admin, anything like that?'

'Apart from signing for deliveries, no. I do all the paperwork remotely.'

Which reminds me. 'I don't suppose you have a laptop I could use while I'm here? I need access to the internet, and I've lost my phone.' Like an idiot, I left it at the rectory. I hadn't realised until I was on the Queensferry crossing over the Firth of Forth, and by then it was too late to turn round and go back. I had to buy a map at a service station to find my way here.

Rachel opens a drawer of the reception desk and takes out a Dell laptop and charger.

'You can use this.' She rummages in the drawer some more to find a notebook. 'The log-in details are in here.' She looks around, pulls a thoughtful face. 'Is there anything I've forgotten? I don't think so. But like I said, my number is in the binder if you need me.'

'I'm sure we'll be fine.'

'Anything you need, don't hesitate to call.'

I wave her off, watching the lights of her car disappear up the long gravel drive. It's only half four, but already pitch dark. I close and lock the doors gratefully against the cold Highland night.

'Bella!' I call her to me. She's looking glum and fidgety again. But I have an idea.

We visit the crèche and bring a haul of toys, games and books down to the housekeeper's quarters. While Bella crows over her new treasures, I explore our latest home. The kitchenette is small, but has a sink, hob and a fridge, stocked with all the basics and also a few luxuries – chocolate pudding, grapes and a half-bottle of white wine. Just off a small corridor there's a shower room and bedroom, where twin beds are made up with deliciously laundered linen. There's a pile of towels and even a couple of bottles of water on the bedside tables. Rachel really has thought of everything.

I'm overwhelmed with gratitude. We've had to rely on the kindness of strangers so much since we left Twickenham – first Roo and Kelly, then the reverend and now his sister, Rachel. What would I have done without them? From the moment I found Polly's note under my bed, my blinkers of wealth and privilege have fallen away. I feel as if I'm now seeing the world as it truly is – more horrifying, dangerous and yet kinder than I could possibly have imagined.

I find some fusilli in the cupboard and make a simple meal of tomato pasta for our supper. Bella's eyes are drifting shut before she finishes. Today has been so taxing for her, waking up in one unfamiliar place and going to sleep in another. I feel a thump of guilt.

'Do you want some chocolate pudding?'

She shakes her head.

'Heavens, you must be tired. Bedtime, I think, don't you?'

She doesn't object as I steer her into the bedroom and help her change into her charity-shop pyjamas.

'Can I have a story?'

'Go and choose one.'

She runs through to the sitting room, bringing back a classic – 'Red Riding Hood'. We snuggle into bed together.

Long, long ago, there was a beautiful little girl who was loved by everyone who knew her. Her grandmother was so very fond of her she never felt she could do enough to please her. One day she gave the little girl a red silk cap, which suited her so well she would never wear anything else and so was called Little Red Riding Hood or just Little Red Cap from that day on.

She's asleep before the big bad wolf even makes his first appearance.

I kiss her on the forehead and tuck her in. She's so small in the bed. So vulnerable. I put my hand on my stomach. There's a new life growing inside me, too. How can I keep both these precious lives safe?

Leaving the bedside lamp on in case Bella wakes up and doesn't know where she is, I go back through to the sitting room. There is a TV, but I don't want to put it on in case it disturbs her. I suppose I could go up to the library to look for a book, but somehow my body refuses to move out of the chair. I find myself thinking about Willow. I have a terrible, heavy feeling about her. I can't think of a good reason why she wouldn't have met me at the station.

I make a supreme effort to heave myself out of the chair and go to fetch the laptop from reception, scurrying back to the warmth and light of the sitting room as quickly as I can. I use the log-in details from the notebook.

How do I find out what's happened to Willow? Could there even be anything online to find? I suppose I could search 'body found London', but I don't think I can bear it. I start in the most obvious place, with her name: 'Willow Schneider'.

It comes up straight away.

Willow Schneider, Beyond actress, found dead aged 35

I have to stifle my cry of shock.

The Metropolitan Police gained entry to Schneider's flat on Thursday morning after concerns were expressed about her welfare. She was pronounced dead at the scene.

The UK actress was best known for playing scatter-brained medium Connie McDonald in the well-loved TV series Beyond, and later took on the role of vindictive tennis coach Belinda Severn in West of Wimbledon. She's also appeared on the stage, most notably as

Ariel in last summer's RSC production of The
Tempest *and, more recently, as Emilia in* Othello *at
the Bath Theatre Royal.*

*Co-stars paid tribute to her, describing her as an
'inspirational' actress who 'cared deeply' about her
work.*

*Authorities said her death was not being treated as
suspicious.*

*In a statement, the Metropolitan Police said, 'Crimi-
nality is not suspected. The coroner will determine
the cause of death.'*

Even though I'd half guessed Willow was dead – in fact,
I'd known in my heart that she was – it's devastating to have
it confirmed. Alex must have made it look like suicide, which
isn't something I can imagine Willow ever doing, even in the
darkest of times. How did he do it? Pills? A noose? A knife?

In my mind's eye I see the congealing pool of blood in
Keira's flat, and my stomach heaves. I vomit onto the floor,
again and again, until my stomach's empty. I take some deep
breaths. My eyes are strangely dry. I don't seem to have any
tears to grieve for my friend, but I feel her loss, deep inside,
as if something vital and passionate has been ripped out
of me.

Alex is a monster. A wolf in sheep's clothing. But how
can I possibly prove that? How can I unmask him? There has
to be a way. I need to avenge Willow, and Polly and Keira
too. But my tired brain is reeling; it refuses to string more

than two thoughts together, stupefied by the fire and the softness of my armchair ...

I WAKE SUDDENLY, jerked out of sleep. The fire is out. Is it the cold that's woken me? I don't think so. I think it was a noise. Bella? I tiptoe along the corridor and look in the bedroom. Bella is still fast asleep, tucked into her pristine sheets.

Then I hear it again. The faint sound of glass shattering somewhere in the hotel.

CHAPTER TWENTY-NINE

I listen, ears straining, for the sound of breaking glass to come again, but all I hear is silence. Did I imagine it? No, I heard it twice, the second time very distinctly. Should I call the police? I don't want to alert anyone to my presence here – least of all the police – but I can't let the hotel get burgled, and I can't deal with an intruder on my own. My heart thuds, loud in my ears. Might we be able to hide down here and hope whoever it is won't find us? Can I take that risk? I don't think I can.

I reach for my phone, then remember I don't have one. How could I have been so stupid! The nearest phone is on reception.

I leave the safety of the housekeeper's quarters and tiptoe up the stairs, feeling my way in the darkness. The electricity is on, but I don't know where any of the light switches are. I don't think I should put any lights on anyway, in case I alert whoever has broken in. I feel my way along the corridor to the green door into reception and pull back the bolt as quietly as I can. I peep through the door into the hallway, but can see no signs of life. My heart thumps with relief as I see the phone on the reception desk. I tiptoe over to it, pick up the receiver and dial 999. It seems an eternity before someone picks up.

'*Emergency services. Which service, please?*'

I'm about to speak when I hear a noise. A footstep? I freeze, peering out over the reception desk into the hallway. There's more light here than there was downstairs because the windows have no curtains.

Something moves in the shadows beside the concrete mixer.

'Lisa.'

My heart almost bursts out of my chest. A dark figure is silhouetted against the light from the windows. I can't see his face, but I'd know his voice anywhere.

'It's okay,' he soothes. 'There's no need to panic. You're safe now.'

Safe? An involuntary bark of laughter bursts from my lips.

'Where's Bella?' Alex steps forward, into the light. I can see nothing of the man I thought I loved in that handsome, faux-concerned face. 'I don't know why you've done this ... this charade, but I'm glad – so glad – you're both alive.'

This is grotesque.

'Stop it,' I say. 'Just stop it. Who is this act for? There's only me here, and I know everything. I know you killed Polly. And Keira. And Willow.' My voice catches on the last name.

'Killed them?' His eyebrows rise in an expression of shock. 'I didn't kill them. Keira isn't even dead. Polly died in a car accident. And Willow ... she never was the steadiest, was she? It's a tragedy, but you must believe I had nothing to do with it.'

'Don't lie to me.'

'I don't know why you're saying these things. You're not making any sense, Lisa. You're not well ... Maybe it's an imbalance. Pregnancy hormones.'

Fuck! How the hell does he know I'm pregnant?

'Come home with me. We'll get you well again, and I'll look after you. All three of you.'

Fuck this. I spin round and dash back through the door. Throw the bolt. I hear him crash against it as I hurtle down the corridor. I run, frantic, bouncing off the walls in the darkness, to the basement stairs, and I almost tumble down them in my haste to get to the bottom. That bolt won't hold for long.

I crash into the housekeeper's quarters and stumble through to the bedroom.

'Wake up, Bella. Wake up.'

She opens her eyes, groggy.

'We're going to play a game. We're going to play hide-and-seek.' I grab her, then bolt back with her through the sitting room into the corridor. As I do, I hear a crash, then pounding feet. Alex is coming down the stairs. I run the other way, towards the delivery entrance. I have to trust in the fact that it's dark, that Alex doesn't know where he's going. I don't have much of an idea either, not really, but I do know more than him. I pause at the point the corridor branches off in different directions. Which way did Rachel say the delivery entrance was?

I choose the left-hand corridor, acting on instinct. I soon

see my instinct was right, because it ends in an archway, hung with one of those curtains made of clear PVC strips. I push through them into the delivery bay. The metal roll-down door won't budge. It's locked. Of course it is. And I've left the keys on the hook in the housekeeper's quarters.

Bella starts to cry, but I don't have time to soothe her. I quickly retrace our steps to the other corridor, the one that leads to the back stairs to the spa. I can hear Alex crashing about, trying to find his way through the warren of dark corridors. The minotaur in his maze.

When we reach the top of the stairs, I have to pause to catch my breath. Bella is a dead weight in my arms, and my legs are like jelly. But I've had an idea. If we can lock ourselves in one of the rooms on the first floor, he'll never find us. It'll be like looking for a needle in a haystack. I can't take a key from reception – it'll be too obvious which one is missing – but Rachel said there are spares in the office. I hurry past the dining room and crèche to the office. I try the handle, but the door is locked. Fuck and double fuck!

The sounds of pursuit are growing louder. Alex has found the back staircase.

I can't run any further with Bella. We need to hide, quickly. But where?

I dodge through the builders' debris, into the conservatory, with its stacks of wrought-iron furniture, closing the doors softly behind us. Bella is crying in earnest now, great snotty sobs that soak into my sweatshirt.

'Shhh. Shhh, sweetheart.' I wipe her face with my hand. 'Everything is okay.'

'LISA!' Alex's voice is close, in the corridor. 'Why are you running away? I'm not going to hurt you.'

'Ali!' Bella's eyes widen in recognition. Is she going to give us away? I put my hand over her mouth.

'I love you! Come out and let's talk this through!'

Bella glares at me over my fingers, her face red with upset and indignation. I take my hand from her mouth, put my finger to my lips.

'We're going to play a game,' I whisper. 'We're going to hide from Ali. Just like we did at the wedding, remember?'

Bella nods.

'We have to be very, very quiet. Like dead lions.'

'Sleeping lions.'

'Like sleeping lions. Do you think you can do that?'

Bella nods again, tears forgotten, eyes alight at the thought of fooling Alex.

We find a spot under one of the tables at the back of the room. Bella lies down. I creep to the French doors to try the handles. Every one of them is locked, but it was worth a try.

'You have to lie down too,' Bella stage-whispers. 'Like a sleeping lion.'

I hurry back to lie down beside her. It isn't easy to do when every molecule in my body is screaming at me to get up and run. If Alex finds us in here, we're done for. The only way out is either through him or through the glass of the French doors.

I try to control my pounding heart, to regulate my breathing. Deep breaths. In and out. In and out. Bella has her eyes squeezed shut.

'Lisa!' Alex is right outside the door now. 'Bella! Where is my special girl? She can't be hiding from me, can she?'

I glance anxiously at Bella, but she just stifles a giggle and squeezes her eyes more tightly shut. Good girl.

'Please come out, Lisa. Let's talk about this reasonably.

Think about Bella. Think about the baby.' His voice isn't quite so loud now. He's moving further away, down the corridor.

How does he know about the baby? I suppose Dr Fulton must have given the police my test results after my so-called suicide. I'd much rather Alex didn't know about it. It feels like a violation. A weapon he can use against me.

'Has Ali gone?' whispers Bella.

'Not yet. We still need to be quiet. Sleeping lions, remember?'

She closes her eyes again.

I lie absolutely still, but my mind is whirring. We're going to have to get out of here, somehow. We'll have to wait until Alex is out of earshot, then try to make our way to reception down the main staircase without him seeing us. And when we get outside, then what? We must be a mile from the nearest neighbour. Will we get that far?

'What's that noise, Mummy?' Bella's whisper breaks into my thoughts.

I listen. A police siren! I never spoke to the call handler when I made the emergency call, but now I realise that I didn't hang up the phone either. Have they come to investigate? If so, I have to get to them before Alex does.

'Stay here, sweetheart. Lie very still. Keep being the very best sleeping lion for me. Mummy will be back in a minute.' I crawl out from under the table, then open the door into the corridor as quietly as I can. There's no sign of Alex, but I can see blue light strobing through the window onto the ceiling. Where is Alex? Has he gone back downstairs? If he gets to the police first, he'll send them away or tell them a bunch of lies. I can't let him do that.

I hurry to the window and peer down onto the driveway.

There is a squad car there, its siren silent now, but blue lights still spinning. Two officers get out and look up at the building. I wave frantically. One of them spots me.

'HERE!' I shout. 'HERE!'

I turn. Pain slams into my head. Fireworks explode behind my eyes, and the world turns black.

CHAPTER THIRTY

'Chief Superintendent McMahon? Sorry to keep you waiting, sir.' Detective Inspector Ian Ramsay, of Tayside division – a wiry man with salt-and-pepper hair – comes into the family room where I've been waiting.

'How is my wife?'

'She's regained consciousness, I'm pleased to say. But she's still very fragile. Confused. We can't interview her yet. How did you say she hit her head again?'

'I didn't.' He can't catch me out like that. 'I have no idea how it happened. I wasn't with her. I suppose she must have tripped. Where's Bella?'

'She's with my colleague from social services until we get this situation straightened out.'

'It's really not that complicated. My wife is ill. Paranoid. She needs taking into care for her own protection.'

'I understand she faked her own death?'

'Yes. About two weeks ago.' I sigh. How many times do I have to go through this charade, with how many different people? Hopefully this will be the last time. 'She pretended to walk into the sea with my daughter, staged the scene, left suicide notes. Then she drove up to Scotland.'

He rubs his nose. 'That seems a pretty extreme thing to do. Why do you think she did that?'

'I have no idea. Like I said, she's not well.'

'Had you been having problems? Marital problems?'

Anger surges, hot in my veins.

'Not at all. We've only been married a few weeks. We are – or were – very happy.' Has she said something to him? I think she must have done, for him to be pursuing this line of questioning. Perhaps a more conciliatory tone would be helpful? I lean forward, confidential. 'When I married Lisa, she was bright, bubbly. I had no idea she had mental health issues. That only became clear when we moved in together. She became depressed. Agitated. Now she's somehow got it into her head that I'm trying to kill her.' I run my hand over my face, the picture of distress. 'I would never, ever hurt her. I love her.'

'It must be upsetting for everyone.'

I still don't like the way he's looking at me. My patience is wearing thin.

'All the details can be verified by my colleagues in London. Call Assistant Chief Constable William Glover at the Met. He'll confirm everything I've told you.' I pause. 'He can provide the character reference you seem to need.'

'I don't need a character reference, sir.'

'Good. In that case I'd like to see my wife.'

'I'm afraid you can't. She's not well enough for visitors.'

'I'm not a *visitor*, I'm her next of kin. Her *husband*.'

He stares at me, assessing, then gives a slight nod. 'I'll see what I can do.' He goes out.

A few minutes later a nurse sticks her head in the door. 'Mr McMahon?'

I follow her through the noisy, echoing corridors to a private room. Lisa is in the bed, eyes closed. She looks serene, peaceful – the woman I married, not the spitting, furious harpy who confronted me in the hotel. That had been a shock. I don't know what I expected, after chasing her the length of the country, but I certainly was not prepared for such venom. I suppose I thought I might be able to reason with her, make her see sense, but she was beyond that. Well beyond it. When the uniforms from Tayside division arrived, I knew things were threatening to spin completely out of control. What if they believed her accusations? I waited for her to show herself and then crept up on her. Maybe I shouldn't have hit her so hard with that lead piping.

'Don't worry,' says the nurse, interpreting my silence. 'Her CT scan doesn't show any fracture or bleeding, but head injuries can be tricky. We want to keep an eye on her for twenty-four hours or so.'

That's good. It means I have time to make arrangements with Bellfield. It won't be cheap to get a private ambulance up from Surrey, but it will be worth it. I'll get her safely tucked away until my baby is born. And after that? She's going to be a liability. I'll have to figure out a way to get rid of her for good.

'You can sit with her awhile, if you like,' suggests the nurse.

'No, that's fine.' Why would I do that? I have too much to do to act the devoted husband, and I don't want to risk her waking up and panicking at the sight of me. 'I'll come back later.'

When I get back to the family room, I find the social worker waiting with Bella.

'Ali!' Bella charges at me.

I scoop her up and hug her. 'How's my best girl?'

The social worker, a thin man with a shaven head, looks on, indulgent.

'We've done all the checks we need to do, and we're happy to release her into your care.' He nods towards a rucksack and shoulder bag. 'We've brought all her things from the hotel. Your wife's things, too.'

'Where is Mummy?' Bella interrupts.

'Mummy's tired, darling. She's just having a little lie-down.'

'Can I see her?'

'Later.'

I have a lot to do. I have to call Bellfield and find Bella and me somewhere to stay the night. But first, I need to make another call.

Danny picks up after a couple of rings.

'Alex.' He's surprised to hear from me. 'Where have you been? I've been trying to get hold of you.'

'It's been a busy couple of days ... Listen, I have something to tell you. You might want to sit down ...'

CHAPTER THIRTY-ONE

I float effortlessly over wet sand and pebbles. My body is light, lighter than cobwebs, lighter than air. And warm. I feel fingers thread through mine. I can't see her, but I know who it is.

'Is that you?'

'Who else?' Willow's voice is full of humour.

'Where am I? Am I dead?'

'Don't be daft. You're just sleeping. But you can't stay here. *While you here do snoring lie, / Open eyed conspiracy / his time doth take. / If of life you keep a care, / shake off slumber and beware: / Awake, awake!'*

Her fingers slip from mine.

'Don't go! Stay with me. Willow!'

'*Awake!*'

I WAKE UP SOBBING, my face wet. My mouth tastes foul, and the back of my head and neck ache like hell, reminding me I am – most definitely – not dead yet. I know

where I am. I'm in the hospital. Willow is dead. And Bella …
I have no idea where Bella is.

The door opens, and a woman – one of the hospital
volunteers – looks in at me, her eyes full of concern.

'Sorry, did I wake you? The nurses thought you might
like a cup of tea.'

I shake my head. The movement sends spears of pain
through my jaw and into the back of my eyes. I must
remember not to do that again. I push myself gingerly into a
sitting position.

'Is Inspector Ramsay here? I need to talk to him again.' I
spoke to him earlier today. Or was it yesterday? I have no
idea what time it is.

The volunteer frowns. 'I don't know. I can ask one of the
nurses, if you like?'

'Thank you.'

She ducks back out. I need to see the inspector; I need to
make him understand what's been going on. I tried to
explain it to him before, but I was in so much pain, so tired, I
could barely string two thoughts together. He must have
thought I was a madwoman.

The door opens again, but this time it's a nurse, with
straight black bangs and a crooked smile.

'Evelyn says you're asking for the Inspector. I've called
him, and he's on his way.'

'Thank you.'

I watch her as she takes my blood pressure and tempera-
ture, then writes it up on my chart.

'Where's Bella, my little girl? Can I see her?'

'We'll see what the inspector says when he gets here. You
seem much brighter. Do you feel well enough for a visitor?'

God no! I shake my head, forgetting it will make pain jolt

through me. Just the thought of seeing Alex makes me want to scream or throw up.

'Are you sure? I know he'll be disappointed. He's driven all this way to see you.'

I frown. My brain doesn't seem to be working properly.

'Your brother?' prompts the nurse.

'Danny! Danny's here?'

'He's waiting in the family room for you to wake up. He's been there a while.'

'Show him in! Please.' My heart swells at the thought of seeing him again.

But as I'm waiting for the nurse to bring him, doubt creeps in. Danny thought I was dead. I wrote him that terrible suicide note, tricked him cruelly. What's he going to say about that? He thinks Alex is his friend. I push my doubts away. Danny and I have always been close. He'll know I wouldn't have done such a terrible thing unless it was absolutely necessary. I'm sure he'll understand when I explain everything, when he sees what Alex has done to me.

The door opens, and the nurse comes back in, followed by Danny. I take one look at his pale, anxious face and burst into tears.

He hurries to the bedside. 'Li, shush. Don't cry.' He hugs me to him awkwardly. 'It's okay.'

The nurse slips discreetly back out again.

Danny and I are both crying. He takes off his glasses to wipe away his tears.

'I'm sorry. So sorry,' I sob. 'I never meant to hurt you.'

'It's okay. It's okay. You don't need to explain.'

'But I do!'

'I'm just glad you're alive.'

I hug him to me again. I don't deserve my brother.

I sniff back my tears. 'I need to tell you what's been going on. Alex isn't who you think he is, Danny.'

Danny frowns.

'I found a note in my bedroom. He kept Polly prisoner there. Tried to poison her. Then he staged the car crash. I don't know how he did it. He's clever, so clever. But he thought Keira had some kind of proof – she told me she had proof – so he killed her. At least, I think he did. Her flat was full of blood. And then he almost drowned Figgy, but I stopped him.'

'Figgy?'

'The puppy.'

He nods, listening intently.

'Willow and I knew we had to get Bella away from him. But we knew he'd never just let us go, so we decided to stage a double suicide.'

'You planned it together, you and Willow?'

'Yes. Yes! I couldn't have done it without her. And now she's dead,' I wail. 'She's dead, and it's all my fault.' I drop my sore head in my hands. 'And I don't know where Bella is, or what I'm going to do now.'

He lets me cry until I'm completely wrung out.

'Listen, Li.' He gently takes my hands from my face and wipes my cheeks with his fingers. 'You don't have to worry anymore. I'm going to look after you both. Make sure you're safe.'

'You believe me?'

'I do.'

Relief courses through me. 'I didn't think you would.'

'You're my sister, Li. My womb-mate, remember? You could have come to me with all of this instead of going through with the suicide thing. Why didn't you?'

'You and Alex are friends. More than friends. The MDMA ...' I tail off, not knowing how to finish the sentence.

Danny nods, regretful. 'I'm sorry. I'm sorry for all of it. But I promise I'm going to do better from now on.' He squeezes my hand.

'What are we going to do?'

'The priority is to make sure your head is okay, and then find you somewhere safe, where you can rest. Where you can get your strength back and think about the future.'

'What about Bella?'

'Bella can come too.' Something flickers on his face, elusive. It's gone before I can pin down what it is, what it means.

'Where will we go? Alex will come after us. I know he will.'

'There's a place I know, in Surrey. It's safe there. Quiet. You can stay there until you get better.'

That jars me. 'Better?'

'Your head.'

'My head's fine. It will be fine. The doctor says so.'

He nods. But there's something tense, something evasive behind his eyes. That's when I realise – this has all been too easy. He should be furious. He should be raging at me for doing such a terrible thing. For writing that unforgivable suicide note, for making him think I was dead. But instead he's treating me like a child. Or an invalid.

I look at him carefully, see the muscle clench in his jaw. He won't meet my eyes.

'You don't believe me, do you?'

'Of course I do.'

'You don't. You always were a terrible liar, Danny. Do

you think I've made all this up? About Polly? About Willow?'

He rubs his hand over his face. He looks tired, suddenly. Tired and ill. 'I think you need rest, Li. That's what I think.'

'Rest,' I say. 'In Surrey.'

He nods. 'At Bellfield.'

I stare at him. I don't know what Bellfield is, but I don't like the sound of it. Not at all.

'You can get the rest you need there. That's where Polly's sister, Keira, is. She isn't dead, Lisa. Alex told me. He's looking after her.'

Looking after her the way he wants to look after me. He's had her locked up in some kind of institution, as if this were a nineteenth-century melodrama!

'Where's Bella?' I ask.

He hesitates, thrown off guard by my question.

'Where is she, Danny?' I can read the answer in his eyes. 'She's with Alex? Dear God! You haven't believed a word I've said, have you? Not a single fucking word.' My voice is rising, but I can't seem to help it.

'Yes, she's with Alex, at Gleneagles.'

'He tried to drown my *dog*, for Christ's sake! He's a psychopath. You can't leave Bella with him.'

'Li—'

'Don't fucking "Li" me!' I'm shouting now. 'Don't you fucking dare!' I make an effort to calm myself. 'You're not my brother. The old Danny would have believed my word against anyone else's. Against the world. You've changed. I don't know if it's the PTSD or the drugs, but I really don't recognise you anymore.'

Danny's eyes are filling with tears again. 'Let's talk later.'

He stands up. 'I'll come back when you're more yourself.' He backs out of the room.

'Don't fucking bother!'

He stumbles out.

My head feels like it's going to explode. My heart is going to explode. I've lost my best friend, my daughter, and now my brother too. Alex has killed them all. I burst into fresh tears, hot and scalding.

'Is everything okay?' The nurse appears in the room. 'The inspector's here.' She sees my tears, my obvious distress. 'I'll tell him you're not well enough to talk, shall I? He can come back later.'

I nod, speechless with grief and the pain in my head. I can't go through all that again. Polly. Willow. Keira. The whole story. It's a waste of time.

No one believes me.

CHAPTER THIRTY-TWO

'That was a nightmare, Alex. A total fucking nightmare.'

I glance at Bella, who's playing in the corner of our luxurious hotel room, and give Danny a warning frown.

'Sorry.' He looks broken. 'I just don't know what to do.'

I know what he can do. He can pull himself together. Get a grip and act like a fucking man for a change. But, of course, I don't say that. 'We need to concentrate on one thing at a time, Danny. We need to get her to Bellfield, where they can help her.'

He throws himself into a chair. 'Where has all this come from? This delusion? She's never had any mental problems before, not even when David died. It makes no sense.'

I raise an eyebrow as I sip my malt. It's good, peaty and intense. 'Who knows. This could have been brewing for a while. The human brain is a complicated thing. As you should know.'

He lifts his eyebrows in wry acknowledgement.

'How are *you* managing?' I'm not that interested, but I need to get him onside, at least until all the paperwork for

Bellfield is signed and sealed. I could do it all myself, with Dr Luca, but it helps to have another family member who can vouch for Lisa's mental instability.

Danny shrugs. 'I'm managing.'

He seems unwilling to share more, which is fine by me.

'I should get Bella to bed,' I say. 'Tomorrow's a big day.'

'What time will they be here?'

'Early afternoon. We need to get all our ducks in a row with Ramsay before that. I hope I can count on you?'

'You know you can.' He pauses. 'Can I ask, though … what's Bellfield like?'

I turn away, ostensibly to put my whisky glass on the table, but really to hide my irritation.

'It's very nice. Very calm.'

'They'll treat her well?'

'Of course they will. Things have changed since the old days. No cold baths or shock treatment. Bellfield's more like a spa, really. A very secure spa. Dr Luca and his team will look after her.'

'I take it it's private?'

'Of course.'

'And you're happy to pay for it?'

'Lisa's my wife. Of course I want the best for her.'

'What about Keira? Are you paying for her too?'

'Polly left some money. I'm using that.' That's a lie. The fact is that Dr Luca owes me a favour. A huge favour. If what I know about him ever became common knowledge, he'd be struck off the medical register. Possibly imprisoned.

'I see.' Danny nods, but gives me an odd look.

'It's late,' I say. 'I really need to get Bella to bed.'

He gets up to kiss Bella. Hugs her to him. 'Night, Bells.'

He looks at me. 'I'm so glad she isn't dead. So glad Lisa isn't, even though ...' There are tears in his eyes.

I nod and put my arm around him. 'Me too, Danny. Me too.' I hug him. 'I'll see you at breakfast.'

It's a relief when he's gone, taking his misery with him. I need him tomorrow, but after that, he can go to hell for all I care. I yawn and stretch wearily. The stress of the day – the driving, the chase through the hotel, dealing with Inspector Ramsay – has worn me out.

'Come on, princess, let's get you to bed.' Should I bathe her first? Does she have a bath every night? I don't know her night-time routine. I can't be bothered to run a bath – it can't hurt for her to go to bed dirty for once. 'Where are your pyjamas?'

She patters to the rucksack and starts pulling stuff out of it. I stare at the growing pile of cheap, faded clothes. I don't recognise any of it. Where did Lisa get this shit?

'Here they are.' Bella holds up a blue and yellow pyjama top with a hideous cartoon dog on it. 'I call him Loopy. Isn't he nice?' She kisses the dog.

'Very nice.' I make a mental note to buy her some decent clothes tomorrow, in the hotel arcade. We're staying at one of the best hotels in the world, and it's only twenty minutes' drive to Stirling, where Lisa is in the hospital. It isn't cheap, but it's worth the money. Thanks to room service, we've already had an excellent supper, and Bella has had her bedtime milk. Tomorrow I can leave her in the crèche while I deal with Lisa.

I help Bella to wash, pee, and change into her pyjamas. She doesn't seem to have a toothbrush, so we don't brush her teeth. Another thing to buy tomorrow.

'Where's Mummy?' she asks.

'You'll see her in the morning,' I lie. 'She sends her love. Come on, into bed.'

As she climbs into one of the twin beds, she looks around with a frown.

'Where's Teddy Pea?'

I look at her.

'I *need* him.'

I go through the rucksack, through the pile of clothes on the floor, but the ridiculous green bear isn't there. I check Lisa's bag, find a couple of hundred pounds in cash that will come in useful, but no Teddy Pea. The social worker must have left it at the West Highland Hotel. Fuckwit.

Bella has been watching, owlish, from her bed.

'Teddy's not here just now,' I say. 'He's gone for a little walk.'

'Teddy doesn't go for walks.' She looks at me as if I'm stupid. 'He sleeps with me.'

'I'm sorry, but he's not here.'

Bella's face crumples. I watch her as she winds herself up to a tantrum. It really is astonishing how children can flash from one emotion to another in the blink of an eye. Astonishing, and inconvenient. I have to get her to sleep. I need my rest, for tomorrow.

I pick up the phone and dial.

'Good evening. Housekeeping here.'

'Hi. I have a problem I'm hoping you can help me with.'

The shopping arcade is closed, and I can't persuade them to open it, no matter how many hints I drop about the money I might spend there. In the end one of the staff volunteers to go down to the crèche, with instructions to look for any stuffed toy that's green. She comes back with a Loch Ness monster wearing a tiny tartan hat. It's absurd, probably covered in God-knows-what from other kids, but it does the trick. Like a fluffy miracle, it distracts Bella from her tears long enough to go to sleep.

By then, I'm totally exhausted. I pour myself another malt from the minibar and sip it in the blissful silence of the room. I know tomorrow's going to be tricky. Emotional. For everyone else, at least. But we'll get through it. And in a few months' time, I'll have a child of my own to look after. Will it be another girl or a boy? I've always wanted a son, someone who will look up to me, who I can mould into a man I can be proud of. I'll be the perfect father. The perfect father I never had. I'd like a few kids – four, at least. It shouldn't be a problem to divorce Lisa with her being mentally incapacitated; then I'll be free to find another wife.

I think about Diana Wilson-Howe, the solicitor I spoke to about Lisa's Declaration of Presumed Death. She was very alluring, in that go-getting, self-possessed way I've always found attractive. I could tell she liked me too. I bet she's a tigress in bed. But I'm not going to make that mistake again. This time I'm going to choose someone softer, more manageable. Definitely not a career woman. Someone who wants kids, someone who is happy to stay home and look after them. What is it they say? Third time lucky?

I raise my glass in a silent toast.

To matrimony.

CHAPTER THIRTY-THREE

'What time did Inspector Ramsay say he'd be here?'

'About eleven, I think.' It's a different nurse today. This one is older than the one with black bangs and not as smiley. But she's told me what I want to know.

I have no intention of being here when the inspector arrives. No intention of trying to tell him about Alex and Polly and Willow again. Why would I waste my breath? I feel much better than I did yesterday. My head isn't aching half as much, and I feel calmer. Calmer and more determined.

I'm not going to let Alex lock me away. I'm not going to let Bella spend one more minute in his company than I have to. I watch the nurse finish writing up my notes on the chart, and as soon as she's out of the room, I swing my legs out of bed. When I stand up, my head swims and the room lurches away from me. I have to steady myself, take some deep breaths until the dizziness passes. When it has, I change out of my hospital gown into the clothes in my bedside locker. I pull them on as quickly as I can; then I find my boots. I don't have a coat – I wasn't wearing one when Alex chased us through the hotel – but there's nothing I can do about that.

I venture out into the corridor, half expecting to see a uniformed policeman sitting by my door, but there's no one there. I suppose there's no reason for Inspector Ramsay to put a guard on me – I'm not under arrest, and I'm too ill to leave. So they think. I can't afford to hang around, in case I'm spotted by one of the nurses, so I hurry out of the ward, then mingle with hospital visitors, down the escalators to the main hospital concourse. It's much busier here, with people coming and going, orderlies pushing trollies, and people making deliveries to the shops. I dodge inside the ladies' loo, where I take a pee, splash cold water on my face and dry it with a paper towel.

Actually, I don't look as bad as I thought I would. There are shadows under my eyes, and my hair is a disaster, my usually springing curls hanging limp and lifeless, but on the whole, I don't think I should attract any undue attention. I tidy myself up as best I can and meet my eyes in the mirror. What now? All my things were left behind at the hotel – my clothes and all my money. Unless … I feel in the back pocket of my jeans and pull out two twenties from when Bella and I went charity shopping. It's not a lot, but it's a hell of a lot better than nothing.

The cold air outside hits me like a sledgehammer, sending nausea rippling through me. Is it because of my head injury or because of the baby? There's no way of knowing, and I suppose it doesn't matter anyway. I just have to grit my teeth and push through it. I find the taxi rank, catching the eye of the first driver in the queue.

'Hi.'

He rolls down his window.

'I want to go to Gleneagles. Gleneagles hotel. How much would that be?'

'Depends on the traffic, but usually between forty and fifty. Fifty-five, max.'

'I only have forty.' I wave my two twenties at him and give him my most charming smile. 'Can you do it for that?'

He scowls at me. It must be a slow morning, however, because he shrugs. 'Go on then.'

I jump in the back. 'Thanks!' I meet his eyes in the rear-view, and he gives me a begrudging nod.

Once we're out of the town, the Perthshire countryside is pretty, with lush green valleys, and purple mountains brooding on the horizon. It's largely wasted on me, though, because my head is elsewhere. Will I be able to get Bella away from Alex? And if I do, what will I do then? As hard as I try, I can't think that far ahead. All I can think about right now is seeing Bella again.

'THIS IS IT.'

I must have fallen asleep, because the taxi has stopped under a massive wrought-iron portico. I rub my eyes and smooth the creases out of my clothes. I wish I'd been awake earlier so I could have seen the building on the drive up to it. I'm too close now to tell what it really looks like. I can sense its size, however, and its grandeur. I hand my forty quid to the driver, painfully aware it's the only cash I have, and now it's gone. There's a doorman on duty, an older man with impressive sideburns and a kilt, but luckily he's busy helping a well-dressed couple take their luggage from the boot of their Mercedes. I'm able to sidle past him up the steps and slip in through the revolving doors without him spotting me.

The entrance lobby is both grand and welcoming, with Art Deco lamps, marble floors and wood-panelled walls. It's also busy. Smart, wealthy-looking guests come and go, on their way to their rooms, to reception, and to the elegant bar I can see through the set of double doors to my right. A woman in golfing slacks gives me the once-over as she passes. I realise I must stick out in my crumpled charity-shop clothing.

There's an alcove off to the left, with leather armchairs and a rack with newspapers. I grab a broadsheet and find a seat, where I can see the reception desk and keep an eye on the entrance. I make a show of reading the paper.

Time passes. Forty-five minutes? An hour? I have no way of knowing. Finally, my patience is rewarded.

Two figures I recognise emerge from the corridor to the right of the reception desk. Alex looks fresh and relaxed, as if he's here on holiday. Bella patters along beside him with a green stuffed toy I don't recognise. My heart squeezes at the sight of her. I want to run and grab her. I force myself to sit still instead, and strain my ears to hear what they're saying.

'It's only for a couple of hours,' Alex is saying in his most persuasive voice. 'There are toys and other boys and girls to play with.'

'But I want to stay with you.'

I can't hear how he responds because they're gone again, into the corridor on the other side. It sounds like he's taking her to a crèche or some kind of children's activity. Which means he's probably leaving the hotel. When he's gone, I can make my move. It might not be easy to get them to release Bella from the crèche if that's where she is, but I'm pretty confident we'll be able to convince them I'm her mother. But first, I have to wait until Alex is safely off the premises. I sit tight with my newspaper, waiting for him to reappear.

Then there's a commotion at the door, making heads turn as Inspector Ramsay strides into the lobby with two uniformed officers. I freeze and sink down behind my newspaper. Is he looking for Alex? Perhaps he's come to tell him I've run away from the hospital? The inspector says something to one of the receptionists, who picks up the phone on the desk. After a few moments she shakes her head. Is she telling him Alex isn't in his room? I think she must be, because the inspector dispatches his men into the hotel in different directions. As they hurry off, he turns back to survey the lobby. I duck behind my newspaper and hold my breath. When I pluck up the courage to peep out again, he has his back to me. I stand up, put down my newspaper, and saunter out through the revolving door. The doorman nods and smiles as I go down the steps, past the police car. I force a smile back and stroll as casually as I can around the corner into the manicured grounds.

I hurry down some wide stone steps and take refuge behind a hedge next to a mini golf course. What the hell am I going to do? The place is crawling with police. I don't have a cat in hell's chance of getting to Bella now. As soon as Alex finds out I'm missing, he'll be on his guard. He'll know I'll come after her.

I need to get out of here, back to London. Alex will have to take Bella home sooner or later.

'That was bloody awful, Johnny!' The plummy, upper-class voice comes from one of the people playing on the mini golf course – a family bundled in coats, not letting the chilly weather spoil their fun. There's someone else braving the cold too, sitting on a bench on the far side of the green. My heart thumps as I recognise Danny.

He has his elbows on his knees, staring at the ground. His foot is tapping. Up and down. Up and down. A stim to soothe his ADD. I feel a surge of guilt. I was so hard on him in the hospital yesterday, but really, I can't blame him for believing Alex. Alex is so smooth, so plausible, and my story is so far-fetched. The space between us is only a couple of dozen yards of manicured grass, but it might as well be a thousand miles. It's a gulf I want to cross, but can't right now.

I hurry in the other direction before he looks up.

There must be another way to get into the hotel. Perhaps I can find somewhere people leave their bags or jackets unattended – a cloakroom, maybe, or changing rooms? I need to steal some cash. The thought horrifies me as soon as I think it. How could I sink so low? And yet … in my mind's eye, I see my mum, cig in one hand and glass of Famous Grouse in the other. She raises her glass to me in a toast.

'Needs must when the devil drives.'

One of her favourite sayings. Her voice is loud in my ear. It sounds so real. Am I hallucinating? Am I still under the influence of the painkillers the nurses were giving me? Or is it just the cold, cutting through my thin jumper, making my brain misfire? I realise I'm shivering violently. I need to get back into the warmth.

The police car is still at the front of the hotel. I give it a wide berth, skirting past a conservatory and tennis courts, looking for another way in. I go through an arch in the garden wall and find myself in a service yard at the rear of the hotel. There's a delivery bay here, with a van pulled up to the dock – the Shoreditch Spice Company. Shoreditch. The number on the side is a London one. I keep out of sight as a young woman unloads a large box and heads into the hotel. I poke my head into the back of the van. It's almost empty, with only a couple of large cardboard cartons lying on their sides. It looks as if she's made her deliveries. Will she be going back to London now? I consider asking her for a lift, but dismiss the idea. It's too risky. I don't know what might be going on inside the hotel, whether Alex and the inspector are asking people to keep an eye out for me.

I sneak into the delivery bay and see a glazed office cubicle at the back. There's no one there. I slip inside, making a beeline for the coat hanging on the back of a chair. I'm in luck. It has a wallet in it, with cash, but I don't have time to count it now. I take the coat and the wallet, and I'm on my way out again when I spot a Thermos flask on the desk. I grab that too. I don't care what's in it, as long as it's hot. I head back to the spice van, crawl inside and hide behind one of the empty cartons. There's an old packing blanket here too, and I make myself as comfortable as I can with it.

Now I'm in the hands of fate.

After what seems like an age, I hear someone jump down from the loading bay and come round to the back of the van. I hold my breath. The door rattles down and locks. I heave a sigh of relief. I just hope the driver's heading south. It looks as if she's made all her deliveries, so I reckon that's a fair bet. The engine starts, and we pull away.

I wrap the big coat tightly round myself. Every minute I go undiscovered takes me further away from Alex. Further away from Bella, too. But I will see her again soon.

I have to believe that. I have to believe that she will be safe.

CHAPTER THIRTY-FOUR

'She's *gone*? Gone where?'

The inspector shrugs. 'Who knows?'

His lack of concern infuriates me. 'What kind of Mickey Mouse police force are you running here? How could you let her get away?'

Ramsay frowns. 'She wasn't actually in our custody. We still haven't seen any evidence that she's done anything illegal. The only evidence we *do* have is of an assault. On *her*.' He meets my eyes, challenging. He clearly still doesn't believe I had nothing to do with that situation in the deserted hotel. I realise I need to backtrack a little.

'We need to get the CCTV from the hospital. Issue a KLO.'

'Is this an official request? If so, you can make it through the usual channels, *sir*. From one force to another.'

I can't do that, and he knows it.

I realise we're putting on quite a show. The toddlers in the crèche are standing with their mouths open, staring at the three policemen, while the nursery staff are pretending to be busy. I can tell they're listening.

The inspector continues, 'I've been speaking to Chief Inspector Mowat, in Edinburgh. He says you authorised a visit to a women's refuge there. That your officer, Officer Becker, requisitioned two of their officers to do it. Is that right, sir?'

'That's right.'

'I assume it was your wife Becker was looking for? And yet he gave a different name.'

'I have no idea why he did that.'

He gives me a long, cool stare. 'I don't think you need any more help from us. Or from Edinburgh. I suggest you go home to London, sir, and settle your marital differences there.' He nods. 'Good morning.' He turns on his heel and strides out, his two lackeys following, leaving me staring after them.

The *fucker*. The ignorant, disrespectful fucker.

'Is everything okay?' One of the nursery staff approaches me cautiously.

'Does it fucking look like everything is okay?' I snap. I go to drag Bella away from the farm set she's playing with. She wails, but I pick her up, ignoring her protests. I have no time for bad behaviour now. I've never been treated so insolently in my life. And by a provincial Scottish plod! When I get home, I'll make an official complaint. He can kiss his joke of a career goodbye.

'I want to play!' wails Bella in my ear as we leave the crèche.

'Shut up.' I give her a little shake. 'Just shut up.'

That does the trick.

We bump into Danny in the lobby.

'I've just seen Inspector Ramsay leaving.' His eyes go from my face to Bella's and back again. 'What's going on, Alex?'

'Your sister's done a runner from the hospital.'

'What?'

'Do I have to repeat everything to you, Danny? Are you retarded?'

He recoils, but follows us up to our room anyway, like a beaten dog.

I put Bella on her bed. 'Sit there and be quiet while I pack.' For once she obeys me.

Danny's eyes slide, troubled, from her to me. 'You're going back to London?'

'Where else would I go?'

'I thought you might stay here. Look for Lisa.'

'I can't afford to spend any more time running after your lunatic sister. I don't need to, anyway.'

I see the question in his eyes.

'I have Bella. Lisa will come to me.'

Danny glances at Bella still sitting silent on the bed. He lapses into silence too, which is a relief. I take my things from the wardrobe and fold them into my suitcase, get my toiletries from the ensuite.

Danny speaks again. 'Can I ask, what's happened to Figgy?'

'Figgy?'

'Your dog.'

I shrug; this man is a genius at rattling my cage. What the hell does that idiot dog have to do with anything?

'I don't know. Willow had it. God knows where it is now.'

Danny says nothing, but his hands are clenching and unclenching. Clenching and unclenching. It wears on me.

'Is there a problem?' I snap.

'No problem. I can take Bella, if you like. In my car? It's a long drive.'

'No., She's my daughter. She stays with me.'

The phone rings. I pick it up, almost relieved at the interruption.

'Mr McMahon? This is Jenny from the front desk. I have someone here asking for you. A Dr Luca?'

CHAPTER THIRTY-FIVE

I stretch, my body stiff and cramped. Something has woken me, but I don't know what. Then I realise – the engine has stopped. It stopped once before, when we filled up at a service station, and the driver took a break. That's when I drank the contents of my stolen Thermos – tomato soup, thick and delicious. But that was hours ago. I have a raging thirst now, my bladder is full, and my head is aching again. I can hear traffic, the beep of horns and the distant whine of an ambulance siren. Are we in London? I scramble to my feet, preparing myself for someone to open the door.

I wait. But no one comes. I never thought about it, but I suppose there's no reason for anyone to open the door. They think the van is empty.

I bang on the door. 'Hello?' I shout. 'Is anyone there? Let me out!'

Nothing. I feel panic rising. Surely I haven't come all this way just to get locked in a bloody van?

I bang again. 'Let me out!'

I pause, listen, trying to quell my rising panic. Then, thank God, I hear footsteps. The door unlocks, then rolls up.

'What the actual *fuck*?' The young delivery woman stares up at me, her eyes round with disbelief. 'What are you doing in there?'

I clamber awkwardly out onto the street. 'I needed a lift,' I say. 'Thanks.'

She stares at me, speechless, as I walk away.

It's getting dark. I look for a sign to get my bearings. St Chad's Street. I don't know where that is, but I don't think it's in Shoreditch or even the East End. I head towards the nearest main thoroughfare and see I'm on Gray's Inn Road. The top end, I think, not far from Kings Cross.

Kings Cross is good. Perfect, in fact.

It's rush hour. The station is at its busiest at this time of day. Anonymous. I visit the toilets, then go to one of the cafés on the mezzanine. I use one of the bank cards in the wallet to pay for my food – contactless, so no one will check it. If they did, they'd see I was supposed to be Mr Iain Spalding, which would be awkward. There's cash in the wallet too, but not a lot. I need to keep it for emergencies.

I eat my burrito as quickly as I can. My head is still throbbing – I must buy some painkillers. But first, I have to find an internet café to look up an address, and then I need a pay-as-you-go phone. I should be able to buy one somewhere nearby. My ride down from Scotland was cold and excruciatingly uncomfortable, but it gave me a lot of time to think.

'BELLFIELD HOSPITAL, how can I help you?'

'Hello. I wonder if I could talk to whoever is looking after Keira Benson?'

'Hang on a minute. I'll put you through.'

I listen to the phone ring and ring. Eventually, someone picks up.

'B ward, Greg speaking.'

'Hello, Greg. This is Georgia McMahon, Alex McMahon's sister.' Georgia's plummy accent is round in my mouth. 'He's asked me to bring a few things in for Keira. Some toiletries, a new nightdress, that kind of thing. Is it okay if I come this evening?'

'I'm not sure. Mr McMahon never mentioned it.'

'Oh dear. It must have slipped his mind. I'm afraid he rather has his hands full at the moment. Can I pop in anyway? Maybe see Keira for five minutes? It's been an age since she had a visitor, poor thing.' That's not much of a gamble. I can't see Alex paying Keira cosy visits, and as far as I know, she doesn't have anyone else who might pop in for a chat.

'Georgia McMahon, you say? You're not on the visitors' list.'

'I know. Sorry about that. I forgot to remind Alex to do it. You can call him, if you like, but I think he's driving right now, so he might not be able to answer his phone.' A huge gamble. Will it pay off?

I can sense Greg's struggle on the other end of the line. I hold my breath, hoping reckless humanity will win out over protocol.

'No. It's okay. Come on in. Five minutes won't hurt. Keira's been doing much better lately, and I'm sure she'll be glad to see a friendly face.'

I WATCH the orderly as he searches my carrier bag of gifts for Keira – an M&S nightie and some Molton Brown toiletries. I'm conscious that my charity-shop clothes are definitely not the kind of thing Alex's fashion-conscious sister would wear, but I hadn't wanted to risk using the stolen bank card too often. I comfort myself that no one in Bellfield is likely to have met Georgia. She probably has no idea Keira is even here, much less cares one way or the other.

The orderly nods and smiles. 'That's fine, Mrs McMahon. I'll take you up to B ward.'

The inside of the hospital looks pleasant enough, with polished panelling and flowers, but I can't help noticing there are locks on every door we pass through on the way upstairs.

'She's watching *Only Fools and Horses*,' says the orderly. 'She likes that.'

There are a few people – patients – in the TV room, but no one bothers to look up as I enter. Keira is sitting to one side, her eyes cast down, not even looking at the screen.

It's hard to recognise the woman who tried to warn me about Alex just a few short weeks ago. Her wild hair has been brushed into a neat ponytail, and all the fire has gone from her face. It's pale and puffy.

'Keira?'

Her eyes widen as she looks up and sees me. 'You're not Georgia. I thought Georgia was coming.'

I put my finger to my lips, a warning for her to keep her voice down until the orderly is out of earshot.

Her brow furrows. 'But I do know you, don't I?'

'Yes.' I pull up a chair to sit beside her. 'You came to my house. I'm Lisa, Alex's new wife.'

Her eyes dart to the door.

'It's okay,' I hurry to reassure her. 'He's not here. I promise.'

'Where's Georgia?' Her thought processes are slow.

'She isn't here. I pretended to be her because I want to talk to you.'

Keira doesn't seem to be listening. Her fingers pluck listlessly at her sleeves as the laugh track on the TV cackles in the background.

'I want to talk to you, Keira. About Polly.'

She turns her head towards me and narrows her eyes.

I press on. 'I know Alex killed her. I know you're telling the truth.'

She turns away again. 'Dr Luca says it's all in my head.'

'I'm not in your head, Keira. I'm right here, and I'm real.' I grasp her hand. 'I'm as real as you are. I'm Lisa. Remember?'

'Lisa?' There's no recognition on her face now. Have I come all this way for nothing?

'Listen to me, Keira. It's important. Do you remember, when you came to see me, you said you had proof that Alex killed Polly?'

She nods. 'He was so mad when he found out what she'd done.' She sees my questioning frown. 'She got rid of the baby.'

'What?'

'She didn't want it. She kept it secret because she knew he'd be angry. But he found out. I don't know how.'

Oh my God. Did Polly have an abortion? Was that why Alex turned against her? He's always wanted a family so badly. That's beyond shocking. But I realise we're in danger of getting off the point.

'You said you had proof, Keira. Proof that Alex killed Polly. Do you remember? What is it? Do you still have it?'

She's trying really hard now to follow what I'm saying, struggling to penetrate the fog of whatever meds she's on.

'I knew he'd killed her. She would never have driven if she'd had a drink. Never.'

'I know that. But what about the *proof*?'

'He cremated her. Even though she wanted to be buried. He rushed it through without asking me.'

She's getting off the point again. I'm so frustrated I could shake her.

'You'd think the heat would burn everything off,' she says. 'Vaporise it.' She gives me an eerie grin. 'Not necessarily.'

What is she talking about?

'He didn't want Polly's ashes. I sent them away. They found traces of poison. In her bones. In bits of her bones.'

I can't stop my hand flying to my mouth in horror. He must have been poisoning her for months.

'Why didn't you take it to the police? Get them to open an investigation?'

'It took so long.' Her eyes are clearer now. Nearly lucid. I can almost see the woman who doorstepped me in Twickenham. 'I only got the results the day before you married him. I had to warn you first.'

Her concern for me was what alerted Alex. Her undoing. And that's why she's been in this dreadful place almost ever since.

'Time's up, Mrs McMahon.' The orderly has appeared in the doorway. 'Keira gets tired easily, don't you, Keira?'

She ignores him. Her gaze is slipping again.

'One more minute,' I beg him. 'Let me say goodbye.'

He nods, but doesn't leave. He stands in the doorway, waiting.

I drop my voice to a whisper. 'How did the lab send you the results?'

She says nothing, just plucks at her sleeve again.

'Keira, this is important. How did you get the results? By email? By post?'

But she's gone, back to wherever she was when I got here. I doubt I'll get anything more from her now. She smiles vacantly at me as I kiss her cheek and leave.

My mind is whirring as the orderly locks and unlocks the same series of doors to let me out. Whatever physical proof Keira had – on paper or on a laptop – will be long gone by now. Alex will have made sure of it. But there might still be traces – if she received the results by email, they could still be somewhere in her email account. And the lab should have a record of it too, if she can remember which lab she sent it to. I'm filled with hope. At last, I have something almost concrete, something I might be able to use to bring Alex down. But that's going to take time. In the meantime, my daughter is home alone with a psychopath.

I hurry to catch the next train to Twickenham.

CHAPTER THIRTY-SIX

'We've just driven all the way up from Walton-on-Thames. Seven and a half hours. And now you're telling me she's not here?'

'That's exactly what I'm telling you. What part of it don't you understand?'

The doctor can't hide his frustration. 'So what are we supposed to do? Just turn around and go back?'

I shrug. 'I suppose so. Unless you fancy a round of golf?'

The doctor splutters. 'That's unacceptable. Completely unacceptable.'

I glance quickly around reception. For once it isn't busy. There's no one within earshot apart from the staff behind the desk, and I don't care about them. I grab the doctor by his scrawny neck.

'What the fuck are you going to do about it, Luca? Make a complaint? Withdraw your services?' I give him a rough little shake. 'You should just feel lucky I don't send your miserable arse to prison.' I release him and smile. 'You wouldn't want that, would you?'

'No. No.' He straightens his clothes and tries to wipe the shocked expression off his face. 'Of course not.'

I don't want that either. He's too useful to me at the moment.

'I apologise if I gave you the wrong impression,' he wheedles. 'I'm happy to help any way I can.'

'Good. I'll be in touch if I need you.'

He can't get away fast enough, barrelling out through the revolving doors as if the devil is after him.

I watch him go, satisfied my threats have done the trick. Now I just have to fetch Bella from the crèche and take her home.

THE DRIVE south is my worst fucking nightmare. In my hurry to check out of the hotel, I leave the Loch Ness monster – Bella's new best friend – in the crèche. Bella moans and grumbles about it for hours. I hope she'll fall asleep – and she does, briefly – but as soon as she wakes up, she starts on about it again. Part of me is impressed by her persistence, but mostly I just want to throttle her. To make matters worse, we have to keep stopping every couple of hours for her to pee and eat. By the time we get onto the M25, it's taken us almost nine hours to drive four hundred miles. Nine hours! I could fucking crawl back to London from Scotland faster.

The house is locked up tightly when I drive in through the gates, with no sign of any intruder. I let us in and switch off the alarm.

'I'm tired,' says Bella. 'I want to go to bed.'

I'm not surprised. She barely slept in the car, and it's way past her bedtime.

'Do you want anything to eat, first?'

She shakes her head. 'I want Nessie. And Teddy Pea.'

Dear God, here we go again. 'I've told you, they're not here. Go upstairs and find one of your other toys. And put your pyjamas on.'

'I want Loopy.'

She means those hideous dog pyjamas. 'Loopy needs washing,' I say. I'll put them in the trash as soon as I get them out of the rucksack. 'Go and find some clean pyjamas. How about the nice yellow ones I bought you in Harrods?'

'You said I would see Mummy today. I want to see her.'

'Mummy's on her way. If you're a very good girl and go to sleep nice and quickly, I promise I'll come and wake you up when she gets here.'

As she thumps off up the stairs, my mobile rings.

It's Bill Glover. He called me a few times on the drive down, but I couldn't speak to him with Bella in the car, so I let his calls go to voicemail. I suppose I might as well deal with him now.

'Bill.'

'What the *hell* is going on, Alex? I hear you've been using unauthorised tech resources for God knows what, and I've had Tayside police bending my ear on the phone. Some nonsense about Lisa. That can't be right, can it? What the hell are you doing in Scotland?'

'I'm not in Scotland anymore. I've found them, Bill. Lisa and Bella.'

'*What?*'

'They're not dead. Lisa ...' I stifle a sob.

There's a shocked, awkward silence on the other end of the phone. I make a show of pulling myself together.

'Lisa's lost her mind, I think. She staged the whole thing. Now she's gone on the run.'

'With Bella?'

'No. I have Bella.'

'Thank God for that. Where are you now?'

'We've just got home. Just driven down from Perthshire.'

'What can I do to help?'

'Nothing, Bill, I don't want to bother you with all this. It's personal.'

'Don't be bloody stupid. Take all the time you need. Use all the resources you need to find Lisa, to get her home safely. Whatever it takes, I'll back you up, one hundred per cent.'

'Thank you.' That's worth knowing.

'My God.' He's still trying to get his head around what I've told him. '*Still alive?* Who would believe it? Wait till Kathleen hears.'

When I hang up, I can't help but smile. That went better than I could have hoped. Bill is an invaluable ally. But I still have one uncomfortable truth to face – I'm probably going to have to ditch my plans to put Lisa in Bellfield. She's not going to go without a fight, and I can't afford a public spectacle. Will I have to deal with her permanently, like Polly? I can say she attacked me, that she turned into a wild animal, and I tried to subdue her ... it was a terrible, terrible accident. With my reputation and the bizarre way she's been acting, no jury would convict me, especially if I'm the sole guardian of poor little Bella.

But ... that would mean losing the baby. Can I do that? I don't think I can. I can't lose another one. I suppose I'll just have to play it by ear and hope things work out.

First, I have to catch Lisa. Could she have got here before us? God knows, we took long enough. I check the

CCTV, but there's no sign of any activity before Bella and I arrived home apart from Mrs T bringing the groceries I asked her to buy. I pour myself a malt, put the lights off and settle into my favourite chair with my phone to keep an eye on the cameras.

Lisa will come to me. I know she will. I just have to sit back and wait.

CHAPTER THIRTY-SEVEN

It's after eleven when my train arrives at Twickenham station. I jump in one of the cabs on the rank, and within ten minutes I'm at the estate. It's only after I've paid the driver with the last of my stolen cash that I realise I don't have my key card for the entrance gates. I'm dithering there, wondering what to do, when a car swings off the main road, catching me in the beam of its headlights. I recognise our babysitter Lianne and her mum, Saskia, in their BMW. Saskia winds her window down. Her face is slack with shock.

'Lisa? I heard that you were ...'

'Dead? No. As Mark Twain said, "News of my death has been greatly exaggerated."' I smile, trying to make light of it, but from Saskia's blank expression, I can see she needs me to spell it out. 'It was all just a silly mix-up.'

'Oh.' She still looks confused, which is hardly surprising.

'I'm so sorry,' I say. 'I forgot my key card. Is it okay if I just come in with you?'

'Of course.' If she's wondering what I'm doing on foot,

she doesn't say so. I go through the gate in the slipstream of the BMW, then head for the place I used to call home.

The big house is in darkness. It feels nothing like home to me now. It's hostile. Seemingly impenetrable. Is Alex asleep, I wonder, or will he be on his guard, waiting for me? I should think he'll be asleep. He'll be expecting me to try to snatch Bella, but I don't think he'd ever imagine I'd have the balls to do it right under his nose.

I push into the shrubbery, which is the same route Bella and I used to escape on D-day. I know it's a blind spot for the cameras. When I get to the utility room door, I find the illicit key I keep under the plant pot there. Then I hesitate. This is where it gets tricky. There's a sensor on the utility door. If Alex has the alarm on, I'll trigger it. Can I get to the key pad in the hall before it wakes him up? I hope I can. I take a deep breath and open the door.

The alarm isn't on. I don't know whether that's good or bad. Alex is either so tired he forgot to set it, or he hasn't gone to bed yet. The utility room is shadowy, supernaturally clean, silent except for the ticking of the central heating timer. I tiptoe through it, push the door open and peek out. There are no lights on anywhere. Alex must be in bed. I creep down the hall, thankful for the wall-to-wall carpet that muffles the sound of my feet. I can smell furniture polish and lilies, but can hear absolutely nothing. It's as if the house itself is holding its breath, waiting. I pause at the bottom of the stairs. Bella is up there. Close, so close. All I need—

The lights snap on, blinding me.

'Hello, Lisa.'

I blink. Alex steps out of the living room, into the hall.

'I've got to hand it to you, I really do. You don't give up.'

There's nowhere to run. He's standing between me and

my escape route to the utility room. The front door is behind me, but I know I'd never be able to unlock it and get out before he reached me. He moves closer, wearing his most reasonable mask.

'There's no need for us to fight. Why don't we sit down and talk about it?'

I say nothing. What does he expect me to say?

'Come and sit down. Now.' He grabs my arm, drags me into the sitting room. I struggle briefly, then give up. He's much stronger than I am.

The gas fire is on, filling the expensively furnished, comfortable room with flickering light. He pushes me into a chair and switches on one of the table lamps. Then he takes a chair opposite, between me and the door.

'This is cosy, isn't it?' He peers at me. 'How are you, sweetheart? I have to say, you've looked better.'

'Cut the crap, Alex. What do you want?'

'Okay.' He holds his hands up, a conciliatory gesture. 'Straight to business. I propose a truce.' He sees my disbelief. 'I want this baby, Lisa. I'm not going to hurt you as long as you're carrying it.'

'So what are you suggesting? That we just carry on as if none of this ever happened?'

'That's it exactly.'

He's mad. Completely delusional.

'Think about it, Lisa. Think about what all this has been doing to Bella, being dragged around the country, being separated from you. Wouldn't it be nice just to let it all go? To look after yourself, look after Bella, eat nice food, get well?'

Tears prickle the back of my eyes. I blink them away. I'd give anything to be out of this nightmare, to live a normal life again. And I do believe him when he says he doesn't want to hurt the baby. Look what happened to Polly. But surely, he must know it's impossible for me to live under the same roof as him, knowing he killed Polly? Knowing he's killed my best friend? If he can't see that, he really must be a psychopath.

I need to keep him talking, to give me time to think.

'What about Bellfield?' I say. 'How do I know you wouldn't just lock me up there the first chance you got?'

'Because that isn't good for the baby. The meds. The lack of fresh air. It isn't healthy. And no matter what you think, I'd much rather my kids have a mother. I still love you.'

I can't hide my scorn.

He smiles his most charming smile. 'There's no accounting for the human heart, Lisa. You've really surprised me these last few weeks. You're so much more than a pretty face. You're brave. Resourceful. You're an exceptional woman.'

Whatever. I can't bear his flattery.

'When the baby's born,' I ask, 'what then?'

He shrugs. 'Then we negotiate a new deal.'

I don't believe him. I know he'll kill me as soon as he gets what he wants. But … he doesn't know I have a potential ace up my sleeve – Keira's lab tests on Polly's remains. I could agree to this ridiculous truce and use the time to track down that evidence. Then I could escape with Bella as soon as the chance presented itself. Or … I don't know what the alternative is. All I know is, right this minute, he has the upper hand. I have to change that somehow.

'Okay,' I say. 'It's a deal.'

'Really?'

I need to make this convincing. 'On two conditions. We have separate bedrooms, and you have as little contact with Bella as possible.'

'How's that going to work? We'll both be living in the same house. She loves me.'

'Those are my conditions. Take them or leave them.'

He looks thoughtful, making a show of considering my terms. I can't believe I once thought this man was handsome. Sexy. He repels me utterly now. He isn't a man at all; he's a monster in a man's skin.

'I'll take them,' he says. He smiles at me, with what looks like genuine pleasure. 'I'm so pleased you can see sense.' He gets up and comes to the table beside me, pours a glass of malt from the decanter. 'Shall we toast to our new agreement?' He offers the glass to me.

I look up at it. He poisoned Polly. But he wouldn't risk that, would he? Not again.

'Go on. I'm sure one little sip won't hurt the baby.' Still, I hesitate. Then it dawns. 'Oh!' He grins and pushes the glass towards me. 'Go on. It's safe. I've just poured it from the same decanter as mine.' He laughs. 'You're going to have to relax a little, Lisa, or these next few months are going to be hell for us both.' He turns away, shaking his head, still chuckling.

I don't know what happens, but something inside me snaps. Without making the conscious decision to do it, I jump up and grab the decanter. Smash it over his head. He drops to his knees.

I run for the door, but he's on me before I get to it.

'You bitch!' He grabs me round the neck, slams me into the door frame. His face, streaked with blood, is only inches from mine, twisted with hatred. His breath stinks of whisky. 'You fucking bitch. I tried to be reasonable.' His hands tighten on my throat. 'I tried to help you!' Lights explode behind my eyes ... everything is growing dimmer and dimmer. I realise I'm losing consciousness. I try to fight it, but I can feel myself slipping ... slipping ...

BANG! BANG! CRASH!

'Police! Nobody move!'

Alex releases me. I slide to the floor and gasp, doubled over, trying desperately to pull some air into my lungs. Through the fog behind my eyes I can see boots. A lot of boots.

'Mbala!' Alex's voice. 'What the hell?'

Someone helps me to my feet. As my vision clears, I see it's a man, a plain-clothed officer. He has three or four uniformed officers with him. Among them I can see Alex's face, white with shock under the blood.

The plain-clothed officer addresses me. 'Lisa McMahon, I'm arresting you for theft, fraud and wasting police time. You do not have to say anything, but it may harm your defence if you do not mention when questioned something which you later rely on in court ...'

CHAPTER THIRTY-EIGHT

'Fucking hell! Be more careful, can't you?'

'Sorry.' The nurse pulls an apologetic face. 'This is the last bit now.'

Another piece of glass rattles into the steel dish.

'There. Now we can get you cleaned up and stapled.'

'How many staples?'

'Five or six. I have to shave the area, I'm afraid.'

'Just get on with it.' I'm anxious to get to the station, to see what's happening with Lisa. I've tried calling Bill, to let him know what's happening, but his phone just goes to voicemail. Hardly surprising – it's two in the morning.

The nurse shaves the wound on my scalp, then swabs it. It stings.

I stifle my gasp of pain. Once again, Lisa has surprised me. I really thought she would accept the truce I was offering. It made so much sense – a chance for her to regroup, for us both to catch our breath before the baby is born. Who knows, we might even have forged something more long-lasting. It seemed as if she'd seen the logic of it, but then, out of the blue, she smashed me with the decanter. She really is unhinged. A crazy, deceitful bitch. I just hope insanity doesn't run in the family. I wouldn't want my son to be tainted with it. I'm almost certain now that the baby Lisa is carrying is a son. He'll make all this trouble, all this ridiculous drama worthwhile.

'Nearly done,' soothes the nurse, busy with the stapler on my scalp.

I curb my impatience. I need to get out of here, to talk to Bill before Mbala gets the chance.

I couldn't have been more shocked when Mbala and his men forced entry into the house. At the time I was furious. How dare he break into his senior officer's home? But now I've had the chance to calm down, I've changed my mind. I think I might even owe him my thanks. One minute more and I'd have killed Lisa. And the baby. That isn't what I want. This way, everything could work out for the best. Lisa won't be able to keep the baby in prison.

The only danger is that in preparing his case against her, Mbala uncovers other things too. Lisa is bound to try to tell him everything. I think I can dismiss most of it – her erratic behaviour clearly shows she isn't right in the head. But does she know about Danny and the MDMA? I can't imagine she does, but if I'm wrong, that would be harder for me to cover up. There's a discrepancy in the evidence stores at Bermondsey to back up her accusation. I would have to frame Danny for it, which wouldn't be too hard and actually not a bad idea – two birds with one stone. But I need to be prepared.

'There. All done.' The nurse drops her equipment into the bloody tray. As she does, the curtains to my cubicle part.

'Chief Superintendent.'

'Detective Mbala.'

He hovers, uncertain. 'I thought I should come and see you. To apologise.'

The nurse exits discreetly.

'No need. I'm sorry too. For this whole bloody mess ... I thought she was dead. I thought they were both dead.'

'I know. But why didn't you tell someone as soon as you realised she wasn't?' He pauses, fixes his gaze on me. 'How did you find out?'

I think quickly. I can hardly tell him that Willow gave it up, with her very last breath before she died.

'I found a receipt. For a car she bought a few days before she killed herself.'

'So you suspected she wasn't dead?'

'No. Not at all. But when I realised she'd bought a car without me knowing, and that car was nowhere to be seen ... one thing led to another.'

Mbala grins. 'A natural born copper.'

I shrug, pleased. 'Where is she now?'

'We have her in custody at Ebbsfleet. We can question her there, then transfer her to Belmarsh or Thameside.'

'Will she get bail?'

'I don't know. She hasn't even got a solicitor yet.'

'You will go easy on her, won't you? As easy as you can. She really isn't well.' I indicate my bloody head and clothes. 'As you can see.'

'I know.' He gives me a measured, sympathetic look. 'You can come and see her, if you like, before we get started.'

'Really?'

'I don't see there's any harm in it. You're the boss, after all, sir.'

From the clock on the wall, I can see I've been in this interview room almost an hour. They seem to have forgotten all about me. They've arrested me for fraud, theft and wasting police time. The theft must be for stealing the wallet, and my fake suicide probably took up a lot of police resources, but I'm not sure where the fraud comes in. I daresay I'll find out soon enough.

But time isn't on my side. Every second I'm wasting here is a second Bella has to spend with Alex, assuming they're still at home together. But what if they've brought him in to help with their enquiries? Who's looking after her? Perhaps they've been in touch with Danny?

The door opens, and as if conjured by my thoughts, Danny comes in. He's the last person I expect to see.

'Oh my God!' I run to him. He envelops me in a huge hug. I can't stop the tears that rise to choke me.

'Are you okay?' he asks. 'Did he hurt you?' He pushes me gently away to look at my bruised throat.

'I'm fine,' I say, sniffing back my flood of tears. 'But Bella. Where is she?'

'Don't worry about Bella. Bev Williamson of social services is with her. She's very nice. And you can see her soon.'

'I can?'

He nods. 'As soon as we get this sorted. Come and sit down.'

I follow him back to the metal table and chairs.

'It's terrible, Danny. I can't believe they arrested *me*, when he was the one who had his hands around my neck. He was trying to kill me.'

'I know. Derek Mbala told me.'

I frown. 'Mbala?'

'Your arresting officer.'

'He *knew* Alex was trying to kill me! Why didn't he arrest Alex? I don't understand.' I'm beginning to wonder whether my throttling, along with the earlier blow to the head, has done some permanent damage to my brain.

'It was the only way we could think of to get you out of there without making Alex suspicious.'

I blink.

'We're onto him, Li. We know he's done some terrible things ... but we have very little actual evidence against him. No hard evidence.'

I have to backtrack. 'So I'm not under arrest?'

'No.' Danny grins at me. He looks more like his old self than I've seen for some time. In spite of the circumstances, that's good to see.

'How did you know?' I ask. 'About Alex?'

'I finally saw through him. Up in Perthshire. He showed his true colours, probably because he was under so much pressure ... I didn't like the way he treated me. The way he treated Bella. It made me wonder whether there might be some truth in what you were saying after all. I came straight here and found Derek Mbala, who, it turns out, is working undercover for the Anti-Corruption Unit. They've had Alex in their sights for some time.'

'Anti-corruption?' I frown; then it dawns. 'The drugs?'

'Among other things.'

'But ... the MDMA? Won't they ...?'

Danny puts his hand on mine. 'Don't worry about that.' His gaze is warm, genuine. 'We have other things to worry about right now.'

I frown. 'Like what?'

'Like how we're going to nail Alex.'

CHAPTER FORTY

'We've put her in interview room three.'

I follow Mbala into the viewing room between room three and room two. Through the one-way mirror, I can see Lisa sitting at the table, her head in her hands. I touch the wound on my head gingerly and wince. With the pain comes anger. Looking at Lisa now, small – almost childish – it's hard to believe she's been such a bloody thorn in my side. Much more trouble than Polly, or even Willow, when it came down to it.

'Who's going to interview her?' I ask.

'Me and Tommy Becker. He's on his way in.'

'That's good.' There's no way Tommy will entertain any nonsense about me. I have him too well trained.

'Are you sure you're okay to see her, sir?' I like the new tone of deference in Mbala's voice. 'You don't think she'll go for you again?'

'I'll be fine.' I summon a sad grin, a plucky attempt at humour. 'She doesn't have a decanter in her hand this time.' I'm aware that I still stink of whisky, even though I've changed my clothes. It's in my hair, on my skin. 'Just give us ten minutes, will you, Derek?' I use his first name deliberately.

'You got it, boss.' He heads out.

Before I leave the viewing room myself, I make sure the audio feed to the interview room is switched off. This is possibly the last time I'll ever talk to my wife in private. There are things that need to be said.

She looks up as I go in. Her expression is despairing. Hopeless.

Good.

'Alex.' She makes a pitiful attempt to wipe her face.

I close the door and go to sit opposite her, wait for her to speak first.

'I'm sorry.'

That's unexpected. But laughable. 'It's too late now.'

She nods, defeated. 'I know.'

'I made you a reasonable offer. A truce. You've only got yourself to blame.'

'I think ... I think ... I think I could have done it. I could have stayed with you until the baby was born, made the best of it. If it wasn't for Willow. Why did you kill her, Alex?'

I don't like how this is going. She should be explaining herself to *me*, not the other way around.

'Forget about Willow. What about us? Why couldn't you have just ... been my wife? We loved each other, didn't we? Life was good, wasn't it?'

'It was.' She sniffs. A single tear rolls down her face and off her chin, onto the table. 'It really was.'

'So what changed?'

'First there was Keira. I didn't believe her, of course, not at first. And I felt so sorry for you, facing those kinds of accusations about Polly's death. It seemed so unfair.'

'It *was* unfair. Polly wasn't who I thought she was when I married her.' Somewhat to my surprise, I find I really want Lisa to understand. I *need* her to. 'She was a murderer.'

'What?' Her eyes widen as she looks at me properly for the first time.

'She killed my baby. In cold blood.'

'I never knew you had a *baby*. Why didn't you tell me? Oh dear God, that's awful, Alex. What did she do to it?'

She's misunderstood, but I don't correct her. I'm enjoying her sympathy too much.

I don't answer her question directly. 'It was terrible, Lisa. Just ... the worst thing that had ever happened to me.' It all comes back to me, the feeling of impotence, of sheer shaking rage when I saw the email from the clinic on her laptop. All the time Polly was playing the devoted wife, she was plotting murder behind my back. The murder of *my* baby. I look deep into Lisa's eyes, am gratified by the shock and sympathy there. 'You can see I couldn't let it go, can't you?'

'Of course.'

'An eye for an eye, a tooth for a tooth. I took my time. She fell ill, at least she thought she did. She had to take to her bed, with sickness and vomiting. She didn't know I was putting thallium in her food.'

Lisa's eyebrows lift in shock.

'She was a murderer, Lisa. She deserved to be punished. To suffer. But when the time was right, I put her out of her misery. I plied her with vodka, took her out to Richmond Park and staged the crash, made sure the car caught fire. The body was badly burned, and the autopsy and inquest were rushed through to save me the embarrassment of it all. Poor

Chief Super McMahon, widowed and humiliated by a drink-driving wife.' Something flickers on Lisa's face. 'You can see I had to do it? For the baby?'

She nods mutely.

'When I thought you and Bella were dead, I thought I'd lost another wife, another child. I was beside myself with grief. I couldn't believe you'd do that to me. Then, when I realised you were alive ... why? Why did you go to all that trouble to make it look like you were dead?'

'I went to Keira's flat. Saw the blood. I thought you'd killed her.'

'No. Why would I? I know you think I'm a monster, Lisa, but I'm not. I'm really not.'

'What about Willow?'

This isn't so easy to brush off. I don't know how much she knows about Willow's death. Probably not much. I don't know why, but I want her to understand. I want to win her round. I want her to love me again. Not because I love her, just to see if I can do it.

'That was an accident. I swear to you, Lisa. She came at me with a knife, and I had to defend myself. She fell. Hit her head. It wasn't my fault.'

'*It is the cause, it is the cause, my soul. Let me not name it to you, you chaste stars.*'

'Shakespeare? You're quoting Shakespeare at me? What the fuck, Lisa? Are you even listening to me at all?'

'I am.' She nods. 'Of course I am. You made the accident look like an overdose.'

She knows more than I thought. 'I had to. I couldn't afford a murder investigation. Not when I was trying to find you and Bella. Willow was ...' I hesitate, searching for the right word.

'A threat? An inconvenience?'

I glance sharply at her. Her expression is stone, all softness and sympathy flown.

The door opens. Derek Mbala comes in, followed by Bill Glover and a couple of uniforms. Bill's face looks like thunderclouds. Before I can get a handle on what's happening, Mbala steps up to me.

'Alex McMahon, I'm arresting you for the murders of Polly McMahon and Willow Schneider.'

The cuffs are clicked shut over my wrists before I can respond. At the sound, I look up and catch the glow of triumph on Lisa's face as she rests her hands on her belly.

EPILOGUE

Pretending to be dead isn't easy.

But it's even harder to live a life that's slowly being poisoned by distrust, violence and fear. That's what the women I met in the refuge – Kelly, Jenna and the others – have to handle every single day.

I'm so much luckier than that.

Alex was an out-and-out psychopath, which in some ways made him easier to deal with, even if it was truly terrifying at the time. So many women have to put up with sly, underhand manipulation, undermining comments, controlling behaviour – death by a thousand uncaring and malicious cuts. And fists too, of course – broken bones and bruises where they can't be seen. Most of their men get away with it unless it escalates to the unthinkable, and by then it's far too late.

88 women killed by their partners in a year.

That headline from the press cuttings on Roo McKellen's noticeboard still haunts me. There but for the grace of God ...

Alex's trial is scheduled for the autumn. I say trial, but they're actually going to try him twice – once for the murders, and again for the bribery and corruption charges the ACU has brought against him. Both trials are likely to be media circuses, given his position in the force. He's trying to get the recording from the interview room ruled inadmissible – his lawyers are claiming it was illegal because it was covert. I'm not sure that's going to make a massive difference. There were four police officers, including Bill Glover, in the viewing room, listening and watching through the one-way mirror as Alex gave himself away. They're all going to testify against him.

Keira is probably going to testify too. With Detective Mbala's help, I managed to get her out of Bellfield. Now she's in a better place and off those terrible coma-inducing meds, she's been able to give Detective Mbala the details of the lab she used to test Polly's remains. He thinks the jury will find the results compelling, especially when combined with the rest of the evidence the forensic team have found. Alex's DNA was all over Willow's flat, and they discovered traces of his epithelial cells under her fingernails. My poor, brave, loyal friend. She must have put up quite a fight.

'Though she be but little, she is fierce.'

I miss Willow, like a part of me has been amputated. The loss is still raw, visceral, and I think it will be for years to come. But I'm sure she'd be happy if she knew Alex is facing prison and that her final action – her determined resistance – is going to help put him there.

Danny is going to testify at the corruption trial. In return for his help, the Met have agreed not to bring any charges against him relating to the MDMA. Bill Glover has taken him under his wing, arranged proper counselling and legal medication for him at last. He does seem to be improving. He definitely looks better than he's been for months.

I have to admit, though, that things aren't quite the same between us. There's still a reserve there. I've forgiven him, but I'm not sure I'll ever forget that he believed Alex over me. The reserve is mutual. I said some pretty terrible things to him too. But we love each other, and we have time. Hopefully, our relationship will evolve into something new – something even stronger, more considered and resilient, if we're lucky.

Alex's assets have all been frozen, and the bank is foreclosing on his mortgage, so Bella and I have moved out of the house in Twickenham. I don't mind at all – it never felt like home. I've found a little flat in Richmond, not much more than two rooms and a kitchen, really. It's cramped and hideously expensive for what it is, but I think we'll manage. We're close to the river for the ducks, and the landlord isn't fussy about pets.

After a bit of sleuthing, I managed to track Figgy down. Willow had given him to her upstairs neighbour to look after while she was in Scotland. When her body was discovered, the neighbour had decided to keep him. He was quite shocked when we turned up on the doorstep. I don't think he wanted to let him go, but Bella's obvious delight in the reunion persuaded him.

So now we're a family of three.

Money will be tight, but not impossible. Bella has started school, so I don't have nursery fees to worry about, and, thanks to some hard negotiating by Dinah, I've just signed to play the lead in a two-part drama for the BBC. It's about a woman who struggles to hold her family together when domestic violence breaks it apart. Not my usual kind of role, but it resonates.

It really resonates.

Tis not a year or two shows us a man. They are all but stomachs, and we all but food; they eat us hungerly, and when they are full, they belch us.

Men might not have changed much in the four hundred years since Shakespeare wrote *Othello*, but women have.

That's something we should hold on to.

THANK YOU FOR READING

Did you enjoy reading *Let's Play Dead*? Please consider leaving a review on Amazon. Your review will help other readers to discover the novel.

ABOUT THE AUTHOR

Elena enjoys psychological thrillers and crime fiction of all kinds, from the coziest of cozies to the blackest of noirs.

She lives in East Lothian, Scotland, with her husband, three kids, and a fat black pug. Born in a colliery village in the North East of England, she cut her literary teeth on the great storytellers of the 70's - Wilbur Smith, Frank Yerby, and Mary Renault. She began her writing career as an advertising copywriter, and has since had novels published by Random House and HarperCollins. She's had an original audio series produced by Audible UK, and also writes for TV.

Please visit Elena on her website:
elenafrost.co.uk

ALSO BY ELENA FROST

Someone Like You

Let's Play Dead

Printed in Dunstable, United Kingdom